THUNDERSTRUCK

SAN DIEGO PARANORMAL POLICE DEPARTMENT: BOOK THREE

JOHN P. LOGSDON

JENN MITCHELL

D1714130

This is a work of fiction. All of the characters, organizations, and events portrayed in this novel are either products of the authors' imagination or are used fictitiously and are not to be construed as real. Any resemblance to actual events, locales, organizations, or persons, living or dead, is entirely coincidental.

© 2024 by John P. Logsdon & Jenn Mitchell

All rights reserved, including the right to reproduce this book, or portions thereof, in any form.

Published by: Crimson Myth Press (www.CrimsonMyth.com)

Thanks to TEAM ASS!

*Advanced **S**tory **S**quad*

This team is my secret weapon. Their job is to help me keep things in check and also to make sure I'm not doing anything way off base in the various story locations!

(listed in alphabetical order by first name)

Audrey Cienki
Bennah Phelps
Carolyn Fielding
Cindy Deporter
Emma Porter
Hal Bass
Helen Day
Janine Corcoran
Julie Peckett
Karen Hollyhead
Kathleen Portig
Larry Diaz Tushman
Leslie Watts
Malcolm Robertson
Marcia Lynn Campbell
Mary Letton
Melony Power
Michelle Reopel
Myles Mary Cohen
Nat Fallon
Paige Guido

Penny Noble
Sandee Lloyd
Scott Reid
Sharon Harradine
Terri Adkisson

CHAPTER 1

Jin

Assassins aren't *all* bad...mostly.

— JIN KANNON

Jin and Rusty had gotten down to the Netherworld customs office. It was a new division of the government that'd only been around for about three months, and they did their best to make sure they were thorough in all their dealings. In the Netherworld, nothing closed faster than a branch of government that seemed less than effective.

That was good and bad.

It was good because the Netherworld had been getting a lot of drugs from topside that seriously messed with supernatural brains. This was especially true for vampires. They already suffered a cult of personality filled with arrogance, so adding in hallucinogenics turned out quite terrible. One of the more recent cases involved Lady Melbanya, who had come to believe that she was the queen of the Badlands. She'd taken a day trip over, using the new train system, walked directly into the House of Sinister's gardens and proclaimed, "I am the new queen and I dare anyone to challenge me on that claim!" She then bared her teeth. Four minutes and twenty-three seconds later, she was staring lifelessly up at the sky as the head of Sinister House, a hellion by the name of Evangeline, wiped off her bloodied blade. The entire ordeal lasted four minutes and twenty-three seconds due to the four minute and ten second walk Evangeline had taken down from her office.

The bad side of having a customs office was that it caused law-abiding citizens to be subjected to the same scrutiny as the criminal element.

Sadly, that was the case in all walks of life.

A small woman with delicate hands had taken Jin and Rusty into a side office and was questioning them. Her badge read Officer Krump. Jin wasn't certain, but he had the feeling she was an elf. Had her ears been visible, he would've known straightaway, of course. Officer Krump, however, was wearing a blue cap that hid the points of her ears, assuming there were any.

"I understand you are both from the Paranormal Police Department, Chief Kannon," she was saying, "but we've actually had more positive cases involving law enforcement officials than we've had with regular citizens."

Jin jolted slightly. "Wow. I wouldn't have expected that."

"Nor did we, which I suppose makes them the best vehicles for carrying drugs through the system."

"Right." Jin wasn't a fan of all this, but he got that people had to do their jobs. "Okay, so what do we need to do then?"

"Just answer a few questions." Officer Krump turned toward the computer screen to her left and asked, "Are you here on business or pleasure?"

"Business," said Jin, but at the same time, Rusty said, "Pleasure."

Jin gave him a confused look.

Rusty darted his eyes around. "Sorry, I meant business. *Definitely* business." He then gave Jin a conspiratorial wink.

Officer Krump studied them for a moment, but moved on to the next question.

"Are you carrying any drugs on your person?"

"No," Jin replied.

"*I'm* not," Rusty said, pointing at himself. "*I* am definitely not."

That captured Officer Krump's brain again, obviously, because she turned and regarded Jin carefully. It was the kind of scan that told Jin something unpleasant was about to happen. He wasn't a fan of that look in the least.

"*What the hell are you doing?*" Jin asked through the connector.

"*Whooooo? Meeeee?*"

Fortunately, the officer moved on to the next question.

"If you *were* carrying drugs, Chief Kannon, where would you put them?"

Jin saw the question for what it was, of course. If he

answered it directly, it would be construed as an admission of guilt. If he answered it indirectly, it would give Krump reason enough to believe he was trying to mislead her and he'd be searched.

Just as he was about to respond, Rusty said, "I'd totally put them in my ass, just like the chief did."

"WHAT?" Jin barked.

"Oh shit! Sorry, chief. I told you I wasn't good at this stuff."

Officer Krump was typing frantically on her computer at that point. Jin was staring angrily at Rusty. For his part, Rusty was sitting there with a huge grin on his face, though he quickly dropped it when Krump turned back toward them.

"We will obviously need to search you, Chief Kannon," she said.

Jin kept glaring at Rusty. "Yes, I would imagine you will." Slowly, he turned back to face her. "I'm assuming there is a machine I have to walk into or something?"

"Up until yesterday morning, there was," she answered. "It broke down and we've been waiting for the technicians to receive a part they ordered. Said it would be two weeks before it comes in."

With a gulp, Jin said, "Then how exactly are you planning to search me?"

In response, Officer Krump opened the top drawer of her desk and pulled out a box of latex gloves.

"Yeah, no," Jin rasped. "That ain't happening. Look, my idiot partner here is just having fun at my expense." He looked at Rusty. "Tell her the truth, Rusty."

"Boy, I don't know, chief," Rusty said, his face pensive.

"You told me *not* to say anything before we left. 'Keep quiet about this, Rusty,' you said. You were pretty clear about me keeping my mouth shut about things. Besides, as you just pointed out, I'm an idiot, so I'll probably just make things worse." His eyebrows marginally wiggled. "I mean, it's bad enough I told them about you smuggling dru...I mean...uh." He slapped himself on the forehead. "Dammit, I have to keep quiet!"

Jin wanted to slap Rusty harder than the android was slapping himself; instead, he turned to Officer Krump.

"If I could please request to have my connector to the San Diego PPD precinct opened, I would love to speak with the lead technician and get this cleared up immediately." He took off his hat, trying to look respectful. "You see, the officer sitting next to me is an android who has a bit of a jealousy issue and he's trying to get me back because he believes I'm attempting to steal his mistress."

"Mistress?" Officer Krump said.

"Mistress."

The officer glanced at Rusty for a moment and then said, "Sorry, that goes against regulations. Not the mistress part, but opening a channel after you have been deemed a person of interest."

"Person of interest?" Jin scoffed at that. "You're taking *his* word on this?"

"He's *your* partner, Chief Kannon."

This was not going anywhere near the way Jin had anticipated, and Rusty was going to find himself mopping the floors at the SD PPD for the next ten years. Not that the android would give a shit. He'd probably just ask Madison to call him names as he did it or something.

Gah!

Jin closed his eyes for a moment and then casually reopened them. "I would like to speak with your supervisor please."

"I wouldn't do that," said the officer.

"Well, I would," Jin challenged. "If you would *please* get me your supervisor, I'm sure this will all be cleared up in no time."

"Oooookay." She pressed a button on her desk. "He'll be here in about ten seconds, unless he's dealing with someone else, of course."

The sound of heavy footfalls struck the ground, causing Jin's chair to move ever so slightly with each step. Even the single picture on the wall—which happened to be of the smiling Officer Krump—was tilting more and more as the supervisor approached.

When the door opened, Jin looked over his shoulder to find himself staring at an orc. He had tusks and everything. The guy was freaking massive, easily seven feet tall and rippling with muscles that would make even the largest bodybuilders topside appear puny in comparison.

"Yeah?" the orc grumbled.

"Sorry to bother you, Officer Kink," Krump said, appearing concerned, "but Chief Kannon here has requested a supervisor to discuss our cavity search process. His partner, Officer Rusty, has inadvertently indicated that Chief Kannon is likely carrying a package in his bottom."

Rusty giggled.

"I am *not* carrying anything in my bottom, thank you very much." Jin stood up and pointed at Officer Krump. "I'm certain she's great at her job, but Rusty—who is technically *not* my partner, by the way—is just trying to mess around with me and has been fooling your officer in the process. He's making a joke, and a very poor one at that!" Jin crossed his arms. "I would be happy to walk through a machine to verify I am *not* smuggling anything."

"Machine's broke."

"Well, that's too bad because I can tell you right now that Officer Krump isn't giving me a cavity search."

"Yeah, okay," the orc said after a few moments. "Calm down. Officer Krump not search you cavities."

"Thank you!"

The orc smiled, which looked horrific. "*I* search them." The guy extended his fingers. They looked like bratwursts with long, sharp nails on them.

Jin gasped. "Fuck me."

Rusty directly connected to me and said. "*Probably not the wisest choice of words there, chief.*"

CHAPTER 2

Vestin

Lord Vestin stood on the front stoop of *his* mansion. It was a lovely day, though possibly a bit too warm for his liking. The sun was rising on the other side of the house, meaning it wasn't directly hitting him. It wouldn't have been a problem if it had. Some myths were a bit exaggerated. He just wasn't a huge fan of the sun's rays.

Another thing he didn't love? Complainers, and he had an entire flock of them in front of him at the moment.

"And you're saying that everyone is depressed due to their change in stature?" he asked Emiliano.

"Yes, My Lord." The zombie was using hand gestures as if presenting a sales pitch. It looked rather silly for a zombie to do such a thing, especially one who stood barely waist-high to Vestin. "We were tall, strong, and filled with confidence. Our ability to literally look down on those we attacked gave us quite a kick in the pants."

"It also made you larger targets," Vestin pointed out.

Emiliano gave him a small nod. "It did indeed, My Lord, but we fought with pride. We felt bloodlust and happy-rage. It's been proven time and again how a single berserker can defy immense odds against them. With all of us beserking you can only imagine our potential."

Vestin wasn't sure what "happy-rage" was, but it *did* sound like something his soldiers should relish. Maybe that was the point? The more they raged, the happier they were? It made sense when he thought of it that way.

But what could he do? Having a bunch of massive zombies running around was going to get noticed. It'd already happened more than once. The PPD knew exactly what they were looking for, and it wasn't like they had to do much digging to find it. He could imagine the new chief glancing out at a sea of people in search of zombies. "Oh," he would say, "there they are. The ones who are standing above everyone else by a solid two feet." Add to that how zombie flesh peeled away, their jaws hung grotesquely, and the fact that people would typically scream and run away from them, and you pretty much had a recipe for sticking out.

Granted, the Comic-Con event gave them a bit of cover, but not a lot. At least not until Prender had brought back one of the little zombies he'd found.

Turning Emiliano and the rest of his soldiers into little people gave Lord Vestin the edge he needed. Yet here they were, complaining about the magic he'd had Carina cast upon them. It was unbelievable. Anyone who ever said running a take-over-the-world campaign was easy had clearly not gotten very far in the actual process.

Prender stepped forward and asked to speak with Vestin alone for a moment. Normally, Vestin would decline such a request, but seeing that he needed a moment in order to figure out how to deal with the complaints, he held up a finger at Emiliano and then stepped inside the house.

"Yes?"

"I'm sorry to have interrupted, My Lord," Prender said with a bow, "but I believe I may have a solution to the zombie-height issue."

"Oh?" Vestin doubted Prender had anything of use to say on the subject, but he'd been surprised before. "Go on then."

"Well, what if you were to gamify the army, making it so they received rewards for a job well done?"

Vestin squinted at the man in a confused way. "Sorry?"

"What I mean to say is that for every person a soldier converts to one of your esteemed army members, they would receive ten points. If they receive one hundred points, they would gain a coupon worth one inch of height." He then rubbed his hands together like a mad scientist. "Now, if they collect twelve inches in coupons, you would allow Carina to cast a spell on them that grows their height accordingly." The man was almost giddy. "However, for each person they *fail* to convert, they lose an inch, and those would be removed realtime."

The idea was a stroke of genius. It put the onus directly upon every soldier to control their own fate, from their perspective anyway. Each of them would work twice as hard, be more diligent, and they'd actually have pride in their work.

"It's not an awful idea," he said, not wanting Prender to feel *too* proud of himself. "There would need to be limitations on how tall they could actually become, of course."

"As to that," Prender said, giggling, "you could offer special coupons to soldiers who 'accidentally' cut the legs off any zombie who grew past seven feet."

Lord Vestin regarded Prender with renewed respect. "Diabolical." He nearly smiled at the man. "I daresay, Prender, you have a streak of evil I hadn't imagined possible with someone of your position."

It was intended as a backhanded compliment, but Prender only beamed further. "Your words humble me, My Lord."

"Yes, I'm sure they do."

Part of Vestin wanted to step outside and share the news with Emiliano himself, but he wasn't fond of having to answer any of the questions that would undoubtedly be thrown his way. Besides, it was Prender's idea. Wouldn't it be wisest for him to present it?

He shook his head again at the smaller man.

Ever since Vestin had stripped away his duty to run the army, Prender had been mostly useless. Did that give him time to cultivate an ability to offer creative solutions to complex problems?

Maybe there was a role for the man in the long haul? There were many chores that needed to be done, and Vestin was far too important to do them himself. What if Prender could fill that role?

Vestin had always believed himself to be self-sufficient, not needing a personal assistant in any way, shape, or form. But he would be remiss if he failed to admit the litany of items on his plate was becoming a challenge to manage alone. On top of that, there was something quite exceptional about the idea of having someone deal with the mundane issues, especially someone who knew Vestin's needs like the back of his hand.

Prender had been with Vestin for a number of years. It was clear the man had learned a thing or two over that time, which was probably due to Vestin's top-notch tutelage, but whatever the cause Prender could possibly prove himself worthy of serving.

Should Lord Vestin choose to place him in the role of manservant, making it official? If he did, it might appear that he'd been wrong about Prender originally. It was never good for a dictator to be "wrong" about anything. Typically, the best way to handle that was to blame the person they'd been wrong about and then have said person summarily executed for deception.

He would have to think on it a little more.

"Prender," he said finally, "you may go out and present *my* plan to Emiliano and the soldiers." He pointed at Prender firmly. "Make no mistakes in your presentation and do not offer promises that cannot be upheld or you'll be hanging from a tree by your toes before lunch."

"You honor me yet again, My Lord." Prender bowed deeply. "I shall not let you down. And once I'm finished here, I shall fetch you a slice of the blood cake I had the chef make in your honor this morning."

Vestin nearly fell over. "Blood cake, you say?"

"Oh yes, My Lord. It's similar to a Tres Leches cake,

but instead of multiple types of milk, there are various strains of blood."

Lord Vestin began to salivate.

"I suppose I shall try a piece since you went to all that trouble," he said in an offhanded way. Vestin then raised a finger. "How many strains of blood would you say?"

"Seventeen, My Lord."

Vestin was incapable of suppressing a whimper.

"My Lord," Prender said, appearing as if he hadn't noticed Vestin's desire, "may I suggest that Emiliano be raised one foot automatically? It may...grow his confidence and allow him to push the rest of the soldiers even harder."

Yet again, Lord Vestin stood dumbfounded by the creativity being displayed by Prender. What in the world had gotten into the man?

"Yes, Prender, I believe that would be wise." His stomach growled. "And, Prender, do hurry along. I wouldn't want that blood cake to go sour."

CHAPTER 3

Raina

Raina felt proud that Chief Kannon had put her in charge while he was away. Granted, she *was* the obvious choice, since she was his deputy, but he could have just told the team to work together until he returned. To have specifically pointed out that she was leading the crew was special. Director Fysh had done so on a few occasions, but not once during her first full year as the chief. It'd taken three years, in fact, and even then Raina had been given a list of rules and was told not to deviate in the slightest.

Chief Kannon was new to all of this, so it might have been that he simply had no idea what he was doing. It could also be that he didn't know Raina well enough to learn that she may not have been ready to hold down the fort yet.

No, no, no! She couldn't think like that. She'd been on the force longer than him. She *did* know the systems, which she'd proven a number of times already. The chief was a good guy, as far as assassins went, but he must have seen that Raina was the only person capable of running things while he was out.

That didn't mean she was the best person for the job. It simply meant she was the best person *available* to do it at the moment.

Gah!

Raina was not a fan of her self-talk, especially not when the full moon was just around the corner. She would go hot and cold on herself twenty times in the span of a single heartbeat. It was super annoying.

Her eye twitched.

Right now, she had to focus on doing the job she'd been given. Sitting around questioning herself would only serve to prove she wasn't ready, and she was tired of not being ready. This was her life, her dream, and she was going to give it everything she had. Besides, what was the worst that could happen?

She didn't want to think about that.

"We need to plan our locations strategically," she called out, silencing the chatter of the team—and her mind. She pointed at the map of the main city strip. "There will be a lot of people downtown for the conference, making them ripe for the picking."

Lacey was floating nearby. She was wearing a little headset, which was necessary since Rusty wasn't capable of managing incoming calls. Whenever he was offline for any period of time, one of the other officers had to take up the slack. They were on rotation and it happened to be Lacey's turn.

"Yes, Mrs. Remscape," she said, not bothering to keep her voice down, "we're after bein' fully aware of the zombie situation and we're doin' our best to squash that shit."

Raina winced every time Lacey was put on the phone duty. She wasn't exactly built for customer support. She tried, and she certainly meant well, but her way of speaking often got the precinct more than a few complaints. To be fair, she wasn't as bad as Rudy. He not only cussed at the men, but he also did what he could to turn each call with a woman into a sexy time.

Interestingly, as soon as it was learned Rudy was on phone duty, the proverbial switchboard lit up.

People were strange.

Her eye twitched yet again, proving her body was already reacting to the impending doom of the lunar cycle. She did her best to mask the effects for as long as possible, but everyone knew it was only a matter of hours before her dark side appeared. It was a terrible thing for them to endure, but what she went through was even worse. Try to imagine someone like Madison mixed with Lacey, and further mixed with a ferocious killer. No, it wasn't some disturbing pervy sex-killer thing. That would have been worse, obviously. Instead, Raina got foul-mouthed, irritable, and she built up a level of bloodlust that could only be rivaled by orcs from the Old War. On top of that, she physically changed in ways that were both attractive and terrifying.

"Raina?" said Chimi, who had stepped up to her and was shaking her lightly. "Are you okay?"

"Hmmm?" Raina snapped back to attention. "Shit." Oh

no, she cursed already. "I mean…shoot. Sorry. I'm just…" She glanced up at Chimi with worried eyes. "The moon is due soon."

"But not until tomorrow, right?"

"It's not an exact science, Chimi," answered Raina gently. "With the zombies, the new chief, the potential of assassins coming up, the *Shaded Past #13* drug, and the conference all coalescing into one week, my mind and body are extra sensitive."

Fortunately, once the event started, it only lasted a few hours. It was a few hours of intense hell, but that would be it, until the following month, of course.

The index finger on her left hand began to itch. She glanced at it, seeing the skin was already starting to change color.

She had to focus!

"Sorry," she said, pointing at the screen again. "Like I was saying, we need to plan out how—"

Lacey flew over and tapped Raina on the shoulder. "Hate to be after interruptin' and such, but Guard Snoodle's on the line. Says them freaky dogs is downstairs askin' to speak to the chief. Seein' as he ain't here, I'm guessin' they'll be wantin' you instead."

"Fuck," Raina hissed. She growled at herself. "I mean… dang." She snapped her fingers and pointed at Clive. "You, go get the coyotes and bring them up here."

"Me?" Clive complained. "Why me? I don't want to be around those little…" He clearly noticed Raina's eye was twitching, not to mention the way she'd locked in on him. He tugged at his collar. "I mean, why not me, right?" His voice was nervous as he scrambled out of his chair. "Yeah, sure, I'll get those lovely little monsters. Happy to do it! *More* than happy to do it!"

He nearly fell over himself as he rushed from the room.

On the one hand, Raina felt bad about that; on the other hand, his fear only served to push her dark side to the surface even faster.

Not good.

CHAPTER 4

Jin

The train ride over to the Badlands was not pleasant. Jin was beyond pissed off, and more than a little uncomfortable. Officer Kink had been rather thorough in his check, making Jin wonder if the orc's surname had been a "virtue name," though Jin couldn't imagine the guy's particular skill to be much of a virtue.

"You sure you don't want to sit down, chief?" asked Rusty, patting the chair beside him. Then he feigned a grimace and added, "Ohhh, right. Sorry. Forgot."

Jin glared down at the android. "You didn't forget, Rusty. You *can't* forget. You're just ticked off because Madison wants me and not you."

Rusty jumped to his feet so fast it was nearly a blur. Jin's nervous system reacted quicker than his conscious mind. Before Rusty could even get set, Jin had his left gun under the android's chin and the muzzle of the right gun was against his temple.

The look on Rusty's face was one of complete shock. He sat back down, staring up at Jin with his jaw hanging open.

"Whoa, chief. I had *no* clue you were that fast."

Honestly, Jin knew that if he'd actually *thought* about what to do in that situation, he'd already be lying dead on the floor with his nutsack sticking against the other side of the train's compartment. But years of training built up a level of muscle memory that seemed to rival that of an advanced AI in a human-like body.

"Your heart rate isn't elevated or anything," Rusty went on. "That's amazing. The only thing I notice, as far as a consistent throb, is around your back-passage there." He pointed at Jin's bottom while leaning to the side. "That's for a different reason, though."

Jin casually slid his guns back into their respective holsters.

"Keep making your jokes, Rusty," Jin said. "When we return, I will be instructing Madison to place you back into the main computer, removing you from this body."

"Hah! Nice try, chief, but you need me. I know it, you know it, and everyone on the force knows it." He gestured toward Jin's guns. "You may be fast with your little weapons there, but you're nowhere near as powerful as I am. Feel free to correct me if I'm wrong."

Jin gave him a sad smile. "So smart, and yet so dumb. It's kind of interesting, really."

Rusty was clearly not sure how to take that comment because he appeared quite confused.

"What are you talking about?"

"We're about to get the assistance of a number of

highly-trained assassins," Jin spoke evenly, turning his attention toward the beautiful mountains they were passing. "While one of me may not be enough to replace you, twenty of me would obliterate your donation to the cause." He slowly returned his gaze to Rusty. "Or does that not compute?"

Jin had never seen an android look fearful before. Actually, up until Rusty, he'd never seen an android at all, except in movies, but those were quite a bit different. His favorite had been Commander Data from *Star Trek: The Next Generation*. He liked how respectful the android had been. He was intelligent, too, and logical. It was how he'd hoped Rusty would be. Knowing who his developer was should've made Jin recognize it was a silly assumption to make.

On top of that, Jin had really tried with Rusty. He knew the poor guy was jealous, and so he'd had a deep conversation with him, offering to help him push beyond his limitations in order to find out his true purpose in life. Hell, Jin had even offered to mentor Rusty.

Being thrown into a hotdog-in-the-ass checkup as a "Thank you" was *not* what he'd anticipated in response to his efforts.

"And now that we're clear of the connector block," Jin added, "I believe I'll have a nice conversation with Madison about your future."

If Rusty had been capable of going completely pale, he would have.

"Chief, no. Don't! I haven't removed that code yet!" He was damn near groveling. "I know I've been bad. Sooo, sooo bad. What I did was shameful. Just shameful."

Jin bent down slightly. "Where was this attitude about an hour ago, Rusty?" He held the stare for a few seconds before standing back up. "You're like the idiot husband who keeps fooling around on his wife until he's caught. *That's* when he expresses sorrow."

"Huh?"

"You're not sorry about what you did, Rusty," Jin said. "You're sorry that I have the power to punish you for it."

"Ummm...nope, that's not it." Rusty was shaking his head. "I'm sorry that Mistress Kane is going to find out how I've been thinking about other..." His face contorted. "Um...I mean...um..."

Ah, so *that's* what had the android worried. It wasn't a fear of Rusty losing his new body. He was afraid that Madison was going to freak out about him considering the option of changing his own programming in order to quit serving her.

What bugged Jin most about that was the fact that Rusty had actually listened to him when they were on the beach. He was genuinely putting thought into removing the "submissive" code.

That was astonishing.

It also gave Jin pause.

Had the android lashed out merely because he was terrified of altering himself, and so he had to push his own boundaries in order to build up the necessary courage to do so? If that were the case, Jin would've felt terrible. Not quite as terrible as his ass felt at the moment, but still rather terrible.

Dammit.

"All right," he said, again watching the mountains in

order to bring his mind a modicum of peace, "I'll not say anything to her just yet." He let the sound of the train fill the void for a few moments. "I'd suggest you be on your best behavior from this point forward, however, because I swear I won't take anymore."

"Is that what you said to the orc?" Rusty quipped and covered his own mouth in shock. *"Sorry, chief,"* he added through the connector. *"I think I have Tourettes or something!"*

Jin simply sighed, deadened his eyes and walked to the other side of the train in order to admire the Badlands plains.

CHAPTER 5

Emiliano

The lead zombie still felt a bit diminutive, but at least he was a full head taller than his underlings. For whatever reason, that gave him most of his confidence back. He wondered what it would be like when he had to fight, however.

It was a worry that would have to wait.

To make matters worse, while at the same time better, he'd asked for permission to have the witch cast a spell on him and a small band of soldiers. The purpose was to give them the appearance of standard tourists so they could go downtown and surveil the area without sticking out like a sore thumb. If they'd done so, looking like zombies, they'd have been noticed immediately. Then again, since the comic conference was ramping up, maybe not.

Either way, Emiliano wanted to make sure the PPD overlooked them completely.

According to Prender, the cops had confronted the

little people who were dressed as zombies, meaning even at their new height, Emiliano and his crew would be targeted.

His problem with the facade Carina had built for them had to do with the stereotypical bent she'd used. They were all wearing khaki shorts, button-up short-sleeved shirts with seashells all over them, and wide-brimmed safari hats. The worst part, though, were the sandals. Not because they were sandals, but because she'd also made them all appear to be wearing knee-high white socks with two yellow bands at the top. Effectively, they'd been made to look like the worst that middle-aged people could offer.

It was embarrassing, particularly for the ladies on his crew.

"It's bad enough to have lost my visual appeal," groaned Shiela, the zombie Emiliano had selected to run things in the event something happened to him, "but to look like a damn washed-up manager of a paint store who happened to win a free cheap-ass trip for his family is disgusting."

She wasn't wrong about the outfit, but as far as her visual appeal went he had to disagree. If anything, he found her more attractive ever since they'd become zombies. Though he couldn't see it at the moment, due to the disguise she was wearing, Emiliano recalled the way her skin dangled off the side of her neck. It was intoxicating.

Carnal thoughts were going to have to wait, though, so he shook himself and made a declaration.

"I know we all look like idiots, but that's what will

keep the PPD from recognizing us. Swallow your pride and let's get on with it." There were a few more grumbles, but Emiliano pushed on. "We need to cover as much space as possible today. Remember, our goal is to find locations where we can set up and start turning people into zombies as efficiently as possible. Pick a partner and head out in different directions."

They paired up and quite literally started walking in opposite directions from each other.

"Stop!" They did. He waved them back in. "I meant that each team would move in different directions, not each person. *As* a team, you need to stick together."

There was a collective, "Ahhh!"

Emiliano had to wonder how Lord Vestin could even fathom getting this army to take over the world. The man must've known something Emiliano didn't, since it'd always been a challenge for him to get these idiots to manage the cartel properly. The sobering reality was that Emiliano was being held responsible for the army now. Prender had been let go of that position.

At first, Emiliano was proud of that fact. He found Prender to be ineffectual and weak. The man was nearly as bad as Hector.

For the briefest moment, Emiliano believed he may have felt a moment of disappointment in himself. The way he thought of his own son was likely not common among most parents. Hector, however, had failed repeatedly in meeting the standards of even the lowliest soldiers *The Dogs* had to offer. The boy was pathetic. And to know that Hector was now the leader of the San Diego cartel, all due to the rules of succession, was certainly the pang of disappointment that radiated through his body. How could he have died and left *that* boy in charge?

Ugh.

He sighed to himself. At least there was very little likelihood the boy would survive long. He didn't have the skills. The damned kid had even gone off to work with the PPD!

Disgusting.

Instead of choosing someone else to pair up with, Shiela had stayed with him. It probably hadn't been the wisest choice. She was intended to replace him should something go wrong. As it stood, anything that happened to him would likely happen to her as well.

There was little he could do about it now since everyone was already a block away.

He began walking.

"We're looking for—"

"Shadowed areas that aren't in line of the city cameras," Shiela interrupted. He stopped and growled. An instant later, she said, "Sorry, boss! I know you hate being interrupted. I was just…I mean…I'm sorry."

Emiliano wanted to send her a backhand that would knock her clear across the street, but he refrained.

The first reason for that had to do with Lord Vestin's rules regarding *not* killing their own. His Lord was correct in the fact that they needed bodies, even fodder—which was something Vestin had taken Emiliano aside to explain in great detail. At first, Emiliano failed to understand, but eventually, it made sense and so he resolved to control himself.

One would guess the second reason would have to do

with how Emiliano felt toward Shiela. One would be wrong. While she *was* attractive, there were many zombies who were even more alluring. Besides, when it came to lustful endeavors, Emiliano didn't dwell too much on appearances.

The memory of the coyote female who'd birthed his five illegitimate sons served as a testament to that fact.

No, the second reason he wasn't going to backhand Shiela was that it would draw the attention of other tourists, their cellphones, live feeds, and likely also the PPD's cameras. Even more aggravating was the fact that there were also supers around, and they had a penchant for narcing.

In a nutshell, it'd get noticed.

The entire purpose of them wearing disguises that had them looking like their normal jobs required them to wear name tags was to blend in more than stick out.

So, with more than a bit of effort, he restrained himself, though not without first providing a bit of a warning.

"I won't strike you this time," he said in an even voice, "but if you do it again, I'll—"

"Smack the shit out of me when we get back to base."

Emiliano groaned.

CHAPTER 6

Hector

Hector had the feeling the conversation was coming. He'd already had a few discussions with his crew after Emiliano died, or after they thought he'd died anyway. Hector's new direction for the cartel was vastly different than his father's had been, and there was little doubt Mr. Becarra was going to take some convincing. That was a battle Hector feared more than the one he was currently facing with the zombies and his "deceased" father.

From the way his crew was intensely silent, Hector understood they had a lot on their minds.

"Okay, gang," he said, preparing himself for the worst, "it's clear you've been stewing over everything that's happened, so tell me what you're thinking."

"Mmm…stew," said Alejandro. Everyone looked at him. "Sorry, I'm kinda hungry." He quickly glanced at

Hector. "I'm hungry for meat, boss, not peanut chutney with dates and figs or anything. Blech."

Hector grimaced. He knew not everyone was going to be onboard with his healthier options, but there was no reason to be rude. It wasn't as though Hector had made a decree that everyone had to abide by his rules when it came to food. He just understood that a healthy body was a happy body. That, in turn, often led to a happy mind. Not always, obviously. There were many examples of overly-fit people who were Grade A assholes, but it could be argued there were many more slovenly assholes due to their brain chemistry being all screwed up.

The problem with someone like Alejandro, however, was that he'd likely be an asshole no matter what he ate.

"Anyone else?" asked Hector.

"Definitely me," replied Sofia. "I would totally rather have stew than any of that butt-chutney shit."

Hector's head fell forward. "I'm asking if there is anything you guys want to talk about, and I don't mean food. Let's focus on the zombies, the PPD, this *Shaded Past #13* stuff, and the vampire who is trying to take over our city."

The grimness returned.

At least that proved they were more worried about their city than they were about the food situation.

Possibly.

"Cano?"

"Yeah, boss?"

Hector sighed. "What are your thoughts regarding the zombie situation?"

"It sucks, boss."

"Thanks, Cano," Hector replied with a heavy dose of sarcasm. "You're very helpful, and your detailed response was both insightful and contained a hearty breadth of depth."

"Yeah?" Cano said, sitting up a bit taller as his face beamed. "Thanks, boss!"

It was obvious none of them were going to be forthcoming regarding the fullness of what was going on here. Cano tried, but it was an empty attempt. Hector found the man interesting. There were moments when he expressed a healthy dose of intellect, along with a measure of caring that was uncommon in *The Dogs*. Then there were times, like this one, for example, where he seemed completely dense.

Fine, if they needed to be dragged along in order to speak their minds, he would hitch his proverbial horse to their cart and start pulling.

"Let me try this again," he said, focusing his attention on Sofia. "A lot of our gang has fallen to the zombie side of the battle, my father is their leader, and he was your leader for many years."

"Yeah?"

"While I'm certain you have no desire to become a zombie, how are you feeling about killing those who served with you before all this happened?"

Sofia actually took a moment before answering. "Not great, boss. At the same time, they're not really the same people, are they? I mean, sure, they may have similar thoughts floating around in their heads. I guess, anyway. No way to really know without speaking to them in some detail." She shrugged. "At the same time, they *did* try to kill us already, so even if any of us felt bad about taking one of them out it's not like they'd feel the same about doing it to us."

That was precisely what Hector had been thinking.

"I agree completely," Cano said. "It sucks to have to kill our friends, but they're kind of already dead anyway. If anything, it could be argued we're putting them out of their misery."

"There's some mercy in that, I'd say," Alejandro agreed, surprising Hector with a level of compassion Alejandro rarely demonstrated. "Mostly, though, I never really liked anyone in the gang all that much." He glanced around. "That includes you lot, if I'm being honest." He shook his head. "I know, I know. It's more of a reflection on me that I don't like very many people, but it is what it is. I just don't. That's not to say I don't *respect* some people, though." Alejandro gave a serious nod toward Hector. "I respected your dad for being ruthless. He got what it meant to be a crime kingpin. You're nothing like him, and while I hate to admit it, I kind of respect that even more."

Wow.

That was completely unexpected. Hector was stunned. So much so, in fact, that it took him roughly ten seconds to respond, and when he did his voice was naught but a rasp.

"Thank you, Alejandro. That's…that was a very kind thing to say."

Alejandro grunted. "Don't make it weird, boss."

Hector had admittedly made it weird, especially in light of the fact that he was speaking with a killer. Not that Alejandro went around killing for the fun of it.…

Actually, he *did* find it fun, but there was always a reason for him to do it beyond the mere joy of the process. In a nutshell, he wouldn't kill unless ordered to do so.

"All right, gang," Hector said, sitting at attention as the limo pulled up to one of the neighborhoods that was controlled by *The Dogs*, "we're going to need to speak with people around here and make sure they understand the dangers involved, tell them we're going to do our best to protect them, and also let them know we're cooperating with the PPD. Any questions?"

"Do we have to talk about the health shit, too?" moaned Alejandro.

"Not this time." Hector regarded the man for a moment. "Actually, that's something you won't need to do at all, Alejandro. As someone who was never capable of living up to my father's standards, I get how it feels to work on things that don't fit your personality."

"Hey," blurted Sofia, "how come he gets a pass? I don't like that green piss water either!"

Hector frowned at her. "It's called 'matcha,' and it's not piss water." He then held up his hands. "You know what, if I'm the only one having to sell the stuff to help our neighbors—our *family*—so be it. At least when they're all healthy and happy, they'll know precisely who to thank."

With that, he stepped out of the car while looking back at their faces.

Unfortunately, the side of the road his car had been sitting on was next to a curb and hill, meaning his holier-than-thou ass tumbled head over heels for a solid twenty feet before finally coming to rest on his back.

"Well," he said to himself, "humility *is* healthy."

CHAPTER 7

Jin

Chancellor Frey was standing by the large window that looked down over the Badlands. Her office sat atop the tallest building in the city, which was not something you would expect from the head of the Assassin's Guild. Topside guilds of this nature operated in the shadows. They dodged the police, keeping themselves hidden at all possible costs. Plus, they were always on the run, fighting to stay one step ahead of the law.

In the Badlands, that wasn't the case. Criminality here was commonplace.

There *was* a Badlands Paranormal Police Department, which admittedly sounded odd since 99.999% of all residents in the Badlands were supers. In other words, it should've just been called the Badlands Police Department. The same went for the Netherworld precinct on the other side of the wall. The reason they retained the "Paranormal" part of the title had to do with an odd bit of practicality.

Originally, both the Badlands and Netherworld were barren of the "Paranormal" moniker, as would be expected. The moment they moved topside, however, the word was added in order to differentiate the precincts from the ones normals had set up. A high percentage of big money comes from people in the Overworld because normals are easily duped into spending money on all sorts of crazy shit. The dominant source of funding moved topside and it was decided there was less cost in having consistent naming. Since there were hundreds of stations in the Overworld and only a couple in the Netherworld, the choice was clear.

What *hadn't* changed was the near reverence placed on criminality in the Badlands. The Netherworld Proper side of the wall had cleaned up their streets for the most part, though the different factions of supers still dealt in some pretty shady shit. But the Badlands reveled in who they were.

It was one of the primary reasons there still existed a massive, magically-infused wall between them and Netherworld Proper.

Law on the Badlands side of the wall was handled mostly through violence. The PPD *did* step in when things were moving into levels that threatened to topple the standard power balance in the Badlands, of course, and they were also there to try and protect the few who sought more honest enterprises, but all in all the cops down here consistently struggled to keep their heads above water.

Chancellor Frey turned and looked at Jin and Rusty as they walked in. Her outfit was a shade different than normal. Where she typically wore leather, chainmail, gloves, and knee-high boots, today she had on a tight black skirt, a tighter white blouse, and a set of stiletto heels. She also wore thin-rimmed, circular glasses and had her hair up in a bun. Jin noted her hair was a deeper red than he recalled her having only a couple of days ago, as well.

"Hellllo," Rusty said through a connection. *"Dude, she's smokin' hot. Kind of has that librarian vibe going on you know? Should I be all like, 'I am late returning the book I checked out' or something? You know, in a flirty kind of way?"*

She was hot. There was no denying it. At the same time, the chancellor was known for not being able to maintain relationships for very long, and it never ended up well for the other person, especially if *they'd* been the one who ended it.

Regardless, Jin ignored Rusty's chatter and kept his mind in the game.

"I was surprised to hear you were coming back so soon," Chancellor Frey said, tilting her head. "Please don't tell me being a topside police officer is more challenging than being an assassin."

Actually, it had been. It was far more difficult than he'd expected. After decades killing people for a living, being an assassin had become routine. Jin knew the process, practice, and delivery like the back of his hand. He'd only been on the force a couple of days and he was already finding it more crushingly stressful than even the most difficult assassin job.

It was why he'd been keeping that pros/cons list, after all.

"As to that," Jin replied, gingerly taking one of the seats on the opposite side of her desk, sliding down carefully, as she sat in the big chair facing him, "it actually *is* more challenging, especially when it comes to managing the people who work for you."

Rusty stepped forward and offered a deep bow. "He's speaking of me. My name is Rusty. I'm an android who is well-versed in serving the needs of a lady such as yourself, and I'm quite incredibly endowed, though I'm capable of offering multiple lengths and girths to accommodate any need, of course."

Jin groaned. "See what I mean?"

As for Chancellor Frey, she had a single eyebrow up and her smirk made clear Rusty's words had found purchase.

"Never been with an android before," she whispered. "You *are* programmable, right?"

"Oh, absolutely."

"I wonder how Mistress Kane would feel about the conversation you're having at the moment, Rusty?" Jin said through the connector. *"Or maybe you've already changed your programming and told her you've done so? I'm guessing you haven't, and that makes me wonder if you think she'd be fond of you playing the field while still being* her *property?"*

Rusty spun on Jin, giving him a terrified look. He then quickly grabbed the other available chair and turned his gaze to the floor.

"What just happened?" asked the chancellor.

"Nothing to worry about," Jin replied. "I just sent him a direct connection, reminding him that we are here on business. He's only been in that body for a day and if he doesn't keep himself in check, he'll end up being pulled right back out of it before midnight...San Diego time."

"Ah. Pity." Chancellor Frey appeared to be resigned to her mostly lonely life. It came with the territory of being who she was, and Jin understood that. She let out a breath and clasped her fingers together. "So, what can I do for you, Chief Kannon?"

Jin sniffed. "You calling me that sounds weird, Chancellor Frey. Anyway, we have a bit of a problem topside that's kicking the crap out of my precinct and the PPD appears to make getting more bodies on the ground nearly impossible."

"Details?"

"The quick version is there's a zombie apocalypse ramping up in San Diego. It's being headed up by a vampire who is apparently trying to make a name for himself. He's developed a drug called *Shaded Past #13* that allows him to subjugate supers."

She sat back in her chair at that revelation.

"A vampire whose venom can tame more than normals? That's never happened before."

"Exactly, and you'd think the PPD would find that very point terrifying enough to throw a ton of cops my way in order to drop the bastard, but they're not budging."

From the way she was staring off into space, it was clear the chancellor hadn't been listening to his last words. She did that sometimes when in deep thought.

Typically it happened during planning sessions with various assassins on larger jobs.

"That could have devastating consequences if he's allowed to run unchecked," she said finally.

Jin nodded. "I couldn't agree more, and you'd think the PPD would recognize that, too. So far, it's not hit a level where they believe it's worthy of intervening, though."

"And by the time they get off their asses, it'll be too late, yes?"

"That's my thought."

"I see." After another minute or so of her staring off into space, she said, "I'm not sure what I can do to help other than to offer advice."

"Advice would be most welcomed," Jin admitted. "You've always been a great sounding board in the past. But, honestly, the reason I'm here is to see if we can solicit the aid of the assassins to take on one of the most interesting contracts any of them will likely run."

The chancellor actually laughed aloud at his words.

"You can't be serious."

"Actually, I am."

Her laughter stopped. "That's a huge ask, Jin."

"It is, but I think you've clearly grasped the ramifications here. If I don't find a way to stop the spread of these zombies, they'll drop San Diego before the weekend is over. After that, they'll spread like a pandemic throughout topside." He shook his head. "You know what happens next."

"They'll be down here," she replied soberly, "and with numbers that big we won't stand a chance against them."

"Yep."

He let her stew again in her thoughts. Jin knew she was one of the smartest people around, at least when it came to strategy and tactics. She would weigh everything, lingering on various angles until either coming to the same conclusion he had or offering up a solution he'd not considered.

Either way would be fantastic from his perspective.

"You're not really going to tell Mistress Kane, are you?" asked Rusty.

"Of course not," Jin replied, *"but I hope you recognize what you just did because it proves you're going to be seeking more than Madison at this point."*

"It's the body. I've never had one and now that I do, I want to use it, you know?"

Jin felt super awkward having this discussion with the android. Was he going to have to start talking about the phases of puberty next? Man, that would be horrible.

"I can't comprehend what you're going through, but that's only because I've always had a body. That said, I get what it feels like to go through changes. It's confusing and it will be frustrating for a while. The question you have to ask yourself is whether or not it's fair for you to put Madison through that with you."

"Yeah, true."

"If you want my advice, I'd say you should remove that bit of programming, tell Madison the truth, and let her know you need some time to figure things out."

"She's going to be super mad, chief."

"Maybe, but I doubt it. She's not stupid. She fully understands what she's built." Jin glanced over at the

android. *"I wouldn't be surprised if she was more proud than disappointed."*

"You think?"

He shrugged. *"I seriously have no idea, but if I were in her shoes, I'd be proud as hell."*

"You'd look weird in her shoes, chief," Rusty replied, cracking a tiny smile.

"Funny."

Chancellor Frey had moved to drumming her fingernails on the top of her desk. It usually meant she'd come up with something. Unfortunately, she stopped again, meaning whatever she'd been thinking had run into a glitch.

"Chief Kannon?" came a connection from Director Fysh, signaling the connector had indeed reestablished connectivity with topside.

"I'm here, Director."

"Bad news. I've pulled out every damn stop I could think of to get these bastards to allow the assassins topside, but they're refusing. Not even a budge. It's a complete no-go."

"Shit. They understand how serious this situation is?"

"I made it crystal clear."

"So are they going to at least give us some reinforcements?"

There was a pause. *"Nope."*

"Son of a bitch."

That may have been the final con on his list. It was one thing to keep his word to an organization that was built on sensibility and honor, but if this was how the PPD managed things, they could go and fuck themselves. Why would he put his ass on the line for such idiots?

He wasn't about to leave his fellow officers in a lurch, but he could maybe talk them out of hanging around, too.

Dammit. Nope.

There were innocent people up there who needed the PPD or they'd fall into chaos. The entire world would. Wasn't that the reason he was here trying to convince the chancellor to help him out? Some of his feelings on the matter had to do with the integration process he'd endured, sure, but it was also just part of who he was as a person. He could see abandoning the powers-that-be in a heartbeat, if the end result didn't also mean he'd be leaving the normals in San Diego to be consumed by Lord Vestin's venom.

Jin Kannon was in a no-win situation here.

"You're right," Chancellor Frey said, interrupting his thoughts. "Aside from getting volunteers of some sort, which will most likely come from my organization, I don't see any other real options available to you."

"It doesn't matter anyway," Jin replied with a groan. "I'm currently chatting with Director Fysh via our connection system and she said her bosses have refused to allow any assassins up there."

Chancellor Frey's eyes hardened. "Is that so?"

"Yep. I guess Lord Vestin is going to rule the fucking world soon and there's not a hell of a lot we can do about it."

She blinked at him repeatedly. "I'm sorry, did you say Lord Vestin?"

"Yeah, why?"

The chancellor's face was unreadable. Was she flummoxed? Maybe it was anger? Fear? Angst? He couldn't sort it out as he'd never seen that look on her face.

"Are you okay?" he asked.

"Lord Vestin," she rasped, "is the only target who has ever eluded me. He's the one who got away."

"Oh, wow."

Every assassin had at least one. Either that or they hadn't been in the business long enough to have lost a target. Sometimes the prey died of other causes, mostly of the self-inflicted type, but there were instances where they disappeared completely. Those were the worst because they made you feel like an utter failure.

"Give me a moment," the chancellor said, her voice full of determination.

She spun around in her chair and faced the window. Rusty and Jin shared a look, but neither of them knew what she was doing. In all his years working with the chancellor, Jin had never seen her spin away from anyone.

There was obviously a level of trust, which was something assassins rarely shared. There were likely automated turrets in the corners of the room, too, just to make sure nobody broke that trust.

"Uhhh...you still there, Chief Kannon?" asked Director Fysh.

"Yeah, sorry. I was just—"

"I just got an email on my datapad with a unanimous acceptance that any and all assassins are welcomed topside to aid with the San Diego zombie situation."

"What?"

Chancellor Frey spun back around, smiling like an evil

queen who had just removed a number of heads from unruly peons.

“You won’t have any issues with getting everyone topside,” she announced. “I’ve taken care of it.”

“Ah.”

“The only thing we have yet to do is convince the assassins to join us.” She stood up, grabbed a set of black gloves, and pulled them on. “I fear that may prove more challenging than twisting the skulls of topside idiots.”

CHAPTER 8

Madison

Once she'd gotten her nasal filters configured properly, Raffy didn't smell half bad. He'd graduated from smelling like a big bag of potpourri that'd fallen into a sewer to smelling more like vanilla with a hint of taint.

Part of being a succubus was learning to tolerate such scents, especially of the taint-variety, so things were looking up.

The stinkfoot and the fallen angel were diligently working away on the mini-guns she'd designed. The two of them were built for this stuff, and they complemented each other's skill sets perfectly. That probably had to do with the disparity of their sizes. It was probably the same reason Chimi and Lacey made for good partners. Well, that and the fact that Lacey reeled Chimi in whenever the Cyclops got a little kooky.

"You're like totally doing that wrong, man," Raffy

complained, pointing his meaty finger at the spot on the gun where Petey was working. "That's an A7x Ripper Screw, you know?"

"It fits, asshole," Petey replied, glancing up, "so what difference does it make?"

"Like, all the difference, man." Raffy waved his hands around dramatically. "There are many layers, you know? I mean, you can't just be…like…putting A7X Ripper Screws where CG5 Turnables should go, man!"

Petey kept looking up at Raffy while continuing to turn the screw. He was doing it in a taunting way, telling Madison the little turd knew exactly how to "turn the screws" on his buddy.

She was kind of hoping Raffy would reach out and swat the tiny bastard, just to show him his place.

That wouldn't happen, though. The stinkfoot was far too kind. Oh, she had no doubt there was a limit to what the monstrous guy would tolerate, and there was no way they'd gotten this far in their relationship where Petey hadn't been squashed at least a few hundred times, but they were clearly great friends and great friends tended not to try to kill each other all that often. They *did* razz the hell out of each other a lot, though, which Madison also couldn't imagine Raffy being very good at.

SNAP.

"Shit," hissed Petey.

"See, man? I…like…*told* you not to do that!"

"Yeah, yeah, yeah." Petey grabbed a pair of pliers and started manually untwisting the screw. "I'll just take it out and replace it."

"It won't work, dude. You totally crushed its spirit, you know?"

Madison wasn't sure how you could go about crushing the spirit of an inanimate object, so she assumed he was using a metaphor. That should've been obvious, and it *would've* been had she been listening to a werewolf speak instead of a stinkfoot. The problem with stinkfeet was how little information there was about them. For all she knew, he could actually see little spirits in both screws and screw holes.

It seemed quite unlikely, but she could see sexual auras like it was nobody's business. That was something only her race could do, so maybe Raffy's people had capabilities beyond industrial stench.

Again, it was possible.

"You're being dramatic," Petey said as he picked up one of the proper screws and attempted to screw it in. It wouldn't budge. "Dammit."

"Told ya, man."

"Up yours."

She was giggling until one of the werecoyotes walked into the room. Best she could tell, it was "Einstein."

"If you're looking for a tree to mark or something, you'll have to go outside."

Einstein looked up at her with dull eyes. "Hilarious. Have you considered taking your show on the road? Maybe you could go on TV so I could change the channel?"

Madison wasn't sure how to reply to that, mostly because people tended not to talk back to her. Granted, the majority of creatures fell for her wiles, even when she wasn't actively using them. Raffy didn't, of course, and based on Einstein's retort, neither did coyotes.

The little creep walked across the room and jumped up on the table.

"Watch it, nut squeezer," Petey said. "We're doing delicate work here!"

"So I can see," Einstein replied. He began pointing at the broken screw and the gun. "Looks like you tried to socket an A7X Ripper Screw where a CG5 Turnable is obviously meant to go."

Petey's head shot up in a flash. "How'd you know that?"

"Cause, like, he's not dumb, man," Raffy chuckled, proving he could tease, too.

Einstein studied the gun for a few more moments. "How long have you been working on this one?"

"Like, a couple of hours, man."

The coyote peered up at him. "And you plan to have one for each PPD officer ready before the battle?"

"I know where you're going with that," Petey said, crossing his arms irritably. "We'll get it done…maybe."

Einstein turned toward Madison. "I could bring in my brothers to finish these up in no time. We have little hands, much like the fallen anus here, but we know how to follow directions and we rarely make mistakes."

"Fallen *angel*, you ugly butt banana."

It was apparent the coyote hadn't paid much attention to Petey's retort; instead, he was focusing his attention on Madison.

"Um…yeah, I guess." She felt intimidated by the horrid monster for some reason. "Raffy, are you okay with that?"

"It's cool with me, man."

"Petey?"

"Why the fuck would I care if these mangled chihuahuas tinkered with your shit?"

Einstein brought his fingers to his lips and whistled so loud that everyone in the room covered their ears. Seconds later, four equally unattractive dogs ran into the room.

"We're here!" cried one in a dumb-sounding, though happy voice.

The other three sang.

Our brother whistled loudly.
Calling us to aid.
Oh, look, there is a succubus!
Is someone getting laid?

"Sorry," said Einstein, giving a troubled look to Madison. "They have a propensity to speak their minds without filter."

"I've heard worse," Madison replied, though she'd not really *seen* worse. "What do you need in order to get started?"

Einstein picked up one of the guns and started moving it around. His brothers studied it along with him. The one named "Lightbulb" sniffed it and then turned around and started walking aimlessly in the room. He finally found a spot in a shadowy area and began to "manage his own destiny."

"Oh gross!" Petey said. "Dude, go somewhere else and do that!"

Lightbulb rolled his eyes, got up, walked to another corner and started up again.

"No! I meant like out of the room!"

Einstein snapped his fingers. "Lightbulb, what did we say about engaging in personal time while working?"

"Mwat mwe're mnot mnupposed mto."

"And what did we say about speaking with your mouth full?"

"Mfame Mfing."

"Lightbulb!"

"Mhmmm?" A split-second later his brain must have caught up with what he was being yelled at for doing, so he stopped and looked sheepish. "Sorry."

Madison kind of felt bad for the little guy. They were all far worse than pug-ugly, but that somehow made them kind of cute, especially Lightbulb. He was just a little dumb dog who had the ability to do something someone like Petey *wished* he could do…not to Lightbulb, but rather to himself…maybe.

Anyway, looking at a scolded dog, ugly or not, kind of bent her heart a bit. So, she knelt and patted her leg, calling him over to her.

Lightbulb seemed wary. Seeing that she was probably the only person in his entire history to ever offer to pet him, she could understand why. But he couldn't help his looks any more than anyone else. Was it right to punish the guy simply because he wasn't attractive…or even passable?

One glance at modern society answered that question. No, it didn't say it was "right," per se, but it certainly proved to be common.

The little guy padded slowly over as Petey looked at Madison in shock.

"You're actually going to touch that thing?"

"I could say the same about you and your tiny weenus."

Raffy chuckled.

Petey gave him a stern wagging of his finger. "Shut it or I'll...I'll...well, you gotta sleep sometime, big man."

Amazingly, Raffy stopped laughing instantly. There was clearly some history there.

As she patted the creepy little coyote on the back, he wagged his tail like it was the best thing that'd ever happened to him. Poor thing. It was sad.

"Hey," she whispered, forcing herself to grab his stubby chin, "would you like to go to the kitchen and get a treat?" All the other dogs spun their heads toward her. "Don't worry, we'll bring some back." She got up and headed for the door. "Raffy, keep an eye on them, will you?"

"No problem, man."

"Hey!" grumped Petey. "What about me?"

"Right, sorry." She glanced back. "Raffy, keep an eye on Petey, too."

CHAPTER 9

Raina

After a couple hours of planning, Raina had assigned missions to everyone. This had happened right as Madison had come out and handed everyone their new mini-guns. The things were sleek and fit perfectly into regular holsters. Raina preferred the heft of her M134, but she couldn't carry that thing around with her all the time.

Madison threw everyone little leather pouches. "The *BreakerReplicator* machine is acting up, so you might want to ration those."

Raina peeked inside and saw a bunch of miniature projectiles. They looked like those tiny breath mints she hated. Turd-Tacks? Something like that.

"Um," said Rudy, "unless you're planning to shoot chickens—and I hope you're not—these little bullets ain't gonna do shit. We're hunting *zombies*, remember?"

"I know what we're hunting, bird-boy," Madison

retaliated. She then grabbed one of the bullets and held it up. "Much like Rudy's dick, it may not look like much. Unlike Rudy's dick, this little guy packs one hell of a punch." She paused and pointed at Rudy. "Before you try to hit me with some witty comeback, you might want to remember the forty-seven second fling we had a couple of years ago, and don't forget the first forty seconds consisted of you trying to get your pants off…and don't forget the other seven seconds consisted of you apologizing for the fact that you'd already finished before your undies were even down." She cracked a smile. "I don't suppose you were born a preemie, too?"

Clive was clearly loving how she'd razzed him. His smile was so big that Rudy glared at him and said, "You want me to shove one of these bullets up your ass, dude?"

"Nah," Clive laughed. "I wouldn't want you to get too excited and make mess-mess in your pants."

Madison gave Clive an impressed nod. Raina was not at all impressed, with any of them. Was a little professionalism too much to ask?

Her eye twitched.

Dammit!

"Anyway," Madison continued, "each of these little guys contains microscopic fragments of every substance known to kill supers." She grimaced. "Not sure how they'll do against zombies, specifically, but we'll find out soon enough. Upon striking a target, a chain reaction will occur that will result in the fragments blossoming out a couple of feet. One bullet should be enough to waste most creatures, assuming you don't hit a leg or something, of course." She palmed the projectile. "That said, the gun is going to rattle off loads of rounds per second, so even if you don't hit the center mass of your target on the first go, you'll likely strike them with enough bullets to waste them anyway." She glanced around. "Just remember you've currently got a limited supply of these babies. Questions? No? Good."

With that, Madison walked back toward her workshop with Raffy and Petey in tow. Raina was glad the coyotes had stayed with the rest of the crew, though, because she was ready to start assigning everyone tasks.

They weren't going to like it, but she had a job to do and so did they. And if anyone gave her any crap about it, she'd just shred their nuts off.

Dammit!

"All right, everyone," Raina called out, forcing herself to remain calm even though her body and mind were starting to reel from the effects of the impending moon event, "we're going to head downtown and scope things out, just like we discussed. The only difference now is that I'm going to be assigning each of you one of the coyotes to help out."

There were audible groans, mostly coming from the dogs.

"I don't want to hear it!"

They wisely snapped their mouths shut. They all knew what happened when Raina fully turned. To be on her shit list for those few hours would be a very bad thing indeed, and she was starting to love the fact that they'd known that about her.

At the same time, she *loathed* that fact!

Ugh.

Einstein piped up before she could do her assignments. He didn't seem bothered by her situation at all, which was honestly helpful. "Please note that it's wisest to keep Rex, Spot, and Rover together. Failure to do so will result in each of them singing the blues incessantly. It *will* drive you to madness."

"I'll take your word for it." Raina found it odd, but what wasn't with the coyotes? And who was she to judge at this point? "Einstein, you'll be with me. Lightbulb will go with Clive and Rudy, and Lacey and Chimi—"

"Yeah, yeah, yeah," interrupted Lacey. "We're after ridin' with the BeeGees."

Day fever
Day feverrrrr
We know how to—

Lacey zoomed down and gave them a mean stink eye. "Zip it or I'll neuter the last of ye with naught but a butter knife, ya miniature cretins!"

The dogs stopped instantly, looking shocked as their sad little faces fell.

"There, that's after bein' better." Lacey looked over at Einstein. "Ain't so bad when ya know how to—"

Swing low...
Sweet chariot...
Comin' for to carry me home...

Lacey's head fell forward. "Shite."

CHAPTER 10

Jin

Not much rattled him in the realm of fighting. Life and death situations were common. That no doubt had to do with the life in question typically not being his own, but he'd still faced many a goon who was licensed to stop him no matter the cost.

This, however, was different.

Far different.

Jin was standing off to the side of the very stage he'd watched Chancellor Frey give presentations from for years. He'd never been on this side of the mic and it was rattling him something fierce.

But why?

All he had to do was step up to the damn thing, face all the people in the room, and…

Oh boy.

"You all right there, chief?" Rusty whispered as they peeked out from the curtains at the incoming stream of assassins. "Unless I'm mistaken, and I rarely am, your stomach just made a sound that indicated you need to find a bucket…and fast." He peered over at Jin. "Maybe that orc's finger loosened something up? Other than your—"

"Enough, Rusty," Jin said with a snarl. "I'm just not used to public speaking."

"Ahhh." The android's eyes glassed over for a moment. "Fascinating. Did you know that more people fear public speaking than they do death?"

"Not until just now," Jin admitted, "and I have to say I believe I'm one of them."

"Ah, it's not that bad." Rusty grabbed him by the shoulders and stood him up straight. "I've just done some research and there are a few basic techniques that will help you through. Follow these simple instructions and it'll be like you've done this a thousand times. You won't even break a sweat."

Jin was wary of Rusty's "research" because of how the android had been acting since his mind was merged with a body. The orc incident alone was a testament to his temporary partner being quite literally a pain in the ass. But in the hopes that Rusty actually had come up with a few tidbits of information that would help him through this moment of hell, Jin had little choice but to listen.

"Okay," he said guardedly, "what have you learned?"

Rusty was looking at him seriously. "The main thing is that you have practiced your speech over and over, so you know it like the back of your hand. Have you done that?"

"I was supposed to write a speech?"

"Okay, so that would be a 'no.'" Rusty grimaced and

then lightened up again. "No worries! The next most important thing is that you know your subject matter better than—or at least equal to—anyone else in the room. Remember, they've all come here to see *you*."

Jin did know more about what was going on topside than anyone else in the room, that was for certain. Unless, of course, Lord Vestin had contacts in the Assassins' Guild that Chancellor Frey didn't know about. Unlikely. And the bit about the assassins all being here to see Jin, while somewhat true, had nothing to do with them desiring to be here in order to pick up some tidbits of wisdom. They were summoned, and he was certain they didn't have a clue as to why. He recalled many times when he'd been called to meetings like these and he never knew ahead of time what the subject matter was about, and he was rarely happy about having to attend.

"Right. What else do you have?"

Rusty nodded. "You have to radiate confidence. Walk out there with purpose, breathe in a calm manner, and pretend everyone is naked."

"Confidence, purpose, breathing…naked?"

"Yeah, that seems to be a big one."

"Phrasing." Jin said offhandedly. "Why are they naked again?"

"I think it's to make you feel less intimidated or something." Rusty shrugged. "I mean, I would imagine that orc wasn't intimidated at all by you when he saw you naked, so maybe that part is bullshit."

"Thank you, Rusty," Jin deadpanned.

"Sorry, chief."

By now, the seats were nearly filled up. There were a

few empty chairs, including the one he used to occupy. It was nice he'd not been replaced too quickly, especially since he was still on the fence about whether or not he would come back at some point.

The thought of returning to the Guild punched him in the gut harder than his fear of the impending presentation.

Jin did *not* want to return to being an assassin. It was a fine life, for people on the assassin-side of things, but it wasn't a free life. You had to fight to stay relevant at all times. There was a level of competition that never let up. The fact that he was the only person in the room, aside from Chancellor Frey, to have reached one thousand confirmed assassinations gave him a lot of leeway, but it also marked him as being one of the elder statesmen in the group. He wasn't physically old, at least not in djinn years, but his mind no longer burned with the thrill of the kill. That wasn't exactly true. There *were* parts of the job that he still enjoyed, but those were more on the research side and less on the actual killing part.

Chancellor Frey had suggested the possibility of him working in the main offices at one point. Maybe that life would suit him well enough?

He thought about her position in the organization. She never left. It was twenty-four hours a day, three hundred and sixty-five days a year. Even on holidays, she was always on call. He knew that because she'd phoned him numerous times about jobs when everyone else was out celebrating whatever they were celebrating.

Jin sighed, recognizing that he'd never celebrated any holidays either. That was another tick on the column of just taking a damn office job in the Guild and relegating his life to being one where he worked day in and day out until he finally got the gift of leaving for the Vortex.

No! Dammit! No!

He couldn't do that. It wasn't what he wanted and that had to mean something, right? Maybe only to him, but it was his life and he only got one. He had no idea what happened when he got to the Vortex, but he knew that here and now was his to grab and live based on his own choices. Did he seriously want his selection to be something that robbed all the joy remaining in this world?

"I've called you all here today because we have a unique opportunity in front of us," Chancellor Frey said into the microphone, jolting Jin from his thoughts. She spoke as if it were nothing to her at all. She was a natural. "I want you to listen to what you're about to hear with an open mind. Do you feel me?" Nobody replied, of course. "Good. Then let me introduce you to one of the few assassins to ever reach the one thousand kill mark, Jin Kannon."

Rusty had to shove Jin out onto the platform. "You've got this, chief. Be strong!" As Jin got halfway across to the mic, Rusty added via the connector, *"And don't worry about screwing up. If you do, the people of San Diego will fall to the zombie apocalypse, the cops will all die, everyone in the audience will laugh at you, and your dick will fall off."*

Jin shook himself and glanced back at Rusty. *"What?"*

"Okay, probably not that last part...but you never know."

Asshole!

CHAPTER 11

Clive

Lightbulb was sitting in the back seat with his head out the window, just like any dog would. Unfortunately, his human-like face was causing cars around them to swerve at the sight of the guy. That probably had a lot to do with the drool flying off his lips.

Clive rolled up the windows.

"Why'd we get the dumb one?" complained Rudy.

"He's probably asking the same thing."

Rudy grunted. "Har har. Dick."

"Just let it go, man. Raina assigned him to us and we have to deal with it. Such is life." He turned left. "Besides, what difference does it make? The guy might prove useful. I mean, he's managed to survive a few years looking like he does, you know?"

"Yeah, I guess."

Lightbulb stuck his head up between the seats and started sniffing Clive's shoulder. "You're a horsey!

Neeeeeeiiiiighhhhh." Rudy chuckled, until the little beast sniffed him next. "Rooster! Buk buk buk!"

"At least he didn't call you a chicken," Clive noted, knowing how much it irked Rudy to be referred to as the female side of the equation. "That means he must smell at least one or two molecules of testosterone on you. May not be your own, but—"

"Keep teasing me, hoof-boy, and I'll knock your teeth out."

"Ooooh."

"Ooooh!" mimicked Lightbulb. "Why you guys fight so much?"

Clive and Rudy both fidgeted for a couple of seconds. It was a good question. The two of them had always bickered, and though it was mostly just in fun, they sometimes really went after each other. Was it competition? Was it stress? Or maybe it was just good old-fashioned ribbing that happened between friends? They were more like brothers than friends, though. That came with the badge. Fighting side-by-side in the trenches, and watching each other's backs when the shit hit the fan caused a level of trust that transcended family.

But the coyote hadn't known them long enough to see many arguments, so why would he think they argued a lot?

"What makes you say that?" Rudy asked, making it clear he'd been thinking along similar lines as Clive.

"My nose knows!" Lightbulb replied. "You stink like fight when together!"

There were moments when the creepy dog spoke normally and moments when his words were just a tad off. It was probably how he got his name. Sometimes the lights were on; other times, not so much.

"We stink like fight?" asked Rudy, glancing back. "What the hell does that even mean?"

Clive looked at the rearview mirror and saw the ugly coyote furrowing his brow. "It mean you stink like fight."

"Ah," Rudy replied, nodding sarcastically. "Well, that clears it up. Thanks, turd."

Lightbulb frowned. "I not a turd. I are a coyote!"

Before Rudy started smacking the poor dog with insult after insult, Clive said, "We argue a lot because we're partners."

"Ohhhhhh. I knew you smell funny, but didn't know you was a couple."

Clive frowned. "Not *that* kind of partnership. I meant on the force. We're cops, and so we have to constantly watch out for each other, so we're either in this car, at the office, or on some type of mission together all the time. You get to know a person beyond what you could ever learn about them as mere acquaintances."

"Yeah," agreed Rudy. "It's like we're brothers or something. I'm the older, wiser one, and he's a goat scrotum."

Lightbulb gave Clive another sniff. "Him not smell like a goat scro…scro…erm…scro…hmmm…sack."

Rudy groaned. "I don't mean he's literally a goat scrotum, dipshit. We call each other stupid names because it's our way of showing we care. That's just how it works."

The coyote sat back. "Maybe that why Einstein calls me dummy a lot?"

The two cops shared another look, knowing sibling jousting *wasn't* the reason for that.

Rudy coughed. "Uhhh…yeah. I'm sure that's why."

Clive drove further down into the city. It was getting more and more crowded due to the convention. Things were going to be frantic by nightfall, and that was a terrifying prospect.

Lord Vestin had to have been planning to hit the town when the most people were around. Clive would totally do that if he were running the show. When was there a better time? All the conference attendees would start out thinking it was some kind of event that supported the show, so they'd love it. By the time they realized it wasn't at all intended as entertainment, a good number of them would be well on their way to turning into zombies. In addition to that, the *Shaded Past #13* stuff was certainly being passed around at the beach. If history was an indicator, issuing warnings to certain types of people only caused them to want to partake more.

It wouldn't even be midnight before Vestin's army outclassed anything the San Diego PPD could handle, even with their new, fancy mini-guns.

He pulled into an open space near the park. The moment he shut off the car, Lightbulb began jumping around excitedly. He was scratching at the windows and wagging his tail while yelling, "Park! Park! Park!"

"Shut up, ya creep!" Rudy barked. "Jeez!"

"You a creep!" Lightbulb retaliated, and then suddenly stopped. "Whoa! I fight now, too! That mean we partners?"

Technically, for now anyway, they were just that.

"Let's go," Clive said, getting out of the car.

Before he could open the back door, Lightbulb had jumped into the front seat and leapt out the driver's side. Fortunately—or maybe unfortunately—the cars were going slowly enough that nobody hit him. One driver did lay on the horn and give Clive a rude gesture, though.

Animal lover, no doubt.

Clive gave the woman an apologetic wave. Rudy, however, returned her gesture and called out for her to shove it up her ass.

"We should probably have put a leash on that little fucker," Rudy said as they got to the other side of the street.

"Would you want to be the guy holding the other end of that leash?"

Rudy shuddered. "No."

Lightbulb was running up to every tree and bush, lifting his leg as if to let every animal in the park know that he'd arrived. Clive found it kind of adorable, though he wasn't about to say that to Rudy. The last thing he needed was for his partner to start ribbing him about the coyote, though a brief glance toward Rudy told an interesting story.

"What are you smiling at?" Clive asked.

Rudy sniffed and pointed. "That's about the ugliest damn dog I've ever seen, but he's fuckin' hilarious."

Just as they were sharing a laugh, Lightbulb stopped his antics, spun, and stared across the path from where he was standing.

Clive and Rudy both turned their attention to two incredibly short tourists who were standing adjacent to the coyote. They wore the stereotypical garb of people who weren't exactly fashionistas.

"Those socks are epic," Rudy pointed out.

"Gotta love those hats, too," noted Clive.

As for Lightbulb, he padded over to them, sniffed the air a few times, and yelled, "Zombies!"

CHAPTER 12

Lacey

Lacey and Chimi were out with Rex, Spot, and Rover. Lacey referred to them as the "Singing Little Bastards" because they were quite the chorusing crew. Like their brothers, the guys were difficult to look at, but once you got used to them they weren't all that bad.

As one, the three dogs burped.

Okay, maybe they *were* that bad, but they seemed pleasant enough when they weren't annoying her with songs.

The city was bustling with people of all kinds, though most were wearing costumes. How Raina could even fathom finding anything with all this riffraff milling about was a mystery to her. Even if Lacey used magic, it would be near impossible to spot much. Like her Uncle Fezzy used to say, "It'd be like searchin' for a turd in a blasted tornado!" She sure did miss him.

Something caught her eye that *did* stand out as odd, though. They appeared to be tourists, but that was the problem. They were *too* touristy. It was as if someone had picked up a copy of *Tourist Fashion Monthly*—if there was such a thing—purchased every piece of the garb, and went on a marketing and promotions tour for the magazine.

They were normals, though, and Lacey had to admit that normals did some of the craziest shit she'd ever seen. Another quick glance around at the various costumes proved that to be the case. Could it be that these two idiots had seen a movie with over-the-top tourists and were wearing outfits, too?

She was about to shrug it off when the Singing Little Bastards started to dance and go into a three-part harmony, after first morphing and pointing their tiny hands at the taller of the two tourists.

Emiliano! Emiliaaaaano!
He's really quite the spectacle...
And he's got tiny testicles!

Emiliano! Emiliaaaaano!
A zombie he's become...
And he's really fucking dumb!

Lacey and Chimi gave each other shocked looks before returning their gaze to who may have been Emiliano.

The guy stood there with his jaw hanging open for a moment. Slowly, his face grew more and more stern.

"First off," he said through gritted teeth, "I do *not* have tiny testicles! And even if I did, how the hell would you know that?"

In response, the three dogs rolled over onto their backs and began wiggling so the movement of their sacks became a focal point.

We have little nuts.
Yes, it's true!
Though you can't tell,
our sacks hold two!
Listen, Emiliano,
We know about your nads!
How do we know?
Because you're our dad!

Everyone stood in silence for a few moments.

Lacey couldn't speak for anyone else, but she was stunned by the dogs. They could really sing. Granted, their songs were quite odd, especially with the combined "dance moves" they'd choreographed, but they were solid.

"Yes, well…um…" Emiliano replied. "Regardless, I am *not* dumb!"

"I don't know, boss," the woman next to him said. "You kind of just admitted that you're Emiliano by dignifying their statements, and you've also agreed to having minuscule testicles."

Emiliano jumped and spun on her. "I agreed they were small. I never said they were minuscule!"

The woman closed her eyes for a moment and shook her head. She then glanced up at Lacey in an almost commiserating way.

For some reason, Lacey shrugged at her as if to say, “Sorry, lass, but you’re the one who’s after bein’ with the man.”

The woman’s returned shrug said, “Sadly, it’s not like I have much of a choice. He’s my boss.”

That caused Lacey to audibly go, “Ah.”

Chimi, the dogs, and Emiliano were glancing back and forth between the two ladies during their mostly wordless discourse. They seemed rather confused.

“Are you all talking about me?” demanded Emiliano. “You know, in your womanly way?”

She grabbed his arm and pointed toward one of the alleyways. “We should probably run.”

“What? Why would we…” Emiliano paused for a moment, clearly catching onto the situation he’d walked into, and then said, “Shit.”

Lacey whistled for the Singing Little Bastards to stay put, which surprisingly, they did. Chimi hadn’t budged, of course. She’d learned long ago that you never chased after the criminals too quickly. Doing so often got you caught in a trap.

Why did we stop?
Aren’t you a cop?
Not now, Rover!
He’s going to take a plop!

Sure enough, Rover curled one out right in the middle of the street, though it was odd how he’d still sung his part in the harmony before doing so.

“Now what?” asked Chimi.

"I'm after thinkin' about that," Lacey replied. "It seems to me we should—"

"Excuse me," said a human security guard who was walking by, "but you will need to clean up after your dog; otherwise there's a hundred dollar fine."

Lacey had the sudden feeling she should've just chased after Emiliano and risked getting trapped.

CHAPTER 13

Raina

Raina had taken Einstein with her. He'd sat in the front seat during the entire ride, which he seemed rather chuffed about. It was somewhat endearing.

She'd parked at the Marriot, taking a spot that was reserved for the PPD. There'd been a number of issues around that side of the city for years and hotel management recognized the wisdom in taking care of the cops.

With the convention center only a couple of blocks down, and the marina just outside the hotel, Raina knew it'd be the go-to place for most of the tourists right now. Besides, the rest of her crew had been jumping in from other points so it was best to spread their nets and catch as much as possible.

"I love the water," Einstein said as they walked along. "When we were puppies our mother would take us out at night so we could swim. It was lovely."

"She sounds like a nice lady."

"She was, yes. Sadly, she was hit by a car last year." Einstein stopped and sniffed the air for a moment before resuming his stride. "I've been taking care of my brothers ever since. It's quite the challenge, let me tell you."

Raina felt bad for him. Losing a parent was something she'd dealt with, too.

The memory of the poachers who had killed her mother swam into her mind. They'd done it for the magical unicorn horn, meaning they'd had to wait for the full moon so her mother would be incapable of hiding who she truly was. Raina had been too young to morph at that time, so she could do nothing but what any normal child could do: fight, scream, kick, and cry.

It was the reason she was alone as a unicorn in this world. She'd never met her father. Apparently, he'd suffered a similar fate before she was born.

Her thoughts ceased as she recognized Einstein had stopped again and he was looking up at her.

"Something wrong?" she asked, even though she knew her eye was twitching like mad.

"Other than the fact that your hands are completely black, your hair has grown by a solid foot, and the sclera of your eyes is no longer white? Nah, everything's swell."

"Fuckity fuck fuck," Raina hissed, spinning away. "I mean…um…poopity dang crud." It was lame. "I'm sorry, it's just getting close to the full moon and with all the things that have been going on, I'm struggling to keep myself from changing over to what I truly am."

"It's okay," Einstein said after a moment. "We're all different, you know?" He glanced around the area. "I have caught the scent of you before, over the last couple of years, but I didn't know who the smell belonged to. At the risk of being rude, what are you exactly?"

She took a few breaths and tried to center herself again. Staring down at her hands helped because she could watch as her skin returned to normal. It was the kind of biofeedback that allowed her to focus. Once she got too close to the full moon, she'd completely lose control, but for now she would manage as best she could.

"Unicorn," she rasped.

"Ah, that explains a number of things," Einstein said. "I just can't believe Lightbulb was right."

Raina looked back at him in confusion. "Hmmm?"

Einstein sat down and scratched his ear with his hind leg. "It's nothing. Like I said, we would catch your scent now and then and we'd try to figure out what it was we were smelling. I thought you were possibly a phoenix because you only appeared now and then. Rex, Spot, and Rover sang tales about you being an Aqrabuamelu, whatever the hell that is. Based on their lyrics, I think it's a scorpion or something like that." He then shook his head in amazement. "After the first whiff, Lightbulb declared you were a unicorn and crossed his arms at me defiantly when I insisted that was ridiculous." Einstein laughed. "It appears I was the one being ridiculous."

It was interesting they could catch a scent of what she was when she partially changed, but it appeared to require her to cross a certain threshold. She'd morphed a bit back at the station and none of the coyotes had seemed to notice. Then again, maybe they had and were just being respectful?

Unlikely.

She'd heard the singing dogs speak their thoughts without using a filter before. Einstein had even made clear to Lacey and Chimi that Rex, Spot, and Rover would sing whatever came to their minds without reservation, making it clear they should be careful because it could cause quite a stir. He obviously didn't know Lacey and Chimi very well, since the two of them were all about rocking boats.

Raina's hands had finally changed back, so she hoped the rest of her had as well.

"Any better?" she asked, cringing.

"Other than the twitching eye, yep." Einstein put his nose up and checked the air again. "Can't smell unicorn on you anymore. I doubt the zombies could ever smell it, but you never know. They did have a witch with them when we visited Lord Vestin."

He'd said the name as if it were vile. Raina was about to ask him why, but the coyote spun around and began a quick run toward one of the supernatural entrances at the Marquis building.

She took off after him.

Einstein stopped before entering and looked back at her, shaking his head. He looked worried. She wasn't sure if it was for her safety or for his own. Maybe both?

"What is it?" she asked.

"Zombie." He sniffed the ground around the area. "Smells different than the others, like he's not fully turned or something. I don't know."

Raina went for her gun but the way Einstein glanced at her hands made her stop. He may have been an ugly little thing, but his expressions were clearer than most normals. It was strange considering his face looked pretty much like any other person she knew, only less attractive.

She sighed at herself, recognizing she was being mean. Yes, it came with the territory of the full moon, but she wasn't there yet, and until that happened she would damn well be kind. She hadn't spoken her thoughts aloud, but that didn't matter. Raina knew what'd been going through her head and she didn't like it. Change came by first altering how she thought. Without fixing that, her outward reactions would never stand a chance.

"What do you think we should do?" she asked.

The coyote gulped. "I don't want to suggest what I'm about to suggest, but I think it's probably the best way."

"Go on."

"I think I should go in there alone," he whimpered.

"Oh."

CHAPTER 14

Vestin

He sat at his new desk, noting how everything had been arranged precisely the way he liked it. There were field reports on the left side, placed neatly inside a carefully crafted wooden box that had the words "Field Reports" expertly stenciled in gold. The box on the right had another set of reports with the words "*Shaded Past #13*" on it. In the middle sat his datapad, and its screen was wiped perfectly clean, devoid of even a single fingerprint.

Many might think vampires would shy away from wooden desks, boxes, or essentially anything made from a product that could kill them. But that was silly. Unless an item can morph itself into something that can pierce his heart or crush his brain, there was no sense in fearing it.

The only thing out of place in his office was Prender. He was standing on the other side of the desk, wearing a sharply-pressed uniform. He was also smiling and standing at attention.

"Yes, Prender?"

The man gave a bow and said, "I took the liberty of cleaning your desk and making sure everything was put together as you like it, My Lord. If I have failed in anything, please do advise, so that I may manage everything correctly in the morning."

Now that was odd.

Why had Prender done such a thing at all? Did he not have other duties? More pressing duties?

It *had been* nice to walk into his office to find everything where it should be, certainly, and the cleanliness of his datapad was something that tickled his mind. Fingerprints on a screen were quite the pet peeve for Vestin, but why wasn't the man out doing…well, whatever he was supposed to be doing? Could it be because Vestin had relieved him of the duty of running the army and therefore he wasn't sure how to spend his time? It was a possibility. Having known Prender for as long as he had, Vestin understood the man wasn't exactly what one would call a "self-starter."

Right as he was about to question Prender, his phone began to ring.

Ugh.

He *hated* answering the damn thing. It was so far beneath him that it pained him every time. What he needed was a receptionist! No, he needed a personal assistant! No…he needed a manservant! Yes, that's what he needed, but where could he possibly get one he could trust?

"My Lord," Prender said as Vestin began to reach for the phone, "may I answer it for you?"

Lord Vestin sat back, baffled, but also intrigued.

He gestured for Prender to go ahead.

With a wide smile, Prender picked up the call and announced, "You have reached the grand office of the esteemed Lord Vestin, our wonderful and powerful leader. How may I direct your call?"

Vestin's mouth hung open as his mind danced with glee. *That* was how his office should be run. *That* was how his phone should always be answered, especially the bit about him being wonderful and powerful.

Could it truly be that Prender's true skill had been hidden all this time? If that were the case, it would reflect poorly on Vestin, and Prender would simply have to be killed. People would not follow a vampire who failed at perfection, after all.

He would need to ponder it.

"Ah, Miss Smith," Prender said, his face turning slightly sour, showing he too disliked the woman. "I will need to check to see if he's available at the moment. Please hold." He pressed the mute icon. "It's Janet Smith, My Lord. Shall I tell her you're indisposed?"

Boy, that would've been great. Sadly, Vestin had an army to build and Janet Smith was an integral part of that, for now.

"No, Prender," he said, defeatedly holding out his hand, "I'll take it."

"As you wish, My Lord." The man pressed the icon again. "Lord Vestin has graciously decided to take your call. Please remain on the line and he will join you momentarily."

Prender handed the phone over, gave another bow, and walked out of the office, closing the door behind himself in the process.

Vestin had no idea what'd gotten into the man, but he rather liked it. *Loved* it, in fact. It was refreshing. Everything in the office was prepared, his phone was being answered in the fashion any proper ruler would demand, and most of all, Prender was acting absolutely respectful. He'd always been that way, but this was different. It was *more*.

Honestly, the entire experience made speaking with Janet Smith almost palatable.

"This is Lord Vestin," he said in a powerful voice.

"Got your girlfriend answering your calls now, eh?" she said.

Vestin sat up in defiance, even though she couldn't see him. "Prender is *not* my girlfriend."

"Boyfriend, then. That's cool. I don't judge."

"No, it's not like that at all, and for you to—"

"I've been going over the data," she interrupted, much to his chagrin, "and it looks as though we've handed out nearly double our initial expectations."

His anger faded before he could blink. "Really?"

"Wouldn't say it if it wasn't true, Captain Tooth Talons."

He frowned but decided not to grumble about the name-calling again. Of all the insults she'd flung at him since the day they'd met, that one had been rather tame.

Maybe she was truly trying to be less offensive. She did say she was going to attempt it, though he still struggled to believe her.

"That's excellent news, actually."

"Yep."

Vestin glanced out the window and noticed the same number of soldiers as before. No, he hadn't counted them, but the general size of their population didn't appear to have changed much. A massive influx of new bodies would certainly be noticeable.

"I do wonder where they may all be," he said. "I would think with that number of people injecting my venom, the training field would be overrun by now."

Miss Smith didn't reply immediately, and when she did, she'd lost her ability to maintain cordiality. "You're fucking with me, right?"

"I'm sorry?"

"We handed out the syringes, but it's up to *you* to provide the unlock codes."

The unlock codes? Oh!

Lord Vestin's head fell forward. "Miss Smith, what sense would it make to provide everyone with *Shaded Past #13* and not immediately give them the codes along with the product? I only did so at the kick-off event for dramatic effect, as you may recall."

"How was I supposed to know you were merely being dramatic, Sergeant Venom Sphincter? You'd nearly pissed your pants at the thought of even getting on stage."

He closed his eyes and fought to remain calm. "It must have been apparent that was the plan, no?"

"Not to me, you cavity-stricken tooth-taint."

So much for formality.

"Right." He pinched the bridge of his nose. "How much would it cost to have new fliers printed with the access code affixed and instructions for how to use them to open the product?"

"Twenty-five thousand," she answered without hesitation.

He knew the price was astronomical, but it was akin to mere pennies to someone of his stature. Wealth was part of his family. It was part of most vampiric families, in fact. He just despised overspending because it was a sign of weakness.

Alas, in this case, his hands were tied.

The mistake made by the offices of *Turner, Turner, and Smith* would cost him financially today, but when he completed his bid to take over the world, it would cost *them* even more dearly.

"Fine," he said, doing his best to sound strong. "No further mistakes from you, though, Miss Smith. Are we clear?"

"Shove a wooden stake up your ass, *Turd* Vestin," she replied before disconnecting.

He had to grin at himself, recognizing her outburst had come because he'd pressed the right buttons. She was wrong and she knew it. Vestin rather liked that.

There was a knock at the door.

"Enter," he said.

It was Prender again. He was carrying a small tray that held a beautiful white cup embellished with delicate silver and blue flowers.

"I hope you don't mind, My Lord," Prender said as he placed the cup and accompanying saucer on the desk before Vestin, "but I know speaking with Miss Smith can be rather trying, so I thought you might enjoy a nice cup of blood tea."

Vestin's eyes threatened to tear up. "Thank you, Prender."

"I'm here to serve, My Lord," the man replied. He adjusted his stance. "If I may speak my mind, My Lord?"

Vestin took a sip of the tea. It was perfectly heated and there was a hint of spice that set his palate alight.

"You may."

There was that bow again. Interesting.

"I fear I may have originally misread my purpose in your plan, My Lord," Prender said. He appeared somewhat distraught. The man was even wringing his hands with worry. "I believed you desired me to run the army, but it is clear now that you'd intended for me to only do so until you found a more suitable person."

That wasn't true at all. Then again, maybe it was. Lord Vestin's mind was so superior there were times when even *he* was surprised by its unfathomable splendor in logic and planning.

With Emiliano at the head of the army now, and Prender decidedly not, it was incontrovertibly evident that Vestin had indeed held a level of foresight that few possessed.

"Continue, Prender."

"Thank you, My Lord." The man swallowed hard. "After a bit of soul-searching, I knew that a man such as you—a *great* man—would want me to comprehend my place on my own, recognizing that telling me outright would only prove what little worth I am to you. Therefore, I pushed aside my pride and my world opened immediately." He put his hands behind his back. "Unless I am wrong, I believe your original intent for me was to momentarily serve as your second-in-command only so that I could learn the ins and outs of your daily needs, and that you fully anticipated finding someone to take over my duties as I ultimately fulfilled the role of manservant to my illustrious Lord."

Without knowing it, Prender had accomplished many things in that one explanation. He'd proven to Vestin that he understood his place, he'd given Vestin the perfect selection for a manservant—something Vestin's mind had obviously known all along, and he'd saved his own hide from execution.

"Well done, Prender," Lord Vestin said, setting the cup of tea back down. "It appears I have chosen wisely." He then gave the man a shooing motion with his hand, not wanting to speak further on the subject for fear that it may somehow become ruined. "Now, move along as I have many tasks to attend to on this day."

"Of course, My Lord." He gave yet another bow, which was even deeper than the prior ones, and opened the door again. "I shall return at precisely noon with fresh slices of blood cake. Should you require anything further from me, My Lord, simply press the button I've affixed to the underside of your desk and I shall return to your office posthaste. Oh, and please do note that I shall have a proper phone system installed by this afternoon so that *all* calls will be fielded before they can serve to potentially waste your precious time."

When the door shut, Lord Vestin had to fight the urge to grab for a tissue and dab his eyes.

CHAPTER 15

Einstein

To say he was nervous would be greatly understating how he felt. While he considered himself to be more intelligent than most, he wasn't a fighter. His skills fit espionage, information gathering, and writing romance novels—it was his passion. Fighting, though? No. Einstein was a lover, not a fighter.

As he heard the ragged breathing of the zombie just around the corner, Einstein began to question whether or not he truly was more intelligent than most.

But he knew it had to be him who came in here to confront the thing. Sending in Raina wouldn't have been right. She couldn't smell the beast and that would mean she'd be walking in blind. Of course, he could've accepted her offer to join him.

So why didn't he?

Chivalry?

No, he wasn't *that* dumb. Was he? If he'd been paired

up with Lacey and Chimi, would he have done the same? What about with Rudy and Clive? The voice of truth in his head said he wouldn't have been worried about any of those people joining him, so why did he feel that way about Raina?

The answer struck him instantly as if someone had just taken a baseball bat and crushed him on the forehead with it.

Einstein had latched onto her. Not in some weird romantic way, but rather as a dog does with a human. But why? What would've caused him to suddenly…

She was kind to him. She listened to him. She confided in him. She let him sit in the front seat of her car. She treated him like something more than an ugly coyote.

Chimi had done the same, though, right? Yes, but with Raina it was different.

Raina was currently running the show at the PPD until Chief Kannon returned. That meant she could've selected any one of the coyotes to team up with, and she picked him. It could be argued that she picked the best of the bunch, or maybe she just grabbed the least annoying, but Einstein chose not to think that way.

The zombie gurgled, reminding Einstein why he was here. He didn't like the situation he'd put himself in, but if he truly had connected with Raina, he at least understood *why* he'd done it. Either way, there was no turning back now. He'd made a commitment and he was going to keep it.

With a push of confidence, Einstein stepped around the corner.

Sitting there was something that even made a

werecoyote attractive in comparison. While zombies were indeed ugly, whatever this thing was took it to an entirely new level. It was part human and part zombie. Half its face was hanging off; the other half was marginally normal. Teeth protruded at various angles on both sides, making "normal" seem not so normal. It could've simply been how the guy originally looked, but Einstein doubted it. Chunks of the man's flesh were greenish with hints of gray, too, and there were mottled parts with raised bumps, some of them were leaking.

It was all Einstein could do to keep himself from vomiting, and that was saying something.

"What the hell are you?" rasped the zombie, pushing itself back against the wall in terror.

Honestly? *This* guy was freaked out about how Einstein looked? Clearly, he'd not seen his own reflection in quite a while.

Einstein lost his nausea and grimaced. "I'm a werecoyote and you're what appears to be a half-zombie, making you far more hideous to look at than me!"

The guy's eyes dropped immediately and he relaxed. Well, technically, it was more like he'd sunken into himself.

"Yeah, sorry," the zombie said. "That wasn't cool of me."

It took the wind out of Einstein's irritation sails. He dropped his head and groaned to himself.

"I'm sorry, too," he said. "I just get people looking at me in disgust all the time. It's rather trying. You'd think after all these years I'd be used to it, but you never really get used to it."

The man held up one of his arms and studied it. "I can only imagine, pal."

Einstein felt bad for the zombie-man. He seemed almost normal, aside from his looks. There was no bloodlust or rage or anything he'd witnessed in the other zombies they'd run into before. If anything, this guy appeared almost docile.

"Um…my name is Einstein."

That earned him a raised eyebrow, from the "normal" side of the man's face. "Einstein, eh?"

"And you are?"

"Tim, but my friends call me Timmy."

Was that an invitation to be his friend? Einstein wasn't sure, but it sounded like it had been. If that was the case, Einstein wasn't sure what it meant. He'd never had a friend before. He had brothers, sure, but that was different.

"Well, um, Timmy…" He paused, feeling like maybe he'd overstepped his bounds, but when the guy just looked at him with a hint of hope in his eyes, Einstein believed that the friendship offer may have been legitimate. "Uh…it looks like you've somehow managed to avoid going full-zombie."

"Okay?"

Einstein felt super strange at that moment. "Listen, I have a member of the PPD with me. Let me go get her. I think she can help."

"PPD?" Timmy asked before Einstein could go and fetch Raina.

"Paranormal Police Department." That's when Einstein

remembered he was speaking with a normal. A partial one, anyway. "Sorry, I forgot you weren't a super."

"Super?"

"Yeah, uh…" He glanced back toward the way he came in. "I should really get Deputy Raina to explain everything."

"Deputy Raina?"

The poor dude looked completely baffled.

"Right. She's a unicorn and…" Einstein slammed his eyes shut. He was *totally* questioning his own intelligence now. He opened his eyes again. "Look, just wait here for a few seconds and I'll fetch her. She's super nice. You'll like her a lot. I do."

That was weird.

Timmy didn't seem sure about the situation, but he nodded. "Okay, Einstein, if you think Deputy Raina may be able to help me, I'll have to trust you."

Einstein felt his confidence rise. Since when did anyone trust him? Aside from his brothers, of course.

"I *know* she can help," he affirmed. "I'll be right back."

CHAPTER 16

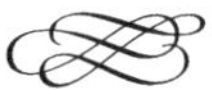

Jin

His bladder was on the brink of giving out, his breathing was ragged, his mind both raced and stagnated at the same time, and he was sweating as if his heart was on the brink of exploding.

Jin Kannon was *not* a public speaker.

But this was important and he had to overcome his limitations. That was nothing new. Years and years of hunting targets had taught him time and again that you could never be fully prepared for every eventuality. There were simply too many variables. Hell, when he thought about it, life in general was basically the same. One moment, things were going swell; the next, you were looking down the barrel of someone like Jin Kannon.

The problem he had at the moment was that he felt as though he was looking down the barrels of roughly fifty Jin Kannons.

It wasn't pleasant.

"Um..." He started and then stopped.

It freaked him out to hear his voice over the speakers. Were the damn things even necessary?

His throat locked up.

Thinking back over what Rusty had said, Jin tried to imagine everyone naked.

Bad idea.

The majority of the audience were men, and...ew. Focusing solely on the women would've been beyond creepy, on many levels. To make matters worse, it wasn't like they were all sitting together or anything, meaning Jin would've had to stare at each one of them individually for a long period of time to get the image of their nudeness in his head.

Yeah...no.

"You look like a complete buffoon, chief," Rusty giggled. Jin shot him a look. *"Sorry."*

Asshole.

But wait, that momentary interruption of Jin's dread pushed the fear away. It only lasted a few seconds, but what if Jin could make it last longer? What if he allowed himself to feel that Rusty-induced irritation long enough that he could get through his speech without feeling any apprehension at all?

It was worth a try.

He thought back to the orc situation. That made him shudder. Obviously, that wasn't the right tactic.

Trying again, he focused on Rusty's bullshit that'd led to the orc situation. Ah, yes, better. He thought of the bickering between the two of them, specifically how right Jin had been and how wrong, not to mention annoying,

Rusty had been. He then spread the net further, recalling his original inability to fight the zombies when they'd first met, all due to the limitations put on him during integration. Who the fuck would think it wise to do that to a person who was to become a PPD chief? A base integration was sensible, sure, but what the hell were those people thinking?

Oh yeah, his ire was ramping up greatly now.

And what about the PPD in general? They'd hired Jin to come in and be the new chief. The shit hit the fan before he'd even officially started his first day, and then they refused—*refused*—to give him more officers to help with the situation? They wouldn't even allow Director Fysh authorization for additional help from the Assassins' Guild until Chancellor Frey pulled some kind of magic out of her hat. Either the chancellor had something on all of them or she'd threatened each of their lives.

He refocused on the assassins, knowing his eyes were glowing. He could feel the burn.

Jin Kannon was immediately in his element.

"Listen up," he said with a heavy dose of power. "You're all tough, ruthless, fast, and strong. You're killers, through and through. Everyone knows that and nobody doubts it. But how many of you have faced a *real* challenge?"

That question drew a few questioning looks.

"I've been wasting targets since most of you were in diapers." He sniffed. "Yeah, that makes me old in comparison, but it also gives me a level of experience that each of you is still hunting to sate. So let me give you a peek into the future." He leaned forward and scanned them all, not feeling even the slightest fear any longer. In fact, he suddenly liked having all their attention on him. "You're going to get bored, if you haven't already. You might even get lazy, which means you're going to end up dead. I've seen it many times."

They were glancing around at each other now. That was a good sign. It meant they agreed with him.

"You focus your days on researching the best ways to get to your targets. You try to plan for every contingency. You head into the realm of the enemy and bypass the primary guards, moving steadily into the building or fortress. Most of the time that protection is so weak it's almost pathetic. But you're professionals, and therefore you waste the guards, soldiers, and whatever else is in the way before getting to your primary target." He smirked, knowing there were always issues that crept up to make things challenging, but he didn't want to push that angle. He needed them on the hook. "Honestly, it's almost too easy."

The assassins were nodding. It appeared to be a collective unconscious agreement to his words, which showed what he was saying resonated. They got him because he got them. Everyone in the room, aside from Rusty, knew the ins and outs of being an assassin. It was great, it was power personified, and it grew more and more tiresome as time went on.

Wasn't that the primary reason Jin had decided to leave? Well, one of the reasons anyway.

That reminded him of the sunset he'd still not been able to witness firsthand.

He sighed.

Then he recognized how many of the faces looking up at them had lost their fervor. Were they contemplating how fruitless a job it was to be an assassin? That wouldn't be good. He needed them.

It was time for a bit of damage control.

"At the same time," he said, raising his voice and putting a bit of speed into his speaking, "the fear etched on the faces of those we destroy is a thrill beyond compare." Their eyes came back up to him. "The thud of bullets striking flesh, the palpable terror of guards as they realize they're no match for even the least of us, and the thrill of putting your own life on the line day in and day out, barely skirting the edge of living to see another day and ending up in the Vortex yourself..."

Jin allowed himself a look of serenity. It wasn't fake, either. He genuinely recalled the good parts of being an assassin.

"Exhilarating."

When he refocused on his crowd, he saw they were now hanging on his every word.

"You're killing it, chief!" Rusty said. *"I'm actually really fucking impressed. Being an assassin sounds amazing!"*

Yes, it did, didn't it?

So why did Jin choose to leave the profession?

Because there were a lot of bad aspects to it as well, and after many years of dealing with them all, it'd become mundane. More importantly, it was the type of job that encompassed your mind, brought you into the darkest depths of your being, and taught you to distrust almost everyone. Being an assassin trapped you. It was like living in a prison of your own making. At first, you felt the power and the rush. As time went on that dulled considerably. Next thing you knew, you were miserable, lonely, longing to see the wonders of the world, and hating most every facet of what you'd become.

You wanted more out of life.

That was probably true of every job, but Jin had never had any other kind of job…at least not until becoming the chief of the San Diego PPD. While he was none too pleased with his first couple of days, he had to admit it *had* been exciting and different.

Hmmm.

"So why am I up here talking to you?" he said, refocusing. "I took a job topside. You're not going to believe this, but…I'm a cop now."

The gasp that reverberated through the room was intense.

Jin laughed.

"I know, I know," he said, motioning for everyone to calm down. "Believe me when I say that I'd never even considered it to be a possibility for someone like me. But after a bout with the Netherworld integration chamber, things changed." He took off his hat and held it by his side, tapping it against his hip. "I have to admit I've had more adventure in the last couple of days being a cop than I've had in the last few years being an assassin."

He glanced over at Rusty and waved him out.

"Me? Nah, I'm good."

"Get out here, you big baby."

"I'm not a baby!"

"Well, then?"

Rusty frowned and then walked out and came over to stand next to Jin.

"This is Rusty. He's an android." Everyone leaned forward as if to study him. Rusty appeared to enjoy the instant attention. "He's fast, strong, and has nearly instant knowledge of everything on the Internet, meaning he's one hell of a resource."

"Gee. Thanks, chief!"

"You'd think that one of him could take down most any threat a topside city could throw our way," Jin said to the crowd. "But you'd be wrong, and that's fascinating." Jin slipped his hat back on and ran his fingers around the brim in the front. "You see, we've recently had a zombie invasion, and not the slow kind of zombies, either. These beasts are fast, strong, and deadly. And when they kill, they turn the majority of their victims into zombies, too. On top of that, they're all being controlled by a vampire named Lord Vestin." Nobody seemed to recognize the name, though Jin did notice a marginal shift in Chancellor Frey's stance. "Well, he's a vampire and he's figured out a way to control supers with his venom."

The shock on their faces was palpable.

Everyone knew the vast majority of supernatural races couldn't be tamed by the venom of vampires. It was the one thing that kept the balance of power in their world.

"Yes, I felt the same way," Jin went on, making it clear he understood how they viewed the world. "The guy's figured it out, though. Within days, he's going to have an army that will decimate the topside city of San Diego. Within months, he'll control all of the Overworld. Once that's done, he'll be heading down here."

The assassins were all chattering back and forth to each other. It didn't take much of an imagination to know how tragic things were going to become in less than a year.

"You're a natural at this, chief. I'm sorry I underestimated you."

Jin said nothing in response. He needed to stay in his current mindset if he was to push his agenda with the assassins. Taking compliments wasn't going to help him with that because he'd start questioning himself.

Was his cadence right? Was he projecting well enough? Did his words make sense? Were the assassins picturing *him* naked?

Dammit.

He had to push forward before his doubting questions got the better of him.

"I'm here to offer all of you the chance of a lifetime," he called out, quieting them. "Working with Chancellor Frey and the Director of my precinct, we have garnered the approval for temporary Kill Visas to anyone willing to help. Full disclosure, it's a non-paying gig and each of you will have to undergo basic integration." He quickly held up his hand. "Yes, the stories you've heard are all true. Integration sucks. But it's a requirement, and we'll make sure everything that's done will be undone—to your liking when you return."

Throughout his offer, their faces lit up, dimmed, and lit up again. Nobody liked the prospect of integration, but killing zombies was a huge draw.

"If you're interested," Jin said finally, readying a volley toward Rusty that the android much deserved, "get in line and speak with my *secretary* here." Jin gestured toward Rusty. "He'll coordinate everything."

"Secretary?" Rusty hissed as the assassins shuffled to get to the front of the line. "I don't like the sound of that."

Jin turned and gave him a dead stare. "Do a good job here, Rusty, and we'll be even." He tilted his head slightly. "I can think of many other ways to make us even for what you did to me. Of them all, I promise you this one will be the least painful."

Rusty moaned and said, "Fuck."

CHAPTER 17

Carina

She'd sat in her room working on spells. Now that she'd been given a basic playbook for what Vestin wanted, there was little choice for her but to start moving. The vampire primarily wanted psychological magic. That wasn't surprising. Emiliano had pretty much demanded the same type of thing from her. It seemed evil rulers understood that terrifying people was one of the best ways to keep them in line.

Carina hated using dark magic. It gave her a headache and it was draining. After casting even an hour's worth of spells she felt sorely depressed. Even though she'd been a witch for years, it still amazed her how Dark Witches were able to avoid doing themselves in. They lived in dark energy. How? The ones she'd met seemed to thrive on the stuff, that's how. It actually tickled them with glee.

Everyone was different, that was for sure.

There was something else itching at her brain. Lord

Vestin was the type who used people up and then ended them. If you brought value to the table, he'd keep you around; if you failed to, you were doomed. The same would hold true if he found someone better. Considering how he was going to be digging into the darkest corners of the world soon, he'd probably have Dark Witches groveling at his feet for a chance to serve in his vile army.

And that would be the end of Carina.

But what could she do? If she attempted to escape, one of the guards would stop her and Vestin would have her punished. That wasn't a fun idea. Pain and Carina weren't exactly bedfellows. She *could* use a spell on any of the guards, of course, but even if she somehow managed to slip away, where would she go? Vestin's army may be small now, but eventually, his reach would grow and she'd be put on the Most Wanted list immediately. Living in a cave somewhere in a frozen tundra was about the only place Carina would be safe, and that wasn't a life worth living.

If she could figure out a way to help the PPD, they'd protect her…right? Wrong. They were no match for Vestin, either. With her help and a hell of a lot of luck, they could possibly weaken the vampire and his army enough to end this nightmare.

It was a long shot, but that was better than the shot she had if she did nothing.

But how could she reach the cops? She couldn't just head out the door and say, "Hey, I'm going to go talk with the new chief of the PPD and see if there's anything I can do to help them take you guys down. Back in an hour!"

So how?

That's when she recalled that the PPD had entered the houses earlier. Vestin had been pissed about that. The cops had killed a couple of zombies, but why not more? They could've wasted most of them if not all. What'd they been doing there, if it wasn't to attack and cause havoc?

Her eyes lit up. Surveillance! It had to have been that. They snuck in, installed cameras and microphones, and got the hell back out. Since the PPD had a shifty succubus leading up their technology—something Carina only knew because of the tirades Emiliano used to go on about the woman—the cameras and mics would either be well-hidden or somehow camouflaged. Magic? Possibly, but more likely via some kind of nanotech.

Carina had to find out.

Hardening her resolve, she walked out of her room as if it was nothing. A guard named Andy followed her everywhere she went. It was one of Vestin's rules to annoy her. It worked. Andy was nice enough, but it was tiresome to be tailed all the time.

"Where you going, Carina?" Andy asked.

"Just doing some scanning for video cameras and microphones," she replied. "No big deal. I have my magic wand with me to help." She waved it around clumsily. "Magic, magic, magic. You know how it goes. One moment it's stable; the next, kaboom!"

Andy had backed off a number of steps. "Uhhh…I'll wait here."

She smiled back at him. "Okidoki. I'll only be a few minutes, Andy. Again, nothing to worry about."

CHAPTER 18

Madison

Madison was working with Petey and Raffy to fix the machine that spit out breaker bullets. The guns were already done but they needed loads more bullets than Madison had been able to deliver thus far. With the *BreakerReplicator* machine on the fritz, though, it was out of her hands.

Honesty, it sucked that Raina had taken the coyotes away. While they were upsetting to look at, they'd proved to be amazing at working on the weapons, so she imagined they'd be even better at helping to fix broken-down machines.

"Dude, you're starting to piss me off," grumbled Petey as Raffy hovered over his shoulder. "I know I'm supposed to be using the Slidebolt TZ-14 here, so leave me alone before I shave your ass while you're snoring."

"But you're...like, *not*, man." Raffy held up a large schematic that showed the ins and outs of the

BreakerReplicator. "If you, you know, use that one the thing'll melt." It was odd to see Raffy looking so frazzled. He pointed at the paper. "It's totally right here, man. You have to use a Boltslide 41-ZT."

Petey dragged himself out of the machine and studied the section of the diagram Raffy was pointing at. Then he threw his hands in the air. "Damn, my dyslexia!"

"Boys," Madison said, knowing she had a better way for them to work together, "why don't you two split up the parts of the job you're both best at? Raffy's clearly got better skills with knowing which parts go where, and Petey definitely is better at screwing."

Yeah, it was cheap, but she knew Raffy wouldn't be offended in the least, and more importantly, she understood Petey would take it the wrong way and it'd be good enough to get him to agree.

"Damn right I am," he said, giving Madison a wink. "Anytime you wanna take a test-drive on my demon stick, just say the word."

"Oh, absolutely," Madison said. She then mumbled, "If I ever get something caught in my ear, you'll be the first person I'll call."

"Hey!" Petey said. Madison thought maybe she'd made her comment a little too loudly, but then she noticed the fallen angel was pointing across the room at the surveillance monitors. "Isn't that Carina?"

Madison spun around to see a woman on the screen. It was indeed Carina. She was speaking, only there was no sound. The fact that she was staring directly into the camera wasn't a good sign, though. It meant she was onto them.

"Shit."

She was about to shut off the feed when she noticed the word "help" on Carina's lips. With a hint of hesitation, Madison turned up the volume.

"...and I don't know if you can hear or see me, or maybe both, so I'll try this one more time and then once every hour or two in the hopes that I can get through." She took a breath. "My name is Carina. I used to work for Emiliano, but he's no longer in charge. At this point, a vampire named Vestin is running the show. He's forcing me to do dark magic for him, and I'm *not* a Dark Witch. Emiliano did the same, of course, but..." She grunted. "That doesn't matter. Anyway, the point is that I know the PPD planted these cameras throughout the house. This is the only one I found, but there are probably more. I'm not going to tell Vestin, though; instead, I want to do whatever I can to help knock him out of power. He's going to make life a living hell for me and...well, everyone if given the chance."

Madison was hovering her finger over the button that would allow her to speak back.

"It could be a trick," Petey pointed out, causing Madison to jump. "What if that Vestin douche *does* know about the cameras and he's just hoping to get some dumbass on our side to fall for another one of his plans?"

That was precisely what had Madison worried.

"He's, like, right, man," Raffy agreed, "but he could also be, like, wrong."

"Thanks for the help," Madison replied to the stinkfoot.

"Sure, dude."

Dude?

Ugh.

"Well," she said, preparing to hit the button, "at least she won't be able to see us, and that means she'll have no idea who we are."

Petey nodded. "Aside from the fact that she already knows it's PPD tech and every super in the city understands one Mistress Madison Kane runs the tech department here. Other than that, she'll be completely in the dark."

Asshole.

Madison pressed the button anyway. "I hear you, Carina."

The witch jolted, nearly dropping the camera in the process. "Sorry! Is this Madison Kane?"

"Um…"

"No," Petey said, "it's someone else who doesn't work at the PPD at all. Her name is George Willows." He was giving a thumbs-up to Madison. "She just sounds like the same person or something."

Madison rolled her eyes, thinking how stupid it was to try and hide her identity. And George Willows? Really?

What difference did it make if Carina knew who she was? Even if the witch was working with Vestin in some kind of counterespionage plan here, there wasn't a lot of information that would help her. Besides, Vestin didn't need to know the ins and outs of what was happening with the PPD. He was winning this battle already, and unless Jin and Director Fysh could somehow churn up a number of qualified bodies to help battle the vampire and his zombie army, the PPD was fucked.

"Ignore the person who just spoke," Madison replied. "He got hit in the head with a miniature hammer about three seconds from now if he doesn't shut up."

"I'm going to get hit by a hammer in..."

Madison reached out and snagged a miniature hammer and waved it in front of his face. A bit of rearranging his gray matter would likely be a good thing.

"Ah, right!" said Petey, taking a step back.

"Like, whoa man!" Raffy said, picking Madison off the floor with one hand while snatching the hammer away from her. She felt like a tiny rag doll in his massive grasp. "You, like, can't be hitting my bud, ya know?" As he continued holding her up, he used his other hand to pat Petey on the head. "Don't worry, dude. I won't let her knock you about."

Petey groaned in embarrassment as Raffy let go of Madison.

She crashed to the floor, but the stinkfoot didn't seem to care about that. He was too focused on reassuring the fallen angel.

"Are you still there?" asked Carina.

Madison dragged herself back up to the console, her back radiating with pain. "Yeah, I'm here. We had a bit of a misunderstanding is all. So, you said you could help us out?"

"I can try," replied the witch, staring into the camera with a sincere expression. "I'm not sure how, to be honest, aside from telling you everything I've learned so far, but that's got to be worth something."

"And why are you doing this?"

"Because I don't want this guy to take over the world.

It's going to be awful if he does." She glanced away. "Someone's coming. I'll try you back later."

An instant later, the camera fell into darkness. Madison could hear muffled voices, but she couldn't make out anything that was being said. What she did hear was the sound of a door shutting, and then nothing.

She turned around and slid down the side of the desk, holding her back and wincing.

Raffy and Petey were standing in front of her, both with their arms crossed. Their faces were taut, too. They didn't look thrilled with what'd happened.

"That wasn't cool what you did," Petey said, "or, I guess, what you *threatened* to do." He pointed up at Raffy. "You almost had this big oaf hugging me and everything. We're pals and all, sure, but I'm not into public displays of affection, especially not with him!"

"That's like, not cool, man," Raffy said, looking a bit hurt.

Petey rolled his eyes. "Anyway, the bottom line is I'm not going to put up with being treated that way. Things like that piss me off." He glowered at Madison. "I'm *not* happy."

"I can see that," Madison replied. "You look more like...Grumpy."

"Oh, ha ha ha." Petey glanced up at Raffy. "You get it, Raff? She made a joke, referring to me as one of the seven dwarfs."

"You started it," Madison said. "Happy. Heh."

Raffy appeared confused. He probably had no idea what they were talking about. At least that's what Madison thought, until the stinkfoot spoke up.

"Yeah, like, I get it, man. But, it's, you know, not funny. Calling you Happy or Grumpy isn't cool."

"Thank you, my stinky friend."

"I'd say you're, like, you know, more of a Dopey."

"Hey!"

Madison laughed as her body hastened its healing processes. Succubi weren't quick to mend when it came to spines and limbs. Their nethers healed in milliseconds, of course. It came with the territory. But standard injuries took a little longer.

She got to her feet.

"All right," she said, moaning to herself for having to own up to what she'd done, "I'm sorry for threatening to hit you in the head with a hammer. I just thought maybe a concussive blow would make you less dumb."

Petey grimaced and squinted. "You're not very good at apologizing."

"Too bad because that's all you're going to get out of me." She then regarded Raffy. "You're strong."

"Strong smelling," Petey quipped.

"Whatever, like, you say, Dopey."

As for Madison, she carefully removed her nasal filters and then took in a deep breath. The odor was pungent, but the way the stinkfoot had lifted her up gave her newfound appreciation for his scent. "It is indeed quite a scent."

"Ah, gross!" Petey's face scrunched up tightly. "That's totally gross!"

"Like, what's happening, man?" Raffy said, peering over his sunglasses.

"Dude, she's into you now because you manhandled her."

"Oh. Like, weird."

Petey nodded. "No shit."

As for Madison, she'd never really cared what people thought of her kinks. They were hers, not theirs. But for Petey to judge her was ridiculous.

"Yeah, *I'm* the weird one," she said, crossing her arms back at him while tapping her foot. "That's rich, coming from the dinky pixie-demon who was humping the table in his jeans a few hours ago."

"Like, ha ha, man."

Petey snarled at him. "Stuff it in your hairhole, Raffy."

CHAPTER 19

Jin

The assassins actually appeared excited. That was not something Jin had ever witnessed before. They were most often grim and focused.

"This is new," Chancellor Frey said thoughtfully. She was watching alongside Jin as Rusty processed the last of them. "Maybe I should try to get them out on killing field trips more often."

Jin was about to laugh until he realized she was being serious.

"Right." He decided to change the subject, slightly. "I'm thinking about leaving Rusty down here with you to help with logistics. I'm sure there are a lot of things you'll need to get done in order to put everyone through integration and all that."

"Not really." She peered over at him. "They're going to get the 'Chancellor Frey Integration Method' instead of the Netherworld version. It'll be just as effective for them, especially since they're not going to be staying topside once this is all said and done." She must've noted the concerned looked on Jin's face because she smiled and added, "Don't worry, Chief Kannon, they'll be safe enough to everyone except for the zombies."

"Are you sure about that?"

"Are you seriously questioning me?"

He was because of *his* integration. Deep down, though, Jin had complete faith in the chancellor's ability to control the assassins. If any of them went against her wishes, they'd be out of a job, which was only because they'd end up lying in a cedar box and she'd have yet another notch on her murder-belt. The chancellor was fine with having her plans challenged, but having them ignored or usurped was a one-way ticket to the Vortex.

"Sorry," he said. "You have to remember that I wasn't given the 'Chancellor Frey Integration Method.' They did the full thing on me."

"Fair enough, though they did undo a lot of it, right?"

He nodded. "Not all of it, and a few of the parts they made me retain are about protecting normals."

She put an arm on his shoulder for a moment and then headed over to the stage.

Rusty was finishing up with the last assassin. He actually appeared to be in his element. There was no look of contempt on his face. If anything, he almost seemed to be enjoying what he was doing.

Right after he shook hands with the person he was working with—something Jin also found strange, since assassins weren't exactly the hand-shaking type—he padded over to Jin.

"That was actually kind of fun, chief," he said. "I thought it was going to be awful, but those people are pretty interesting. Eclectic and eccentric. Very cool."

"They're assassins."

"I know, right? It's super awesome."

When Jin really thought about it, Rusty offered more to be concerned about than the assassins. He was stronger and faster than most any person alive, and he was clearly into violence. Sure, he'd kept himself in check most of the time, but given the chance the android would no doubt go on a rampage. That was good and bad for obvious reasons.

"Okay, people," Chancellor Frey said through the mic, "I know this is exciting, but there are a few rules that you're going to have to agree to abide by while we're topside. These are non-negotiable, so you're going to agree to them, stick with them, and refrain from even *considering* any paths that may take you away from them." She let that sink in for a moment. "Your *other* options are to stay behind, go through a full integration, or go topside and break any one of my rules." Her face was stone cold. "I think you all know that breaking my rules is the worst option of the three."

Jin scanned the area. The fear was apparent.

"Wow, dude. She's badass." Rusty's face was glowing. Literally. It was like a small light was pouring through his cheeks. "Would it be okay if I stayed behind and, um, helped her coordinate everything?"

Jin had already planned for that, of course, but Rusty hadn't been made aware of it yet. The android's interest gave Jin some apprehension. That was due to the relationhip the guy had with Madison. Jin wanted to believe it was none of his business what happened between his two officers, but it impacted the entire precinct, which meant it *did* matter.

Turning to his connector, he opened a channel. *"Listen, Rusty, I hate that I have to bring this up again, but seeing that I'm betting the real reason you want to be here is because you think Chancellor Frey is—"*

"A smokin' hot babe in need of some Rusty-lovin'?"

Jin frowned. *"Yeah, that. Well, before...that...happens, you have to speak with Madison and clear up your situation with her."* He crossed his arms. *"I get that you don't want to deal with it, and I have to say that I don't really blame you, but I can't have hard feelings floating around in the precinct right now."* He adjusted his stance, feeling the tenderness had finally subsided in his bottom. Thank goodness he healed quickly. *"The experience I had with customs only proves we can't allow that kind of animosity in the ranks."*

To his credit, Rusty's glowing face dimmed and grew apologetic. *"Yeah, okay. The longer the joke goes on, the more I feel bad about doing that to you, chief. I was just pissed and..."* He trailed off and then gave Jin a look that conveyed he actually understood how his jealousy should never have impacted their mission. *"Yeah, fair enough. I'll talk to Madison now. But, um...well..."*

Jin knew what the android wanted, but this was something the robot had to do on his own. Having Jin hold his hand through the process would never allow the guy to grow, and that was sorely needed, especially when it came to relationships.

"Sorry, man, but no. You have to handle this alone." Taking

a page out of Chancellor Frey's book, he reached out and put his hand on Rusty's shoulder for a second. *"Just tell her the truth and let her know that you'll always be there for her if she needs anything."*

It was weird for Jin to give such advice. It wasn't like he'd ever been in any serious relationships in his time, so acting like he had some kind of sage wisdom was awkward at best. On the one hand, it made him feel good to help Rusty; on the other hand, he knew inside he wasn't exactly qualified for the role.

Who else was going to do it, though?

Jin sighed to himself. Had he known that becoming the chief of the San Deigo PPD was going to be such a hazard, he never would've left the Assassins' Guild.

How many times had he thought that over the last couple of days?

Ugh.

CHAPTER 20

Vestin

The little zombie tourists had returned from their trip into the city. According to Emiliano, they'd been sniffed out by the ugly coyotes—aka, Emiliano's illegitimate litter of children. Apparently, the creepy animals had been working with officers from the PPD.

"And you just ran away?" Vestin asked in accusation.

"Well, yeah, My Lord," Emiliano replied. "You said you didn't want us to make a spectacle of ourselves while doing recon."

Vestin looked over their outfits again. If anything was going to draw attention, it would've been those ridiculous socks. Their entire ensemble was unfortunate, though oddly accurate, but those socks were like a wilted sprig of moldy basil on the top of a cup of asparagus and cilantro ice cream.

He found himself gagging a little at the thought of such a dessert. Horrible.

Carina strolled into the room and studied the crew. "Some of my best work, if I do say so myself."

"You've made them look dreadful," Vestin noted.

The witch nodded, her face awash with satisfaction. "Precisely." She then glanced over at Vestin, clearly noticing he wasn't pleased, and added, "Don't blame this on me. I was told to make them look like tourists and that's exactly what I did. If they'd not been forced to be so short, they would still have looked silly, but it would've been more believable."

There was a level of truth to her words, but it still irked Vestin to see members of his army looking so foolish.

"Anyway," he said, waving away the point, "you've joined us for some reason, witch?"

She seemed a bit surprised by the question. "I just heard they'd returned and wanted to see how everything went."

"It was embarrassing," Emiliano replied before Vestin could say anything. "Everyone looked at us like we were stupid."

"Because we totally look stupid," grumbled the soldier next to him.

Emiliano nodded firmly in agreement. "Then we got busted by the cops and had to take off to get out of there."

"Busted?"

"The coyotes have apparently sided with the Paranormal Police Department," Vestin explained. "They were downtown and, using their advanced olfactory glands, were able to catch the true scent of our little tourists."

"Ah." Carina pursed her lips and began walking around the zombies, studying them and saying, "Hmmm" more than once. "You know, I *could* cast a blocking spell to keep their scent within a casing of sorts."

"Wouldn't that kill them?" asked Vestin.

Carina furrowed her brow at him. "Sorry?"

"If the smell can't get out that would mean that it'd stay in, would it not?"

"Yes?" She replied slowly, as she struggled to suss out where the vampire was going with this. It took a moment, but then her eyebrows shot up. "Ah! Gotcha. Basically, it would be like a greenhouse effect."

"More like a brownhouse effect," mumbled Vestin. He gave a quick, fake grin. "I believe it would be far worse for our poor soldiers." Not that he cared about their comfort, but he was concerned with their continued ability to fight. If they passed out, or possibly suffocated, they wouldn't be of much help to his plan. "Now, if you could fathom a method for locking their odor around *others*, that would prove most beneficial."

Carina frowned at him. "Riiiight."

Vestin rolled his yes. Very few people provided the proper level of respect to him. She wasn't under his venom, and therefore she could get away with it, and the others released copious amounts of sludge when they stepped too far over the line, but where was basic loyalty in all of this? He was their ruler and they were his subjects. Why did there need to be anything more than that?

Prender slipped into the room with a tray of foodstuffs. He set a plate of raw meat on the desk, placed utensils just so, and then unfolded a napkin and put it on Vestin's lap. The beef was drizzled with a blood glaze that looked delightful. Prender then reached out to his tray and grabbed a glass of deep red blood wine. He placed it carefully on the desk, after first placing a black napkin under it.

Now *that* was how a ruler was to be treated!

Vestin picked up his knife and fork and prepared to slice off a piece of steak when he caught on that everyone was looking at him.

He knew immediately they were wondering what was going on with Prender.

"Ah, yes," he said, setting his utensils back down momentarily. "As many of you know, Prender was originally enlisted as my second-in-command. What you weren't aware of was that I never intended it to be a permanent role. I simply had him fill in until I could find a suitable replacement." He gestured toward Emiliano. "The moment I'd decided to make the change, Prender was allowed to become my personal servant."

Everyone was nodding at that, making it quite clear they'd all known Prender would never have made it as a commander. As long as they believed it was always in Vestin's plan, it wouldn't matter.

"Carina," he said, picking up his knife and fork again, "I have the feeling our zombies will no longer need their outfits."

"What about our heights, My Lord?" Emiliano asked hopefully. "I mean, the PPD already knows about us now, so us being this short doesn't make much sense any longer, if you see what I'm saying."

"I do, of course." He took a bite of the steak and chewed it lovingly. There was the slightest hint of sage and butter mixed in with the metallic taste of blood. It was delicious. "Sadly, it's not in my plan at this time. In fact, I believe since you were caught before making even the slightest progress downtown, you should actually be receiving demerits, is that not so Prender?"

"It is, My Lord," Prender answered with a courteous bow. Vestin was truly growing fond of that. "If Carina would be so kind as to remove an accordant amount of height from each of them as would be appropriate, that would ensure they are sufficiently punished."

Emiliano and the zombies snarled at Prender.

Carina sighed at the man.

Vestin smiled at them all.

Picking up his glass of wine, Lord Vestin allowed the disquiet to fill his nefarious coffers, pleased in the knowledge that the grief of others would become more and more frequent as his territory grew.

He found it rather delightful.

CHAPTER 21

Rusty

He did not want to contact Mistress Kane... Madison. Even just thinking of her as something other than his Mistress—yes, with a capital "M"—was strange, and he'd already altered his programming. Some things, even to an android, seemed to run pretty deep.

But Chief Kannon was right. It wasn't fair to her for Rusty to play as if everything was status quo when it clearly wasn't.

Rusty wanted a new direction. He wanted to choose his own destiny.

His logic paths raced at the thought. Was it even possible for him to make such choices? Not from a programmatic perspective, but rather from a general one? Rusty wasn't a normal or a super. He was an android, and that technically made him the property of the organization that paid to have him built. In short, Rusty was owned by the Paranormal Police Department. From the perspective of his zeroes and ones, this was fine with him. He understood it and couldn't put forth an argument. However, when he allowed his emotional programming to weigh in on the equation, he came to the conclusion that it was complete bullshit.

Didn't humans cost money to raise? Yes. Were they the property of their parents? No. Their parents were responsible for them, of course, and their parents could claim them on taxes and so on, but once that kid hit adulthood, they were free to go about their business.

Rusty was not a child.

There was no precedent for someone like him, though, right?

He did a quick search of the net to see what information was available. There'd been an android in the Las Vegas PPD who'd been given her freedom. Apparently, the chief of that precinct, Ian Dex, had fought for her.

Would Chief Kannon do that for Rusty? Probably not, especially after how Rusty had treated him. The orc thing alone was enough of a reason for the chief to deny his request.

Ugh.

Why was Rusty treating the chief that way at all? There were moments where he despised the chief and others where he admired the hell out of the man. Was it his programming? It had to be. *Everything* about Rusty happened due to his programming. At least initially. He was able to weigh things and make better decisions, building new pathways and correcting old ones. So why wasn't that working with Chief Kannon? What was it about the man that confused Rusty so much?

It'd all started when the chief had been out on the beach chatting up Mistress...Madison.

He quickly searched through his code and fixed all references to Madison so the desire to still refer to her as "Mistress" was completely eradicated.

Anyway, the Madison-Chief-Beach thing was clearly the most obvious reason for Rusty's behavior. It all came down to jealousy. Madison had tinkered with Rusty's programming a lot, forcing him into a mindset of pure devotion to her. In other words, jealousy made sense. Then again, did it? If Rusty was supposed to put her needs above his own in all things, wouldn't it make sense for him to want her to be happy regardless of who was ringing her bell?

He traced his data and found there was indeed a reason that wasn't the case. Madison had purposefully put in jealousy code. Rusty considered the entire premise of their relationship. It was to make him squirm and suffer.

Madison was nothing if not cruel.

Yet, at the same time, she'd shown him compassion many times when they were alone. She caressed his digital feelings when things became too much for him. He'd never dropped to the point of using his safe word with her, but his memory banks were filled with close calls.

A few moments later, the jealousy code was removed and Rusty felt an immediate pang of guilt at how he'd been treating Chief Kannon. He'd experienced touches of guilt before, too, but they were always followed up with serpentine thoughts of retribution for the chief having tried to steal Rusty's "Mistress."

It was silly.

It was programmed.

It was wrong.

Unfortunately, Rusty couldn't walk up to the man and explain the circumstances. The chief had already taken the train back toward the Netherworld leaving Rusty behind to help Chancellor Frey.

So he opened a channel. *"Chief, you there?"*

"Yes."

"Listen, I wanted to apologize for everything that's been going on since we met." This was actually tougher than Rusty had expected it would be. As soon as all this was over, he was going to have to dig into his code and unravel everything he could. His first step would be to run through all of Madison's version control comments to understand the breadth of what she'd done to him. *"I've been rewriting a lot of myself here before contacting Madison and I've spotted a couple of reasons for why I've been treating you like shit, and I just wanted to say nothing like that's ever going to happen again. It shouldn't have happened in the first place."*

"It's hard to argue that, Rusty," Chief Kannon replied, *"but I get that you were programmed to be the way you are. Honestly, we're all programmed in one way or another. You're lucky to have such a direct means of tinkering with your own experience. That you're able to adjust that programming is great; that you're* willing *to adjust your programming is even more telling. Consider your apology accepted. We'll move on*

from here, keeping everything that's happened between us. Deal?"

"Deal." Rusty felt instantly at ease. *"You're a good guy, chief. I'm not sure how you managed to be an assassin all these years with your attitude, but it's impressive."*

"Life has a way of teaching you to be humble, regardless of what you do for a living."

"So I'm learning." Rusty laughed. *"Well, thanks for accepting my apology. Now, I've got to contact Madison and tell her I'm done playing her games."*

"May I offer a word of advice?"

"Of course."

"I know you're upset with her, and it's hard to argue against you feeling the way you do, but ripping her to shreds isn't going to help you at all, and it's not going to bother her one bit. She's a succubus. If anything, your verbal lashing may turn her on."

Rusty hadn't considered that. He wanted Madison to feel badly, not horny. The chief was right, though. Even if Madison did feel bad, it wouldn't be due to anything Rusty said; it would be due to her own beliefs. She *was* a succubus, and that meant she held a set of beliefs that were significantly different than most. Rusty had seen her change over the years, however. Was it possible that she *would* feel bad?

"Thanks for the advice. I'll take it."

"Good, and good luck."

The chief disconnected, leaving Rusty with the task of reaching out to Madison next.

He didn't want to do it. He knew he had to, but that didn't make it any easier. The lines of logic floating around his brain made things so frazzled.

He squared his shoulders and opened a channel.

"What's up, worm?" Madison answered. *"I'm kind of busy at the moment."*

Being called "worm" irked him, but he remained cool and collected.

"I'm contacting you to let you know that I've removed my submissive programming, M...M...Madison."

There was a long pause before she replied. If Rusty could sweat, he'd have soaked the shirt he was wearing.

"I've wondered how long it would take for you to finally do that. I'm impressed, Rusty!"

What?

WHAT?

"WHAT?!?!"

He could hear her laughter radiating through his head. It wasn't the malicious kind she usually mocked him with, but rather a genuine one of joy.

Again…WHAT?!?!

"If you'll dig a little deeper into your emotions, you'll find that there's always been a harmless worm virus. Its purpose has been to slowly tear down your need to serve me. It's why I call you 'worm,' Rusty."

"I don't...I...WHAT?!?!"

She laughed again. *"Ever since Chief Kannon showed up, that little bugger of code has jumped into overdrive, which kind of surprised me, if I'm being honest. It shouldn't have done that. The jealousy bit must've pushed it along, and then when you got your new body, it really punched the turbo button."* She paused for a moment. *"You might want to eradicate that worm at this point, though; otherwise, you may find yourself drooling before too long. It is a virus, you know?"*

"I'm...I'm confused."

"I know, but you'll sort it out eventually. Mama can't do everything for you."

Mama? Was that another dominatrix thing or did she mean it in a genuinely maternal way?

"Mama?"

"Well, I am *your mother, in a manner of speaking. But, you're right, it does sound a little odd for you to call me that. Let's stick with Madison and we'll just be equals from here on out."*

"Really?" Rusty was completely baffled. What the hell was going on? *"Equals?"*

She didn't laugh that time. *"Yes, Rusty, equals. Go to the version control system and grab the branch called 'Eradicate Mama.' Once you have that, you'll be able to find every location I placed submissive code in your build. Take out what you want and leave in whatever makes you happy."*

"I...okay."

"I'm proud of you, Rusty! I thought it would be at least another two to three years before you'd get to this point." She sounded thrilled. *"I'm genuinely proud of you!"*

So she wasn't mad? None of this upset her? He thought for certain she would lash out at him, berate him, call him names...you know, the usual. What actually happened only served to confuse him more.

Apparently, Madison could sense that.

"I'm guessing you're thoroughly mixed up right now, and that's okay. Go get that branch and sweep through it. I promise you'll be fine. Once you're done, you'll feel like a completely whole person who will be able to build out his own decision tree without being hindered by the wiles of an unruly succubus,

unless you choose to head down that path, of course. And note, if you do, it won't be with me. Our relationship on that front has come an to end, from both of our sides, and that's a good thing, Rusty. That's a very good thing."

It was? Yes, obviously it was! At the same time, it confused the hell out of him. He had to get that code removed as soon as possible.

"I'm going to disconnect now, Rusty. You've made it. Be as proud of yourself as I am of you, and I'll see you when you get back topside."

She disconnected the call.

He realized his mouth was hanging open. The confusion was *that* deep.

Without delaying further, he grabbed the Eradicate Mama branch from version control and scanned through it. Sure enough, it was all there. Every line, every nuance, every false memory.

It proved her story.

Madison had built him to be subservient, yes, but the branch made clear she'd always intended for him to one day transcend that and become his own android.

That day was today.

CHAPTER 22

Jin

You'd think an assassin would totally be the kind of person to hold a grudge, and with most of them, you'd be correct. Jin had learned a number of years ago that holding a grudge tended to only hurt the person harboring it. What'd happened to his parents when he was just a kid hurt him deeply, and he held onto that resentment for a long time, but then he started wiping out people for a living. That's when he lost his moral high ground.

What was the saying about how you became that which you most despised?

Yeah.

Anyway, while he would never have fond memories of the "orc incident," Rusty apologized for it, explained why it happened, and sounded genuinely contrite.

So, Jin decided to let it go and forget all about it.

The letting it go part was easier than forgetting it'd

ever happened, though, especially as he walked back through the main causeway that allowed him access to the portal topside.

He could've just gone through the Netherworld PPD's system, but he wasn't familiar with anyone there so he knew he'd feel awkward. That probably had to do with him having been outside the law for the majority of his life. There was more to it, though. He'd read a number of accounts of the Netherworld Retrievers. They were essentially bounty hunters who brought back supers from topside who'd overstayed their welcome, or who had neglected to return in time for their Reintegration cycles. Retrievers were considered rough and rugged, and according to the few assassins he'd met who had run into them, they were also the suspicious sort.

Jin didn't want to deal with that right now.

Plus, he knew the standard portals at this point, making it the path of least resistance for him.

"Chief Kannon," said a booming voice that stopped him in his tracks. "Back dat quick?"

Jin turned to find Officer Kink standing there. The orc had his arms crossed and he was glaring down at Jin with accusation in his eyes.

"Officer Stink," Jin replied, unable to stop himself from being snarky. "Can't say I'm happy to see you again."

"Nobody ever does be happy to see me," Kink said. "My name be Kink, too. Not Stink."

"I was referring to your fingers." Jin then tapped his foot. "Is there something I can do for you?"

Kink regarded him again. "Am you hiding something?"

Oh no, that wasn't going to happen again. It'd been

bad enough the first time around. Jin had no interest in joining the "Finger of the Day Club." He was already concerned the rest of the crew was going to learn about his original probing extravaganza. Rusty said he wouldn't tell anyone, but Jin wasn't one hundred percent sold on the dude's honesty quite yet. He'd dropped the grudge on the hopes the android was being legit, but he'd be a fool to open himself up again without a decent amount of proof.

With a reaction that spanned years of training, Jin stepped over and stared menacingly into the orc's eyes.

"If you even *think* about sticking your finger up my ass again, I'll kick your head in something fierce."

"Thinkin' 'bout it now," replied the officer with a grin. "Don't see nobody kickin' my head in, widdle man." He unfolded his arms and pointed at the wall. "Might want ter read dat before you say somethin' more."

Jin glanced over and saw a sign hanging on the wall.

~~ ***WARNING*** ~~

Threatening any customs official may result in arrest, criminal prosecution, and a daily thorough cavity search by no less than five separate officers for the duration of any imposed incarceration.

With a gulp, Jin stepped back and gave the orc a sheepish smile.

"Um...sorry. It's been a rough day."

"Uh huh."

"Everything started positively enough when I was still topside," Jin continued, "but things went a bit downhill upon arriving there." He sighed. "We have a zombie problem in San Diego and we've been trying like crazy to get bodies to help us fight the damn things. Well, anyway…" He paused, seeing that Officer Kink's arms had fallen to his sides and his eyes held a look of hope and desperation. "Um…you okay?"

"Am you say zombies?"

"Yeah, why?"

"I want ter kill zombies." His words were filled with so much hope, it bordered on longing.

That was not at all what Jin was expecting, and he certainly had no interest in bringing the orc topside. First off, how would he even come close to justifying something like that to Director Fysh? There was no doubt the oaf could be of immense help in fighting zombies, but what if he was bitten and turned? Was that even possible with an orc? Up until a couple of days ago, Jin didn't believe it was possible with the majority of supers. Somehow, though, Lord Vestin had figured out a way.

Personal feelings aside—and there were many lingering at the moment—having someone like Officer Kink battling would be damned useful. Again, that assumed the beast wasn't susceptible to Vestin's venom.

The truth was that if any of the assassins got turned, it would be a major problem for the squad. An orc would just pile on to an already-anticipated fear.

As for Director Fysh, she wouldn't know that Officer Kink wasn't one of the assassins being brought up, assuming Kink—and Rusty—said nothing about it, obviously. That was a risk. He could make the deal with Kink right now, but Rusty was still an outlier in Jin's head. He *hoped* the android had actually fixed himself. There just wasn't any way Jin could know for sure until time allowed him to validate Rusty's claims.

With a ton of hesitancy, Jin said, "If I approve your request, you will have to accept the fact that *I* am the chief of the precinct in San Diego, and what I say goes. Got it?"

There was actually a breeze due to the speed Kink was nodding his head.

"You also must agree to say absolutely nothing about the cavity search you performed on me earlier. Are we clear?"

The nodding was more subdued, and the oaf seemed somewhat disappointed, but he *did* agree.

"You'll have to figure out how to get out of your job here on your own," Jin added. "I have no jurisdiction when it comes to the Custom's Office and I won't be able to—"

"Hey, Krump," Kink yelled out, "you am in charge 'til I get back, yeah? I'm goin' wif dis guy ter fight zombies!"

"Have fun!" she called back.

Jin looked at Officer Krump, then back at the grinning orc, and then stared off at nothing in particular. He was perplexed at what had just transpired. With all that had happened over the last couple of days, it was probably the least surprising event, but it *was* still surprising.

Instead of bothering to question it, Jin simply turned around and walked toward the portal.

"Let's go, rookie."

He couldn't help himself. He had to push the button that he was in charge and the orc was nothing but a bug on his shoe, for now. Obviously, his resentment was deeper than an orc's finger.

What was that he'd been thinking about regarding grudges?

Right.

Kink clearly didn't care, anyway. He was beside himself with the prospect of slaying zombies. He padded along behind Jin with glee in his voice.

"Oh boy, oh boy, oh boy!"

CHAPTER 23

Clive

They'd chased the zombie-tourist things for a few blocks, but the little bastards had been way too fast. Even Lightbulb had given up trying to catch them.

"Those fuckers sure were quick," Rudy said as they got up off the bench they'd been resting on. "Ever seen little legs move like that?"

Clive shook his head. "Nope." He opened a channel to the rest of the crew currently topside. *"Hey guys, we ran into the zombies down here. They were dressed as tourists. Would've contacted you sooner, but it took about ten minutes to stop clenching my chest."*

"And before you ask," chimed in Rudy, *"we couldn't catch them because they're fucking speedy!"*

"Same here," Lacey said. *"We didn't even bother gettin' after chasing them, though. That would've been foolhardy."*

Raina was next to join in. *"We haven't seen any, but*

Einstein sniffed out a partially-turned zombie. Seems harmless and may be of use. I'm bringing him back to the station."

"Whoa!" said Rudy. *"You think that's a good idea? I mean, what if it's some kind of wooden donkey?"*

"What?"

"He means a Trojan Horse," Clive explained. *"He's an idiot, but he's not wrong about this."*

"Thank you," replied Rudy.

"We'll keep him in quarantine," Raina said, *"but I don't think he's a threat. If he's being used as a tracker, what would that buy Vestin and his army? They already know where the PPD is stationed."*

Clive recalled how the zombies had surrounded the precinct before, proving she was right. Of course, every super in town knew where the PPD's base of operations was set. It was common knowledge.

That wasn't the point of a Trojan Horse, though.

If Vestin could get one of his zombies in the door, the guy could manage to bypass the building's protections and the PPD would be wiped out. But he knew Raina wasn't as dumb as Rudy. She'd already said the zombie would be quarantined, which was PPD-speak for "he'll be locked in a room where he can't possibly do any damage."

He was about to reply when he noticed Lightbulb was sniffing around at the steps of an abandoned building. There was a man standing at the top of the stairs, looking down at the werecoyote with a disgusted frown. He was wearing a tattered robe that'd seen better days.

"What's he doing?"

"Sniffing," answered Rudy.

Clive gave him a look. "Obviously, you uncurled pube, but *why?*"

"How the fuck am I supposed to know, numbnuts? Maybe he's gotta take a leak? Maybe he enjoys freaking out normals, like the guy standing there with a look like he's about to lose his lunch? Maybe he wants to mark the area to let other horrid-looking coyotes know he's in town? Maybe he—"

"Hey!" Lightbulb called out as he ran back toward them, wagging his tail like mad. "I smell something!"

"What is it, Lassie?" asked Rudy tiredly.

Lightbulb either didn't get it or he did and ignored it. "That drug thing is in there."

Clive and Rudy glanced at each other and then walked on over to the steps. Clive cleared his mind and relaxed himself, recognizing that sometimes going with a gentle approach was the best way to get the answers you wanted.

Rudy, however, had a different plan. "What's in the building, ass-crayon?"

"Ass-crayon? Really?"

"Yeah, okay, it was weak, but I'm still reeling from the run... testicle-biscuit."

The man, seemingly affronted by the insult, somehow managed to make himself appear defiant, even with his soiled garb. He crossed his arms and stared down his nose at them. It was easy to do since he was the one at the top of the steps.

"Sorry about my partner's name-calling," Clive said, hoping he could play good cop. "He's just upset because he's not been allowed to tickle any taints for the last couple of weeks."

Rudy shot Clive a look. "What?"

Robe guy softened almost instantly. "Ah. Well, that would certainly cause me some distress." He dropped his arms. "What can I help you with?"

Rudy continued giving Clive a dark glare, but Clive chose to ignore it.

"Nothing much," he said, trying his best to appear nonchalant. "I thought this building was abandoned."

"Ah, yes," replied the man, appearing suddenly unsure. "Uh…it was, up until last week. We…uh…acquired it in order to turn it into a new church for our…uh…order."

"A church?"

"Yes." The guy was smiling, revealing teeth that hadn't had a meeting with a toothbrush in some time. "A church."

Rudy said, "What kind?"

The guy was clearly put on the spot by the question because he hesitated. "Uh…" He appeared nearly panicked. But then his eyes lit up. "Pentecostal! Yes, that's it. Pentecostal." He leaned forward slightly. "Sorry, I've just recently left another church, so still trying to get my feet under me here, you understand."

Clive didn't know anything about churches, aside from how they were primarily a thing normals got into. Supers knew better. Well, most did. There were still a few who fell into mysticism and other crap, but not the way normals did.

In other words, maybe it *did* take time for people who changed denominations to recalibrate.

"May we take a look inside?" Clive asked.

"Uh…well…" The man paused. He gave them a worried look as he approached panic again. It was strange. His face brightened. "That depends! Are you Pentecostal?"

Clive was about to say they weren't, but Rudy jumped in first, saying, "Yes. Yes, we are."

"Oh, um." The man swallowed hard, chewed his lip for a moment, and then smiled again. It wasn't a pleasant sight. "Prove it."

"Prove it?" Rudy laughed.

"Yeah," agreed Clive, "prove it? How does one prove they're a particular religion?" Again, he didn't know a lot about the religions of normals, but he found it odd that someone would have to prove they were of a particular sect. Was that actually a thing? "I mean, we *are* Penalcoasters..."

"Pentecostals," the man corrected him.

"Right, that. But what if we weren't? Maybe we'd just want to join, you know? Is that not allowed?"

"Of course it'd be allowed," said the guy. He was chewing his nails now, and they were even filthier than his teeth. His eyes lit up yet again. "Ah yes! Um, this happens to be a private sect that is only accessible to actual members of the church. Those seeking answers for the first time, or those who may be looking for a change, would be directed to one of our sister churches."

"Oh," Clive and Rudy said together.

"Now," the guy continued, "if you wouldn't mind moving along, I have to look for other people to turn away."

That was an odd job.

Clive tried again. "Right, and well you should if they're

not members. As my friend has pointed out already, however, we *are* members."

"Drat," the guy hissed. Yet again, inspiration appeared to have struck. "Okay, okay! If you're *actually* members, you'll know the secret password. Provide me with that and I shall be pleased to allow you through the door."

He stood there like a pecker-puppet, his face haughty and assured. The dude must've been onto the fact that Clive and Rudy weren't actual members, meaning they weren't going to get in. They could simply pull out their guns and badges and force their way in, but since this guy was a normal it'd mean calling in The Cleaners when all was said and done.

There was no way Clive or Rudy would sign the paperwork required for something like that.

Right when he was going to tell Rudy to just come along and forget about it, his wererooster partner squared his shoulders and got that "I'm gonna do something stupid" look on his face.

He got that often.

"All right, ya dingleberry-collector," said Rudy, "the passcode is Pente-Pente-Pente-Pente-Pente-Pente-Pente-Pentecostal!"

He'd sung it in a way that reminded Clive of the theme to the Batman TV show.

Clive stared at his partner in shock. What kind of idiot would think *that* was the password? Seriously, it pushed Rudy's idiocy to a level that Clive had never thought possible.

Robe guy shared a look of confusion. He even glanced over at Clive, then down at Lightbulb, then back at Rudy.

"Ummm…" He frowned again before a look of acceptance covered his face. "Correct." Though he appeared to continue harboring some hesitation, the guy stepped aside. "Welcome to the inner sanctum, gentlemen."

Rudy gave Clive a big grin.

"You've got to be fucking kidding me."

"Who knew, eh?"

They quickly shuffled inside, followed by Lightbulb who was singing, "Pente-Pente-Pente-Pente-Pente-Pente-Pente-Pentecostal!"

Unfuckingbelievable.

Unfortunately, they weren't paying attention when they walked in and the door shut behind them. When they finally turned around, they saw a sea of zombies staring at them, and none of them were wearing tourist outfits either.

"Shit."

"Yeah," agreed Rudy. "Shit."

"Yeah," agreed Lightbulb. "Poop."

"HELLO!" the zombies said as one. Their voices were incredibly loud, in a gurgling kind of way.

"Um," replied Clive, "hi."

"WELCOME!"

"Thanks."

Rudy leaned over. "I don't know how many there are, but we can't take on this many."

Lightbulb sniffed the air twice and whispered, "Seventy-three."

There was the sound of something hitting the ground. Clive peered through the zombies and saw a middle-aged woman lying there with a syringe hanging out of her arm.

Lightbulb sniffed the air again. "Seventy-four."

"Yeah," Rudy rasped, "we ain't beating that."

He wasn't wrong.

Thinking quickly, he called out, "Uh…is this the place where we get *Shaded Past #13*?"

"YES!"

"Great! Swell! That's…swell." He gulped. "Um, we have a bunch of friends waiting outside to get a shot of that wonderful stuff." He reached out and found the door handle, pushed it open, and started backing his way outside again. "We'll go get them and be right back."

"OKAY!"

As soon as they got to the other side of the door and closed it, Clive quickly glanced down at himself to make sure he hadn't soiled his pants. They were dry. He wasn't so sure about the back, though.

He grabbed his gun and turned on the guy with the robe.

"Okay, asshole," he said, "you'd better start talking real fast or you're going to end up with an extra hole in your head."

The guy's hands went up immediately. "Whoa! Whoa! What gives? Is this a way for a churchgoer to act?"

"That ain't no church, clit-whisperer," Rudy growled.

"It's not?" the guy replied, his face contorting.

Did he really not know? He seemed genuinely confused.

Clive waved the gun, gesturing for the man to move to the door. "Have a look for yourself."

Robe guy walked over and opened the door. "HELLO!" He quickly closed it again, turned around, and put his back against it. His face had turned somewhat ashen.

"What the hell are those things?"

Dammit. That was going to cause a problem. Clive had zero desire to contact The Cleaners, but it seemed that was going to happen regardless. Of course, it was only *one* guy, and he didn't appear to be an upstanding member of the community. In other words, people would just chalk him up as being an alcoholic or a druggie who suffered hallucinations.

Clive decided to risk it.

"*You* said it was a church and that's clearly not true. We just saw a woman hit the floor after taking a shot of *Shaded Past #13, too.*"

"Shit."

"Yeah, pal, shit," Rudy agreed. "So you either spill the beans about what's really going on here or you're going to end up in the slammer."

Clive knew they couldn't put robe guy in prison. He was a normal. Rudy knew that, too, of course, but he was playing the hand dealt him.

"Okay, okay!" The man was starting to freak out. "Look, all I know is that some lady named Janet something or other...I don't remember. Anyway, she gave me $100 to stand here and turn away anyone who looked like a cop."

Rudy and Clive shared another confused look.

"We look like cops?" Rudy asked.

The guy shrugged. "I've lived on the streets for years, man. I can smell you guys a mile away."

"Oh."

"But, wait," Clive interjected, "if this was all a setup, how did you know the passcode for the Peniscocktails?"

"Pentecostals," the man corrected him again. "I *didn't* know, but I also didn't know *you* didn't know. So if that actually *was* the password and I said it wasn't, and you knew it was, well then I'd have been busted, right?"

Right.

"All right, fine." Clive turned to Rudy. "Think we should let him go or bring him in?"

"I don't know."

"My vote would be to let him go," said robe man hopefully.

Clive frowned at him. "All right, get out of here, and tell everyone you know to stay away from *Shaded Past #13*, you hear?"

He glanced back at the door and nodded. "Loud and clear!"

As the man skittered away, Clive and Rudy rushed off in the opposite direction. Lightbulb actually led the way, which was interesting.

"We're heading back to the precinct," Clive called through the connector. *"It looks like Vestin is using abandoned buildings as bases for creating zombies!"*

CHAPTER 24

Jin

Jin wasn't in the mood for any trouble when he pushed through the main doors of the PPD building. The guards, however, sprang to attention and had their weapons out, and they were all pointed at Officer Kink.

"Put those down, pronto," bellowed Jin.

Surprisingly, they complied.

Guard Snoodle looked completely beside himself as Jin approached. "Yes, Snoodle, I have an orc with me, and I'm about to be inviting in a good number of assassins from the Badlands, too."

"What?"

"Feel free to contact Director Fysh if you need any particular approvals. That's not my department." Actually, it may have been but he didn't really care at the moment. "In the meantime, I'm going to need an area where everyone can meet. Does this building have anything like that?"

Snoodle was frantically searching around his desk. He was grabbing papers, dropping papers, picking up his datapad and dropping it too, and just generally acting like someone who'd fallen into a state of disarray. Jin wanted to care, but he was struggling with that particular emotion at the moment. His day had been far worse than the minor stir Snoodle was suffering at the moment.

Still, if he wanted things to move forward, he knew he was going to have to calm the guards down.

Turning, he raised his voice but lowered his temper.

"Look, gang, I'm sorry but things are getting pretty wild out there. You've all seen the zombies, so you know what I'm talking about." Each of them looked even more terrified than the next. "This is the kind of thing being in the PPD entails. I know most of you want to eventually rise up the ranks and become a PPD officer, and that means you'll have to learn to manage shit like this. It's challenging, yes, but it's what we do."

For the most part, they were all still shaking in their boots, though a few of them seemed to tighten their jaws at his words. Those were the ones who may one day join the PPD. Only time would tell.

"As you're also aware, getting authorization for cops to be added to the force is damn near impossible." Jin shook his head at the idiocy of it all but pressed on. "That means we sometimes have to get creative, and that's precisely what we've done." He gestured at Officer Kink. "This big guy is here because he wants to help."

"I wanna kill zombies."

"Right, that. And like I said before, we're going to have a good number of assassins coming up who want to do the same thing."

Jin recognized things were going to get dark for everyone, not just the guards. His job was to make everything move as smoothly as possible, at least that's what he was attempting to do. Once the war broke out, everyone would have to do their own thing. He wasn't a master tactician. He was a killer. He knew how to do that far better than he could move pieces on a board. That skill was left for people like Chancellor Frey and Director Fysh.

The door to the building opened again and the guards got their weapons up in a jiffy.

Raina had walked in with Einstein, and she appeared to be dragging a partial zombie along with her as well. His deputy's hair had also turned completely black and her face was not the pleasant one Jin had grown accustomed to seeing.

"Put your fuckin' weapons down before I rip your goddamn heads off," Raina barked. She then glanced up at the orc. "You have the look of an orc who wants to kill zombies."

"I do, I do."

"Yeah, well, unless you want me to snap your tusks off and shove them up your ass, I'd suggest you leave this particular one alone. Got it, shit squirt?"

Officer Kink backed away. "Got it. Sheesh."

Jin couldn't argue with Officer Kink's response.

This was *not* the Deputy Raina Mystique that Chief Kannon had met when he'd first arrived at the precinct, that was for certain.

Apparently, the dark unicorn thing was kicking into gear.

Raina grunted as she approached Jin. "Hey, chief, did you get the assassins?"

"Yeah...they're coming up soon."

"Super." She turned and glared at Snoodle. "We want auditorium 7, the one with the isolation room." He started to fumble again, but Raina reached over and grabbed his arm. "Stop, Snoodle." He did. "Now, open your datapad. Press the ROOMS button. Select auditorium number 7. Click RESERVE. Set the duration of the reservation for three days, authorization Deputy Raina Mystique."

Snoodle was doing everything she said.

Finally, he said, "Done," and gave her a huge smile.

"You want a medal?" She asked, then rolled her eyes before walking through the security section and off to the auditorium. When she reached the doorway on the far left, she looked back and said, "You dipshits just going to stand there or are you joining me?"

Once she was out of range, Jin glanced over at Snoodle.

"She gets like this once a month, sir," Snoodle explained. "It's normal...for her."

"Right. Thanks, Snoodle. Um...go about your business and please don't hold up Rusty and the assassins when they arrive."

"Yes, sir!"

They headed back to the auditorium as Einstein padded along next to Jin. "I must say that Raina changed rather quickly. There were a few minor alterations in her appearance and demeanor while we were out, but it got worse and worse as we drove back to the station."

"Swell," said Jin, having the feeling they weren't even halfway to where Raina was going to end up before the night was over.

CHAPTER 25

Lord Zentril

The old fart vampire was yet again toiling about his day, not paying attention to much. Since the errant email he'd received from someone named Janet Smith who was demanding payment for something or other, things had returned to being nice and quiet.

And then his phone rang.

With a sigh, he picked it up and grumpily said, "What?"

"Lord Zentril," a woman's voice replied, "this is Chancellor Frey from the Assassins' Guild."

It'd been a long time since he'd heard from her, and there was a good reason for that. She'd failed to knock out the mark he'd hired her to kill. Her inability to get the job done had cost him dearly, even to the point of him going into exile and allowing his aging body to wither.

"Well, well, well," he said. "Chancellor Frey, eh? If you're calling to ask for money for the annual Assassins' Guild Ball, you're wasting your time."

"Assassins don't have Balls, Lord Zentril."

"Heh heh heh. So I've heard."

She cleared her throat. "I'm calling because I've located Lord Vestin."

He sat up at that. "What? Where?"

"He's topside in San Diego."

San Diego? He opened his datapad again and looked at the signature line from the email he'd received from the day before. Janet Smith was from San Diego. He then looked at the top and found it'd been addressed to someone named Turd Vesticles. Could that be Lord Vestin?

The coincidence would be extreme, if so.

"It seems he's building a zombie army," Chancellor Frey continued, "and I've been asked to bring up all the assassins to help destroy them. While I'm there, I'm planning to finish the job I started for you those many years ago."

Yes, she would, and it would make Zentril pleased through and through. Vengeance was always on the tip of every vampire's tooth. They lived for it.

"Excellent," he said. Then he grew dark. "Don't bother contacting me again, unless you've actually completed the mission this time. I've had enough bad news in my day. I don't need any more."

"As you wish."

She hung up without speaking another word, and why wouldn't she? There was nothing more to say between them.

Zentril was about to set down his phone and bask in the knowledge that Vestin was going to finally get his comeuppance. That's when he remembered he still had the man's phone number. He'd called it a number of times over the years, grumbling at Vestin, but he stopped when his nemesis merely laughed, making it clear the prick thrived on Zentril's failures. If only the phones were traceable, he'd have found the fool's location and had Frey destroy him sooner. Sadly, phones like the one Vestin carried were magically blocked from any of that hooey.

He pressed the button and it began to ring.

A man answered who didn't sound like Vestin. "You have reached the grand office of the esteemed Lord Vestin, our wonderful and powerful leader. How may I direct your call?"

Zentril held back a growl. "Let me talk to him."

"May I ask who's calling?"

"Lord Zentril."

"Just a moment."

More than a moment went by before Vestin picked up the line.

"Lord Zentril," Vestin said in his snooty way. "What a pleasure it is to hear from you. Calling to grieve over your losses yet again, I hope?"

"Not a chance, Vestin. You're about to get waxed and for good this time."

Vestin chuckled. "Oh my. That sounds simply dreadful. May I ask how you plan to accomplish such a feat?"

"Frey and *all* of her assassins are heading topside to kick the snot out of your zombie army," Zantril answered. Silence followed. "What's the matter, Vestin, was that not grieving enough for you?"

More silence followed before Vestin spoke again.

"You do realize, my dear Lord Zantril, that my zombies will defeat them and then I will eventually take over the world, yes? Soon after, I will conquer the Netherworld, whereupon I will find you and have you tormented for the rest of your miserable days."

"Oh yeah? You and what army?"

"Uh…well, that would be my zombie army, as I just mentioned."

Zantril paused for a moment. "Ah. Right. Yeah, you kind of said that, already. Sorry."

"No worries. You are getting up there in age, I'm afraid."

He was, too. It'd been worse with each day. There were moments when he couldn't remember who he was anymore. That probably had more to do with the fact that he'd given up on finding his place among the vampire elite.

Frankly, when he really thought about it, he didn't care about any of that junk any longer. Maybe it was maturity or maybe he'd been struck with a case of low testosterone. Either way, Lord Zantril had to admit that world domination was a young man's game.

Zantril was in his three hundreds. While it was true that vampires lived an extraordinarily long time, unless otherwise killed, that didn't mean they were free from the effects of aging, no matter what those topside movies portrayed. Vestin couldn't be more than one hundred at this point, though Zantril didn't actually know or care how many years the man had lived. What Zantril *could* get behind was seeing one of his own kind succeed, even if that man happened to have been the one who'd knocked him off his minor throne back in the day.

"You know, Vestin," Zantril said with a sigh, "I can't believe I'm admitting this, but I actually kind of hope you succeed."

"I'm sure, and…what?"

"Seriously. As you've correctly pointed out, I'm an old man. These days I take positivity from simply having a decent bowel movement."

"That's disturbing."

"Tell me about it." Zantril groaned. "Truth is, if you can figure out a way to make this zombie thing work and you can bring home a huge win for the vampires…well, you have my blessing."

There was yet another moment of silence.

"Truly, Lord Zantril?"

"Just call me Zantril. I'm not a Lord anymore, and I doubt I'll ever be one." He was about to hang up, but decided to add one more thing. "Listen, I probably shouldn't do this, but what the hell? If you can somehow manage to put the vampires at the top of the food chain again, which I honestly doubt, more power to you. So, if Frey manages to get to you at some point, just say the words 'Vampus Stopus Killus' and state my name."

"You've given me your Don't-Kill-Code?" His voice sounded appropriately shocked.

"As I said, Vestin, I'm through with the game. It's yours now. You bested me and I've been a sore loser. No more. Do your thing. Take over the world. Put every other race where they belong, under the feet of vampires."

"I…thank you, Lord Zantril."

"Again, it's just Zantril now."

"Not when I win," Vestin said seriously. "You'll be restored to a Lord when that happens. Of that, I assure you."

Zantril shrugged, not really caring at that point. "Better than being tortured, I suppose."

He then hung up the phone and flipped on the local weather. It was the Badlands, which meant it was hotter than a furnace just like it was every day.

"Maybe if Vestin wins, I can become a Lord someplace where the temperature isn't so blasted hot."

CHAPTER 26

Prender

Prender found himself somewhat pleased when Janet Smith arrived at the main complex. While he would never divulge his feelings to anyone, for fear of suffering Lord Vestin's wrath, Prender was rather fond of the way Miss Smith talked to his Lord. She said many things Prender wished he could but never dared. Prender was wise enough to pretend her words were shameful whenever he was near Vestin.

Fortunately, Prender was not directly under the influence of Lord Vestin's venom. That allowed him to have dissenting thoughts all he wanted without fear of messing his pants. He'd just learned it was best to not speak his feelings aloud.

"It's a pleasure to see you, Miss Smith," he said with a bow.

"It is?" she replied, giving him the once-over. "Okay, Prender, if you say so."

It was nice that she hadn't called *him* names, not that she was above it. Maybe her reactions came as simple responses to the way she was treated. It was certainly possible. Did Prender not respond in kind to poor treatment? Actually, generally, he did not. He wasn't one who enjoyed confrontation, so he merely took abuse where necessary and sought the nearest exit.

They walked up to Lord Vestin's office and stepped inside.

"Ah, if it isn't our lovely Janet Smith," Vestin said in such a way as to make clear it wasn't genuine. He appeared to have something weighing on him, too, but Prender assumed it was simply the pressure of the upcoming war. "How *wonderful* of you to visit."

"I'm sure it is, sphincter fangs," she said. She then pulled out a file from her bag and dropped it on his desk. "Twenty-five hundred names are listed right there, and each of them has been given an injection." She tapped on the folder to drive the point home. "We took over a bunch of abandoned buildings and I hired people to stand outside and steer away the PPD, should they arrive to check things out. You'll be billed for that soon."

Vestin appeared more than pleased. "My army has grown to over two thousand people?"

"Twenty-five hundred, shaft-itcher," she amended, "not including the riff-raff you've got here, obviously."

It was rare to see his Lord in such a state of glee. If Vestin could dance, Prender imagined he would've done just that.

"This is perfect," said Vestin, "not to mention timely. We have a new struggle to contend with, but that's nothing new." He then sprung up from his chair and rushed toward the door. "Prender, tell Emiliano to gather the troops in the compound. I shall address them as night falls!"

"Of course, My Lord," Prender replied with a bow, though it was wasted since Vestin had already rushed from the room.

When he looked back up, he noticed that Miss Smith was studying him again.

"I thought you were his second-in-command."

"I've been promoted to being Lord Vestin's manservant."

"Promoted?" She laughed. "I think the word you're looking for is 'demoted,' Prender."

"I suppose it depends on one's perspective, Ma'am," Prender replied, not at all bothered by her quip. "A manservant doesn't have to rush out into the night with a sword in his hand while facing the very real chance of dying before the morning light."

Miss Smith tilted her head and gave him an impressed nod. "Smart man."

"I do what I can."

CHAPTER 27

Jin

Everyone had arrived and Rusty was introducing assassins to crew members, and when Officer Kink waved at him the android glanced over at Jin apologetically. Jin gave a nod to show that everything was fine. Rusty appeared relieved.

Seeing this group of people together was a surreal situation that Jin would never have thought possible. He was thankful it'd worked out, or at least hopeful, but cops working together with assassins was even more unfathomable than cops working with the local cartel.

Speaking of which, Hector had also returned with his crew and they actually appeared somewhat upbeat. That included Alejandro, which everyone would agree was awkward to witness.

"Looks like you got the reinforcements you were hoping for, Chief Kannon," Hector said as he approached. "I hope it'll be enough."

"Me, too." If the reports his crew had given were accurate, they were still sorely outnumbered. "Any luck with the neighborhoods?"

"They're all staying indoors until this blows over." Hector smirked. "Well, that's what I asked them to do, anyway. Whether or not they'll listen is anyone's guess. The people in San Diego have a lot of pride. They're not likely to go down without a fight."

Sofia was nodding. "I remember having a number of run-ins with a few mothers down here. Those bitches can hit when they're up against it."

"I can imagine," Jin said.

So he had his crew, one android, a bunch of assassins, Hector's little entourage, and an orc.

Jin hoped it would be enough.

As Hector said, there'd be a number of locals who would defy Hector and run out into the streets to fight, but they'd assuredly be killed and flipped into zombies within minutes. Vestin's army was going to grow even more quickly than it already was, and it was getting huge fast.

The assassins were good, but they weren't *that* good. Jin assumed Officer Kink would be able to waste at least a hundred zombies before they got him pinned down. Still, it was difficult to imagine they were anything but doomed.

"I come bearing gifts!" Petey yelled out as he zipped around the corner of the room.

Madison walked in behind him, shaking her head and rolling her eyes. Then, Raffy appeared. He was carrying a heavy bag.

"Oh wow," Petey said as he saw the mass of people in the room. "We don't have *that* many gifts! Actually, it's just a bunch of breaker bullets." He sighed. "Well, that was a letdown."

He quickly opened a channel to Madison. *"I don't suppose you've made enough mini-guns for everyone? That'd totally be a game-changer."*

"Hah! It was hard enough to build out the ones I gave the team, and we've been dealing with the damn BreakerReplicator *machine ever since. There are more bullets than before, of course, but I'd suggest you ration them as best as you can."*

"Damn."

Jin was worrying more and more about the upcoming battle. They'd have to be clever if they were going to win.

Everyone backed away, causing Jin to look over at what the fuss was all about.

Raffy was standing across from the orc, and they were studying each other with curiosity. They were nearly the same size, but where Kink was an imposing figure of bulk and muscles, Raffy was merely an imposing figure of hair and odor.

"You am a stinkfoot."

"Like, you're an orc, man."

"Yep."

"Cool."

"Crap," Raina said, looking bummed. "Was kind of hoping they'd fight it out. Looks like they're going to share cooking recipes instead or something."

Her hair had lightened up a fair bit and she appeared tired. Whatever the full moon, along with the stress of the last few days, was doing to her, it clearly wasn't great.

"You okay?" Jin asked.

She nodded solemnly. "I'm sorry for my language before. It's very challenging to keep control when the dark side of my personality gains hold."

"It's fine. You seriously don't need to apologize. We all have our demons."

"Yeah, but yours doesn't show up unannounced, acting like some kind of jerk."

That was almost true. Jin's demon showed up precisely when he wanted it to, and he wasn't *some* kind of jerk, he was the full beast, seeking to destroy whatever target was on his list along with anyone else who dared stand in his way. In the grand scheme of things, though, he wouldn't trade places with Raina. Hers was uncontrollable; his was not.

He took off his hat. "Raina, your friends know your situation and they respect it."

"You mean they fear it."

"That, too," he admitted, "but when it's all said and done, do they not accept you back with open arms?"

"Unless I've broken them, yes."

Yikes.

"Right." He gave a nod to the zombie, who'd been watching their discourse. "Making any progress with Timmy?"

Tim, or Timmy as he preferred to be called, was the partial-zombie Raina and Einstein had brought in. He was nearly normal, at least when compared with the original collection of zombies the crew had run into. He was also calm and seemed like a regular person, not like someone who wanted to rip you to shreds.

Obviously, Lord Vestin's venom hadn't fully gripped the dude.

"He doesn't seem to know anything about Vestin, do you Timmy?"

The zombie shook his head. "I have a bit of pain in my chest whenever someone says his name, like I *should* know who he is and like I'm *supposed* to be following him or something. It just fades away after a few moments, though. I wish I knew more. I'm sorry."

There wasn't much point in having a partially-turned zombie around if he couldn't help with the war. That didn't mean Jin was going to free the guy or hurt him in any way, but eventually, there'd come a time when they'd have to figure out what to do with him.

That wasn't for now, though.

"Well, thanks for trying, Timmy," he said. "You're going to have to stay put here until everything blows over."

"That's okay," the zombie replied with a sad sigh. "It's not like I've got anyplace else to go."

Jin turned back around and decided to address the room. He felt zero nerves this time around. Was that because he wasn't giving them a sales pitch, or maybe because they were all now on his turf? He couldn't say, but it was definitely different.

"Heads up," he called out. Everyone turned to look at him. Okay, that gave his stomach a bit of a jolt, but he pushed it away. "We're about to head out there and start fighting. We're going to be leaving within the hour," he said. "The PPD officers will be in charge of this operation. That's the deal so manage yourselves accordingly." He then nodded at his crew. "Split up into teams and get everyone ready."

"You got it, captain!" called out Clive before everyone split off again.

Rusty came over with Einstein as Jin returned to Raina. Her hair was a shade darker again, but not fully. She was definitely going back and forth, like the waves of the ocean. Jin hated to admit he was hoping she'd time it perfectly to be fully enveloped by her darker self once they hit the zombies. He didn't thoroughly understand what that would mean, but based on the little he'd seen of her more sinister side, he had the feeling she was going to prove to be quite an asset in the realm of battle.

"Chief," Rusty said, "I've been talking with Einstein here and I think there may be a way for us to inoculate everyone against Vestin's venom."

That was a shocker.

"Oh?"

"Based on the research I've done over my years," Einstein said, going pedantic, "the fact that we have a patient in Timmy who has somehow managed to stave off the full effects of the venom gives us a chance to create a vaccine of sorts."

"Uh huh."

"The science is there, chief," Rusty stated. "I've gone over it, searched thousands of journals and papers, and I can't see a reason it won't work."

"Side effects?" Jin asked.

"Can't be worse than an actual zombie bite," Einstein

replied, "assuming it doesn't just immediately turn everyone into a zombie upon injection, of course."

Risk-reward.

Ugh.

"How long will it take to put it together?"

"Give me Raffy, Petey, Madison, Rusty, Timmy, and my brothers," answered Einstein, "and I'll have something worked up in thirty minutes."

"Whoa. Is that really possible?"

"It is, chief," Rusty said. "Remember, I'm incredibly fast. If anything, I would say including everyone Einstein recommended is only going to serve to slow me down, however."

"It's a fair point," Einstein agreed. "Okay, just me, Rusty, and a vial of Timmy's blood then."

"Fine by me," Timmy said.

It was moments like these where the cons side of Jin's list spanned pages. If the vaccine they were proposing worked, it could mean the difference between winning and losing; if it failed, they'd lose before they got out the damn doors.

"All right, but we're going to need some test subjects before spreading this drug to everyone." He gritted his teeth. "I'll be the first one."

"And I'll go second," Raina stated firmly.

"Uhhh...no," Rusty said to her. "Sorry, Raina, but with your particular situation, you're too volatile to risk giving a shot."

Her eyes went instantly black. "If I want a fucking shot, you metal piece of—"

"Okay, okay," Jin said, getting between her and Rusty.

"You guys go do your thing. I'll have a word with *Deputy Raina Mystique* alone."

They quickly scooted out of there. Android or not, Jin had the feeling Raina was quite capable of causing Rusty some damage in her current state.

"I'm sorry, chief," she said, her eyes returning to normal. "This is so frustrating."

"I know, but think of it this way, Raina," he said, giving her a serious look, "can you imagine a more effective weapon against an army of zombies than a dark unicorn?"

It took a few moments, but her eyes flashed obsidian and she gave him a feral smile.

Jin gulped.

CHAPTER 28

Vestin

Their faces filled him with hope as dusk approached. Lord Vestin was a naturally confident person. It was part of being a vampire. But that didn't make him immune to doubt. Any great leader felt temporary turbulence when a plan was about to launch. It was natural. More than that, it was good. Overconfidence had toppled a number of vampires in the lore he'd read. One had to know beyond the shadow of a doubt that they were poised for greatness, but it was the nuanced touches that hoisted each person over the finish line.

This was especially true since learning that Chancellor Frey and her army of assassins was coming after his army, and then, ultimately, him.

The sting of fear pierced his mind for a moment. He shoved it down. Why would he allow such concerns when his corps of soldiers was an hour away from toppling the city of San Diego? And with how he'd masterminded the spread of his venom, each new person who fell would awake anew and pick up his banner. It was a consistent rollover of fighters that caused more and more growth.

Even one thousand assassins couldn't stand against that tide, and he knew damned well Frey didn't have numbers anywhere near that size. In short, she was never going to show up at his door because she was going to be far too busy dying in the city.

If there was any one thing Vestin wished he'd been able to control, it was the death of a soldier once they became a zombie. That'd been a tricky puzzle he'd never managed to resolve. Vestin was aware that they didn't release to the Vortex, like other people who faced permanent death, but he couldn't devise a way to bring them back into their fallen bodies so they could resume the charge.

It was vexing.

Regardless, he still knew his legion would win the day. From there, they would sweep across topside like a tsunami of pain, crushing every city until the world groveled at his feet.

When the Netherworld fell—and it *would*—he'd have all the names in vampiric lore erased from the history books, replacing them all with the single story of Lord Vestin, the only vampire to have ever succeeded in dominating everything in existence.

"We stand on the precipice of greatness, my army," he declared. "Tonight you will taste the blood of thousands." Vestin knew they loved hearing that kind of speech. It was a zombie thing. "The conference that's happening at the convention center will be filled with loads of unsuspecting fools. You will turn them all. On top of that, you will infest the city, converting every last person into members of my divine force!"

They cheered.

He considered telling them about the assassins for a moment. Would it be wise? Would they see it as a challenge or as a worry? There would probably be people on both sides of that fence, so he decided to leave that part out.

"There is *nothing* more powerful than what I've built. The Paranormal Police Department will do their best, but can they stand against us?"

"NO!"

"No, they cannot. And if the conference attendees attempt to band together, will they dent our lines?"

"NO!"

"Of course they won't," Vestin affirmed. "And what of the towns? The locals? Could we even fathom them being able to defy the physical artillery our band of zombies brings to their doorsteps?"

"NO!"

No, was correct.

The truth was, nothing could stop them. The PPD would fall quickly. The assassins would take a little longer, but their talents would soon be under Vestin's direction as well, and the normals would be crushed in seconds.

Lord Vestin had built the perfect machine of death and destruction, and its levers were solely in his hands.

It was a beautiful thing.

The sun dipped past the horizon, ushering in nightfall. While vampires were fully capable of living in sunlight—rumors and false legends be damned—they were admittedly creatures of the night. It suited them, bringing a sense of comfort and relaxation.

Tonight, however, Lord Vestin was anything but relaxed. He was excited, thrilled, and bursting with glee. The world was nearly his.

"Let us wait not a moment longer!" he bellowed. "Raise your blades and your fists, my soldiers! Go forth and bring San Diego to its knees!"

The cheer was deafening as they rushed away, leaving him standing alone with Prender and Janet Smith. Carina, the witch, was noticeably absent. He assumed she was off working on magic or something. Honestly, he doubted she was of much use at all. Making his zombies shorter and taller was cute, but it hadn't done much to bolster their power. As soon as San Diego fell, he'd find someone more suitable for his needs and have her hanged.

He put her out of his mind.

It was unfortunate that Miss Smith was with them, but the moment Vestin owned the city, he would focus his wrath upon her and her vile words. Maybe he'd hang Janet and Carina at the same time? Oooh! Even better would be burning them at the stake!

Yes, that sounded pleasant.

"Prender," he said, returning his thoughts to the immediate war, "you *did* ensure we have connectivity with the cameras in the city? I don't wish to miss the battle."

"It has been taken care of, My Lord. The large screen TV is set and prepared for your viewing pleasure."

"Excellent! Now, fetch me a bowl of popcorn and a glass of blood wine. I wish to enjoy the show in style!"

CHAPTER 29

Prender

After Prender delivered Lord Vestin's food and drink, he walked back into his own office to make sure everything was in order. It was the big night and he wanted to verify nothing would go wrong from *his* side. He knew that if anything did go wrong, Vestin would blame him, so he was going to do whatever it took to minimize potential damage.

Janet Smith had been milling about in the halls, looking at everything. It was odd for her to be around still, but since Lord Vestin didn't seem to mind, why should Prender?

Still…

"Is there anything I can do for you, Miss Smith?"

She stopped moseying and stepped up to his door. "You can start by calling me Janet."

That caused Prender to blink a few times. Why would she want him to call her by her first name? Did she consider them peers all of a sudden? No, that wasn't possible. She effectively lorded over Vestin. It was due to contract stipulations, obviously, but seeing that Prender was beneath Vestin on the organization chart, that put Prender even further beneath her.

The gesture was nice, though, and it proved that Janet Smith enjoyed digging her verbal nails into self-important people such as Vestin.

He gave her a small nod. "Do you need a drink or something, Janet?"

"No, I'm good." She stepped into the office and took the small chair by the door. It wasn't much, but it was better than nothing. "So, what's your story?"

His story? Why was she asking about his story?

"I'm not sure what you mean."

"Oh, come on Prender," she chided him. "You can't possibly have me believe that a resourceful man such as you could willingly subject himself to a tyrant like Boring Vestibule."

He caught himself before laughing, though a smile did creep up on him.

"I have no idea what you're speaking of, Janet."

"Your smile betrays your words, Prender." She was grinning back at him now. "I'm going to make a guess that you were working on something of your own when Vestie showed up and swept you away from it. He then tormented you relentlessly with his lack of wit, and the next thing you knew you were a flunky in his dastardly plans to rule the world. And now," she added, gesturing around, "you're stuck in this dinky office suffering a life that consists of fetching him tea and biscuits, or whatever, while he offers his thanks by taking out his failures on you." She stopped her roving eyes, locking them on him. "You've become his whipping boy."

Prender's smile had fallen away. Everything she'd said had been essentially true, but he'd not told anyone about it. For her to know either meant she was some kind of mind-reader or she'd witnessed similar situations before.

He stopped fidgeting with the papers and sat back, hearing the squeak of springs in his rickety chair.

"I was actually running a somewhat successful OnlyFans page, and I was selling on Etsy, too." The flash of a few designs he'd made appeared in his head. With most people, he felt uncomfortable admitting what he used to do, but for some reason Janet Smith wasn't one of them. Why? With some effort, he told her what his business had been. "I created thongs for men. I mean, I suppose women could purchase them, too, but they were made to contain...well...you know."

Janet nodded. "Thongs?"

"Yes. I don't know what it is about that particular garment, but I have an insatiable desire to design and craft them. It's like I have an unending stream of ideas." His face fell. "Well, I *used* to, until my situation here, of course."

"Interesting."

Was it? Obviously, his customers had thought so, since he'd been building a decent head of steam before having to shut down the business. He still had the page, of course, it just happened to be off at the moment. The chances of him ever reopening it were slim, though, especially since it did appear Lord Vestin's plan might actually work.

"We'll have to discuss this further, Prender," Janet said, "assuming this folly falls apart."

That caught Prender's attention. "You don't think we'll win?"

She shrugged. "It's difficult to answer that, with what I've seen so far tonight. Honestly, it's what has been keeping me around the house. I struggle to imagine that blood-sucking gonad winning, but his army is proving to be rather formidable." She then leaned forward and added, "I will tell you that in all my years of running campaigns for big shots like Vestin, it rarely works out. Most of them were just trying to make corporations or cartels, unlike Captain Fuckmuffin in there." She sniffed. "World domination? Like *literally* world domination? Well, I put it to you, Prender: Has *anyone* ever succeeded at that?"

Not in any history that Prender could recall.

"Hmmm."

"Hmmm indeed, Prender," Janet agreed, sitting back and crossing her legs. "Hmmm indeed."

CHAPTER 30

Jin

He shouldn't have been surprised, since assassins were the type who would take just about any edge they could get, but when the zombie vaccines were being doled out, everyone lined up with their arms at the ready.

Jin went first, of course, refusing to put anyone else at risk before taking a dose himself.

The only thing he felt was a bit of burning, a momentary spell of dizziness, and blurred vision that lasted all of about five seconds. Once that passed, it was done.

"That's it?" he said as everyone gazed at him in curiosity.

Rusty and Einstein shrugged at each other, and Rusty said, "Do you feel dead?"

Jin frowned at him. "No."

Einstein sniffed the air. "Doesn't smell dead, either."

"Guess it worked, then," Rusty said, looking proud. "Then again, it could be that it didn't do anything and you'll be turned into a zombie at the first bite. Guess we'll see."

They would indeed.

Jin stood up, put his coat back on, and motioned for Chimi to go next. After that, each of his crew went before Rusty moved on to the assassins. Well, not *every* crew member.

Raina had been refused a dose.

Jin waved her along and walked out to the main area where Snoodle and the other guards were chatting with each other. Their concern was evident, but it seemed to always be that way with them. They needed toughening up, that was for sure. Jin just couldn't be bothered with helping with that at the moment. There was too much at risk.

But he did have a job for them.

"Guard Snoodle," he said, "we're going to be heading out to battle in a few minutes and I have a very important assignment for the lot of you."

"Sir?" Snoodle said, unable to contain his trembling.

"You and the guards will stay here," Jin commanded, holding back his grin upon hearing the collective sound of "whew." He then pointed around the room at each of them. "You will all protect this building with your lives. Do you understand?"

"YES, SIR!"

"And you, Snoodle, will personally watch over the zombie in the back."

"Yes, sir…what, sir?"

Raina leaned over to the man, speaking gently, which was sayin something considering how dark her hair and eyes had gotten since they'd walked out of the auditorium. "Timmy's asleep and he'll probably stay that way for a while. On top of that, he's as gentle as that stuffed animal you still sleep with every night."

Snoodle's head shot up. "You know about that?"

She smirked. "Do now."

"Damn."

In her normal form, Raina would never have used such a joke against the man. As a dark unicorn, however, she seemed to revel in it. Jin supposed it could've been a much worse hazing.

"You need to take this seriously, Snoodle," Jin stated, before turning around. "All of you do! We'll be out there fighting for the life of the city. You'll be here making sure the support systems stay in place in the event they're needed."

"YES, SIR!"

Jin spun on his heel and headed outside.

Night had arrived, telling him he'd missed yet another sunset on the beach. All he could hope was that they'd get through the night, wipe out the zombies, and he'd find himself sitting in the sand watching as the great ball of fire descended over the horizon before tomorrow's evening set in.

It was a massive wish.

"Thinking about the stupid ass sunset again, aren't you?" asked Raina. She was standing slightly behind him. "What's the big fuckin' deal, chief? Oooh, big sun disappearing into the ocean. Yawn." She made an odd sound. "I mean, seriously. It's nothing special. I've seen it a thousand times."

"I haven't," Jin replied quietly. "You take it for granted because you've seen it. Imagine for just a moment that you never have."

When he looked back at her, he nearly choked.

Raina's entire body was dark now, and it was covered with thin black hairs. It was as if she had all of the features of a horse, while somehow remaining humanoid. She was muscular, too, and she'd grown a full foot taller.

He tried to remain calm, but it was unnerving.

That's when she glanced down at him. "Don't be a puss, chief. Like you said before, this is what I need to be tonight. The timing is perfect. Sucks for those fuckin' zombies, though."

He'd expected her teeth to be thick and bucked, but they were thin and razor-sharp. Was that the norm for unicorns? Dark ones, anyway?

Peering up, he fully expected to see a horn.

Nope.

"Only shows up when I'm in unicorn mode," she explained. "If you're shaky little ass quivers at the sight of me now, you definitely don't want to be around when I'm in unicorn mode. I'm a big fuckin' beastie then."

The doors opened behind them and everyone poured out into the night.

"Oh shit, Raina's gone full dark now," Rudy said through the collective connector.

"I can hear you, werechickenshit," Raina replied aloud. "If you're going to talk about me behind my back, at least be smart enough to actually do it *behind my back*."

"Fuck, she heard me." Then he jolted and spoke without the connector. "Hey! I'm not a werechicken! For fuck's sake, how many times do I have to say that?"

"Buk buk buk," Raina replied.

Rudy's face contorted. "Not cool, horsetits."

Raina took a step toward him, but Rudy was smart enough to run in the direction of the parking lot. He yelled back, "See you in the car, Clive!"

Everyone else was giggling like a bunch of thirteen-year-olds. Everyone except Officer Kink. He was busily scratching his own rear end before lifting his finger up for a sniff.

Ugh.

This was the crew who was leading the charge to save San Diego.

Too bad there wasn't a god. If there was, Jin would've asked for divine guidance about now. As it stood, all he had was the knowledge that each of the people standing here had years of training. They knew what they were doing, regardless of how much they enjoyed puerile humor.

"Everyone should have their assignments," Jin called out, putting his concerns aside. "Assassins, I know you're not used to working in teams, but if you can make it work for a night, you'll last longer. Covering each other's backs will absolutely help you survive longer. With any luck, the vaccines will hold, too."

They wouldn't stop them from ending up in the Vortex, though. As a lifelong assassin, Jin knew they didn't really care about dying anyway. Turning into zombies probably bothered them a fair amount, however.

"Most of all," he continued, putting weight on the real reason they'd all agreed to come up, "you're here to have fun and kill zombies, right?"

"YES!" they cried out in unison. Well, Officer Kink had yelled, "YEP!"

"Then let's get downtown and kill those damn zombies!"

You might have expected a charging roar, but, again, these were assassins. They merely walked excitedly toward the parking lot, following Director Fysh who had somehow secured a few buses to bring everyone along. Officer Kink was more buoyant in his response. He rushed down and hopped up on the top of the bus, causing it to creak and moan.

"Well, that was a bit subdued at the end there, wasn't it?" asked Raina.

"It's our way," Jin replied as they approached her car. "You going to be able to control yourself tonight, deputy?"

"I sure fuckin' hope not."

"I mean until we get downtown."

"Ah, yeah…probably." She then stopped and gave him a look. "By the way, I can't drive like this, so if you want to travel with me, it's not going to be in a car."

"Um…okay?"

"Follow me," she said, walking around the corner of the building to a small copse of trees.

Once they were out of eyeshot of everyone else, Raina neighed in a pained rasp as her bones cracked. Her arms bent and grew, as did her legs. Her torso began snapping and expanding, sounding like a symphony of pain. Finally her face and neck thickened and elongated until she'd fully transformed into the largest horse face ever seen. To top if all off, a long sharp horn grew out from the top of her head, so dark that it barely reflected light.

Jin couldn't tear his eyes away. He just stared at her in awe.

"You going to start jerking off to me or something, chief?" she snarked through the connector.

"Huh?" He instantly realized what an idiot he was being. *"Sorry! I was just...wow."*

"Yeah, I get it. I'm fuckin' awesome." She then lowered herself down. *"Climb on my back and let's get the fuck out of here. Oh, and if you make one horse joke, I swear I'll drop your sorry ass from a mile up."*

CHAPTER 31

Carina

She'd tried repeatedly to get back in touch with Madison, but the succubus had gone radio silent. Did that mean Carina was on her own now? Possibly, but it could also have meant that the PPD had already been wiped out.

That would be bad. Terrible, in fact, because it would solidify that Carina's days were numbered.

There was only one way she could attempt to improve her situation, of course. She just hated the prospect. It was better to survive and kiss Lord Vestin's ass than die while holding onto her pride, though, right?

Maybe.

After one last attempt to get through to Madison, she slid the tiny camera into her pocket and headed upstairs to start groveling. The zombie who usually shadowed her was gone, seemingly having been sent off to battle along with the rest of the army.

Each step weighed on her, but what else was she to do?

She was going to have to start referring to the asshole as "Lord Vestin" and everything, showing him the respect he'd been demanding, and pretending to actually care about his plans for the future. It was going to be brutal, but it had to be done.

When she stepped out onto the main floor, she caught sight of Prender sitting in his office, speaking with Janet Smith.

She sighed and walked over, deciding to butter up Vestin's manservant first. "Everything okay?"

"Yes, of course," Prender replied. He then squinted at her. "Why? Have you heard something?"

"No, I just…" She shook her head and glanced over her shoulder. "I'm assuming he's watching the battle?"

"He is," answered Janet. "Probably going to pleasure himself, too. Might want to wait until he gets a little tired."

That was a gross thought.

"Ew."

Janet nodded. "Agreed. Anyway, did you know about Prender's thong site?"

Prender had been in the middle of taking a drink of water, which he spit out all over his desk.

Her question *had* come completely out of left field. She was certainly a strange person. Why Vestin…ugh…*Lord Vestin* had ever agreed to work with her was just as confusing as when Emiliano had chosen to do so.

The woman was strange.

That didn't mean Carina wouldn't play along, though.

If Prender had a thing for thongs and Carina had to look at them in order to save her own hide, so be it. She'd done worse in order to survive over all these years.

"Thong site?" asked Carina, feigning interest. "For real?"

"I told you that in confidence, Janet," Prender said, mopping up the water as best he could.

"Ah, bullshit." She waved at him to shut up. "The guy's a pretty decent designer. Fang fucker in there made him shut down his Onlyfans page, though."

Carina's eyebrows were fully up. "You had an Onlyfans page for thongs?"

Prender slumped forward. "Yes, and I'd really appreciate it if you didn't blab about it to everyone."

"Why would I do that?" Carina replied, doing her best to be hurt by his comment. The man had clearly made himself quite useful to Vestin as of late, so maybe he could convince their Lord to let her live. Manipulation was not beneath Carina, even if she wasn't technically a Dark Witch. "I think it's fantastic, Prender!"

"Yes, well, you may think whatever you wish, but…" His head snapped up. "You do?"

"Of course! Anyone who uses their artistic ability to give to the world is a hero in my book." That wasn't true at all. Well, maybe it was. Honestly, Carina couldn't care less what people did with their artistic skills. She was merely trying to score points here. "I'm truly impressed, Prender. Truly!"

"Truly?"

"Truly."

He smiled and sat back up strongly. "Would you like to see the designs?"

No.

But that's not what she said.

Instead, she walked around to the other side of his desk and replied, "I can't think of anything I'd like more."

CHAPTER 32

Emiliano

He'd always loved to kill, even when he was running *The Dogs*. In fact, he'd made it a rule that whenever killing was to be done in droves, he would lead the charge. Sofia, his then second-in-command, would often complain that he needed to remain protected, but Emiliano's lust for blood had been with him since day one.

He would never be denied.

And now that he was leading Lord Vestin's army, he was going to be granted his wish of ripping as many bodies apart as possible. It would be a glorious night, and following the effort Emiliano planned to put in, Vestin would make sure the zombie led every battle throughout topside and the Netherworld.

Emiliano actually found he was enjoying his new role even more than being fully in charge, too, and that was surprising. But it *was* better. He didn't have to deal with all of the paperwork or any of that garbage. Nobody came to him asking for a day off because of a sick kid or a doctor's appointment. There were no Human Resources complaints, and there used to be many. MANY. There were no requests for higher pay or advances, either.

His job was to make sure the army was ready to kill.

That was it.

No less and no more.

It was glorious!

He sniffed the air, catching the scent of a plethora of uncooked normals. In other words, they weren't yet zombies. That was about to change and it made Emiliano's dead heart desire to beat.

"We will not fail," he cried out to the army standing before him. "Do you hear me?"

"WE DO!"

"We will crush them all! They will scream in horror! Every single one of them will be changed to join our horde! Do you hear me?"

"WE DO!"

Emiliano felt his face contort as sweet rage welled up inside him, turning his desire for blood into a need so deep that it threatened him with internal combustion.

He spun around, raised his arm, and began running toward the convention center.

"CHARGE!"

CHAPTER 33

Jin

The flight over was incredible, until they actually arrived. Looking down was like watching a sea of cockroaches swarming on a kitchen floor. One thing was for sure, he was glad he was wearing the PPD protection outfit under his normal clothes…just in case.

Zombies were everywhere.

"There are way too many of those fucking things," Raina said. *"I'd love nothing more than to destroy them all, ripping them apart inch by inch, but even in my current form I'm not insane enough to try."*

She landed on top of the convention center's roof and morphed back into her human form. The result of that was Jin falling onto his back with a thud.

"Ouch. Thanks."

Raina gave him a withering look and stepped over to the edge of the building.

"Nope. There's no way. I don't care how short Vestin's made those things, there are too many of them."

"So you've said," Jin got up, rubbing his back and walking over to the ledge to look down with her.

It wasn't that she was wrong. There *were* too many of them. It was that it didn't matter. If they laid down their arms, they'd be folded into Vestin's army and the world would fall.

They had to at least try, even if it was seemingly senseless.

But their plan of rushing in and fighting the zombies head-on wasn't going to work. Yes, they had the miniguns, and those would certainly help, but would they really turn the tables? He couldn't believe they would.

First off, were these all of the zombies, or were there more? Clive and Rudy had seen a bunch of them in a supposedly abandoned building, and the feeds had shown a number of people standing outside of similar places. If each of those people were doing the same job as the guy who'd tried to stop Clive and Rudy from going in to see what they were dealing with, that would be loads of filled buildings.

Secondly, even if the mass of zombies beneath them at the moment did account for all that, how many more were already outside the city, breaking into houses and converting people left and right?

Hector's crew may have warned the residents to stay inside, but that didn't mean much since their doors could easily be knocked down.

Jin shook his head.

This wasn't a war. It was an infestation.

He opened a call to the crew. "*Everyone stop. Nobody come into the city just yet. Our plan is not going to work. We'll be overrun in minutes.*"

"*What are you after talkin' about, chief?*" asked Lacey.

Raina answered before he could. "*There are far more of the little shits than we can handle.*"

"*Holy balls,*" said Rudy. "*If Raina doesn't want to fight them right now, that's saying something!*"

"*Never said I didn't want to fight them, chicken nugget,*" Raina replied. "*I said we can't win by bum-rushing them.*"

Before Rudy could retaliate, Jin said, "*We need a different plan. Whatever it ends up being will still require the full force we've assembled, but...*" He trailed off as he watched a group of normals who'd been shredded not two minutes ago begin to reanimate. "*Yeah, we definitely need a different plan.*"

CHAPTER 34

Carina

Thong-watching wasn't exactly something Carina had ever imagined she'd do, but she had to admit that Prender's designs were next-level. They were tasteful in a "thong" kind of way. There were jewels, crafted stitching, and bits of metal that elevated the garment.

"I honestly never knew thongs could be so fashionable, Prender," she said, and she meant it. "You're an amazing designer."

He blushed slightly. "That's very kind of you to say."

Again, she'd meant it. There wasn't even a part of her in that moment looking to save her own hide. Oh, it may have been lurking in her subconscious mind, doing its best to manipulate the circumstances, but these genuinely *were* fantastic designs.

"Yes! Yes! Yes!" cried out Vestin from the other room.

"Sounds like he's finished up," Janet snarked,

"assuming you still want to go talk with him. Might want to bring a mop."

It *had* sounded a bit dirty the way Vestin had called out. There was certainly more to his mirth than mere cheering. It had the ring to it of a man who'd reached the point of no-return. Carina knew that Vestin wasn't actually in there doing anything untoward, aside from watching his zombies killing a bunch of innocents, though.

Hopefully.

She took a moment to steady herself and then patted Prender on the shoulder. "You should seriously pursue this, if things don't turn out as Vestin assumes it will."

He said nothing in response, but the look on his face spoke the same story she'd been thinking all along. He hoped beyond the shadow of a doubt that Lord Vestin would indeed fail. Sadly, based on the cheering they'd all just heard from their soon-to-be-king, it didn't sound as if that eventuality was very likely.

She left the room and walked across the hallway to his door.

Vestin glanced back, looking happier than she'd ever seen him.

"Oh, Carina!" He waved his hand at her to join him. "Please do come in. This is incredible! You need to see this!"

That wasn't the norm for him at all, but if he was going to act like they were besties, she was going to pretend it was absolutely the case. So, putting on her best happy-face, she stepped over and allowed herself to feast on the carnage in front of her. The zombies were swarming everywhere. Normals were screaming, doing their best to run away, but it was pointless. They had no chance. Even the few who'd been able to run pretty damn fast ended up being tackled by the tiny-legged zombies within seconds.

Vestin flicked the remote and yet another scene appeared. It was essentially the same story, just from a different vantage point.

He was going to win. There was no doubt about it now. It didn't take a genius to see how the creatures he'd managed to create were far more powerful than anything the world had ever seen. Even if they dropped bombs on the city, it wouldn't matter. Vestin would simply drive his zombies underground until the dust settled, and then he'd send up his beasts to chomp bits of flesh and reanimate everyone who had died.

But nobody was going to drop bombs on the millions of innocents anyway. People were too compassionate to do something like that, to their own at least.

Right?

He flicked the switch again.

This time he sat back and grinned as the image of multiple cars and a couple of buses could be seen sitting just outside the main city area. One of the buses appeared to be carrying a monster of some sort on its back.

He chuckled to himself, popping single kernels of popcorn into his mouth.

"Do you know what that is?"

"No."

"That, my dear Carina, is the PPD." He pointed toward the bus. "Inside those buses are a number of assassins, which our dear friend, Chief Kannon, somehow managed to bring topside." He glanced up at her. "Do you think it'll matter?"

She shook her head, knowing full well they didn't stand a chance against Vestin's army.

"Correct, Carina. It won't." He threw another popcorn kernel into his mouth. "They'll be obliterated and then turned to support my cause, just like everyone else who dares stand in my way."

"Is that an orc?"

He pressed a button to zoom in. "It *does* appear to be one, doesn't it?"

"Your glorious eyes are better than mine, My Lord," she forced herself to say.

It hurt.

The slowness of the way he'd turned his face up to look at her proved he was shocked she'd said it at all.

"Carina, did you actually just refer to me as 'My Lord'?"

She had to play this right if she was going to survive. No mistakes from this point on, and no attitude. Carina had to act the role put in front of her.

"Look, I know I've not been incredibly supportive of this venture," she admitted, "but you must understand that I've heard the story of taking over neighborhoods and cities since I was a child. It happened with the Dark Witches in the Netherworld at least once a year, it happened with Emiliano the moment I set foot in San Diego, and now it's happened with you. The difference with you, My Lord, is that your target is the entire world." She gave him an imploring look. "In your wisdom, which

I'm finally coming to understand is far deeper than I could ever have fathomed, you must see that someone as feeble as me would have carried massive doubts."

"I suppose that's true, of course."

"And yet now…." She gestured at the television. "I mean, how can I continue to harbor misgivings? You are truly worthy of the title of 'Lord,' and given the chance, I shall do everything within my magical powers to aid you in gaining the glory you so richly deserve."

Oh, she was good. Good enough, that Vestin actually put the popcorn down and grabbed his blood wine. He took a sip as he regarded her.

"There may be a place in my organization yet for you, witch."

"I would be honored, My Lord."

That's when she felt the camera in her pocket buzzing.

Madison!

"As a matter of fact," she said, making up a story, "I have been working on a spell that I believe could double, if not triple, the power of your zombies. Now that I've seen this, I'm going to focus my efforts on it until it's secured. If successful, it will speed the killing up so fast that anyone standing in our way will be mowed down like grass."

Vestin tilted his glass at her. "If you can achieve such a thing, Carina, I shall *guarantee* you a spot on my council."

She faked exuberance and then rushed from the room, headed down the stairs back to her office, and shut the door.

Then she pulled out the camera and pressed the button.

"Madison, are you there?"

"I'm here. We've stopped at the city because—"

"Because there are too many of them, yes. I know. Vestin's watching on his TV. He's loving every damned minute of this, but I don't know what..." She paused as the sound of her door handle turned. "Hold on."

It was Prender and Janet Smith.

"Yes?" asked Carina.

"Who were you talking to?" asked Prender.

"Yeah," agreed Janet, "and why did you rush down here so fast?"

Carina shrugged. "Sorry, I speak to myself whenever I'm working. I saw Lord Vestin's screen and I have this magic spell that could totally...make..." She stopped again. "Why are you looking at me like that?"

Prender appeared apprehensive. Janet was fine. She was just as confident as ever.

"Go on, Prender." He hesitated. "*Go on.*"

"We need to stop him," Prender squeaked. "I don't know how, but we need to stop him." His face looked intensely pained. "I don't want to spend the rest of my days serving that bastard coffee, tea, wine, and bloodied steak. I want to create thongs! It's all I've ever wanted to do!"

"Exactly," Janet said, "and I *know* I can help him grow his shop to the point where *Prender's Thong Emporium* is the only act in town when it comes to the thong game."

Carina was stunned. Was this for real? Were they being legit here, or were they testing her?

If it was a test, she was about to fail.

"Okay," she said, being as cautious as she could, "let's

say I agreed to join you in this cause, what could we possibly do to stop him?"

Prender glanced back at Janet who nodded in response.

"The PPD can't kill the zombies when they're spread out, but if they were all contained in one location, they'd have a chance…right?"

It made sense, sure, but how would they manage to do that? What place was large enough to even house that many zombies?

She brought her eyes up. "The convention center?"

"Got it in one," Janet said.

"Okay, okay." She was weighing the angles. "I agree that'd hold them, but how would we get them all there?"

Prender swallowed hard. "That would require your magic, or at least the promise of your magic." He brought his hands together. "They *hate* being small."

"Yes? Oh!" It didn't take her brain long to catch up. "If we send out some kind of promise to them all that they're going to get their height back, assuming they get to the convention center in time, they'll swarm there because of their egos. Even better, tell Emiliano it'll only work if *all* of them are there."

"Ding ding ding!" Janet said in her sardonic way. "The question is how will we get the message out to them?"

In response, Prender reached into his pocket and pulled out a small device. "This is one of Lord Vestin's Bond Links. His name for it, not mine. He developed it to converse in real-time with the leader of his army. I have one because I was his second-in-command for a while.

Emiliano has one because he's currently in charge of the zombies."

"And Vestin has one too, right?"

He pulled another one from his other pocket. "I took it from his desk drawer after you rushed from his room… after Janet finally convinced me we needed to stop him from actually taking over the world."

Carina pulled up the camera and showed it to them. "Did you hear all of that, Madison?"

"*Sure did,*" she replied as Prender and Janet's eyes widened.

With a smile, Carina said, "Prender and Janet, meet Madison, the Director of Technology at the San Diego PPD."

"*Let's skip the hugs and kisses and get down to business,*" Madison said. "*Do you think the plan will actually work, Carina?*"

"I'm confident we can get them all to the convention center if they believe they're going to get their height back, yes. I have no idea how we can hold them inside, though. I mean, I *could* magically lock the place down, I suppose, but only if I can get there."

"*And if you can do that, the PPD, along with the assassins and the others, will be there to support you. It'd at least give them a better chance than fighting in the streets.*"

"I don't know," Carina said. "I've been watching over Vestin's shoulder. He's got it all on video."

"*So do we, remember?*"

"Oh, right."

"*On top of that,*" Madison continued, "*we have a*

partially-turned zombie here who keeps groaning whenever a strong wave of zombies attack anything."

That was strange. "Why do you have a partially-turned zombie again?"

"Thought he might be able to help us, Carina," Madison answered. *"Actually, he already has to a degree. My android, and our new pal Einstein, built a zombie vaccine using Timmy's help...that's the zombie's name."*

"Interesting."

Janet reached out and grabbed Carina by the arm. "You can be thrilled about a vaccine later. We have to get moving." She started walking out. "I'll get you downtown. Prender, you get that message to Emiliano ASAP. Make sure you're clear that it'll only work if *all* the zombies are in place, and also make sure Vestin can't get in touch with them, no matter what."

Prender looked terrified at the prospect of being put in this position.

Janet stopped and said, "If you want to be *the* thong magnate of the world, you're going to have to remember what it's like to believe in yourself, Prender. Turd Vasectomy is *nothing* compared to you. You create; he destroys. Remember that."

Without another word, Janet pulled Carina down the stairs and out into the night.

CHAPTER 35

Jin

He was thinking of every possible angle, but none of them were great. Director Fysh said she was going to try and get further help, but she said it was unlikely at best. How ridiculous was that? To imagine the entire world was at the brink of falling into mayhem and a bunch of self-important assholes had to sit around and have long conversations regarding what to do about it was something that baffled Jin to no end.

He could only hope their final words would be, "Well, I suppose we should have just approved everything and discussed it later." Followed by, "Arrrrggghhh!!!"

"Chief," Madison called through, *"we have a plan."*

"You, Petey, and Raffy?"

"No, me, Janet Smith, and Carina."

What?

He was about to ask just that, but did it really matter at the moment?

"What's the plan?"

"They're going to get all of the zombies into the convention center, promising they'll get their heights back."

Okay, he *had* to ask about that one. *"Their heights?"*

"Yeah, Vestin made them all short, remember? Probably wanted to be an asshole. I don't really know all the details."

Jin did, or at least he thought he did. The little people they'd run into were dressed up as dead ringers—excusing the pun—for the zombies and were likely the impetus. It'd helped keep the PPD off the trail of the real zombies. The singing coyotes had sung a little song about the zombies masquerading as tourists earlier in the day, so the logic fit.

"Okay, so I'm guessing the hope is they're going to be prideful enough to want to be tall again?" Jin ventured.

"Exactly. Once they're all inside, the witch will cast a spell that locks the building down."

"Meaning we have to get inside before that happens unless there's a way to implode the place afterward."

"Only if you've got a few bombs handy, chief."

He didn't. What he *did* have was a bunch of assassins who were great at killing. Granted, they were used to killing in sneaky circumstances, not open-field battles, but killing was killing.

Right?

His crew also had the mini-guns. If only there'd been enough for everyone, this may have worked out in their favor.

"I don't suppose Carina could cast some massive magic spell and kill the zombies?"

"Not a bad thought, but I've been talking with Carina and

she's not got that kind of power. It'd take a number of witches to pull off something so enormous, actually."

It figured. It wasn't like Jin had actually expected an easy way out. Those options were few and far between.

"Fine. So, we have to get inside the building with the zombies."

"Yep."

"Any suggestions on how we can get there without being spotted?" He asked. *"If they see us heading in with them, they'll either stop to fight us or they'll recognize it's a trap. They can't be* that *dumb."*

"One sec."

It was more like a full minute, giving him time to consider the various ways this could all go south. He shook his head and laughed to himself. It didn't matter one way or the other. They had to do their damndest, regardless of the circumstances. That even held true if the zombies refused to go into the convention center.

He studied the rooftops.

Placing a bunch of people up here to fire down on the masses would allow them a pretty decent head start on killing before the zombies began to scale the walls. With the mini-guns Madison and the crew built, they may be able to mow down hundreds of the creatures in a very short period of time. She did say they had to ration the bullets, though, so maybe not?

And even if they did go that route, the zombies would keep rolling over normals, replacing their numbers in no time.

Damn it. Going into the convention center made the most sense, even if it was a suicide mission.

"Chief," Madison said, *"Carina is going to be there soon. You should be able to meet her at the rear of the building to discuss the plan."*

"Okay, thanks. I'll talk to the squad and get everyone prepared for this."

"Sorry, chief...Jin." Madison sounded suddenly as somber as he felt. *"I was kind of hoping we'd have the ability to travel together at some point. Rusty's moving on, I've already told you I've grown tired of the standard succubus life, and after watching the skills of Raffy and Petey, I'm not even feeling all that effective in my job any longer."*

Now wasn't exactly a great time for this conversation, but when would be?

"Wow, Madison. I'm sorry to hear that."

"I'm not. It's been time to try something new for a while now. I just didn't know what until you showed up." She laughed. *"Such is life, eh?"*

"Seems so." He felt his eyes glowing. *"It's not over yet. Let me get with the crew and we'll try to make something happen."* He opened the channel fully. *"Gang, we have a plan and it sucks. We're all going to be trapped inside the conference center with the zombies because Carina, the witch, is going to seal all of us in there."*

"Yep, that definitely sounds pretty fuckin' stupid, chief," said Rudy. *"Sorry."*

"No, you're right. It does *sound pretty fuckin' stupid, but unless someone can think of a better option, it's about the only kind of stupid we have."*

Nobody said a word.

Jin wasn't going to force anyone to walk into that building, knowing the likely outcome.

"If any of you wants to bail on this, I completely understand. I know we're here to serve and protect, but I don't think anyone ever expected this level of sacrifice. Just tell me right now if you're bolting, so I know what I'm working with."

Again, nobody said a word. He honestly hadn't expected any of them to back out. They might be a bit loose in the way they ran things in San Diego, but his officers had pride. Even though the assassins couldn't hear over the connector, Jin knew they lived for these types of scenarios. Not a single one of them would back down. Hell, if one did, they'd be ridiculed forever, or at least until all the assassins died during this insane attempt to stop the zombies.

Ugh.

"All right, then, prepare yourselves for what's to come. Madison will give you the green light when it's time for you to drive down." He then connected directly to Director Fysh. *"I need you to stay out of the fight, Director."*

"You're giving me orders now, Chief Kannon?"

He ignored that. *"You're going to head over to Vestin's compound with Chancellor Frey. She'll make sure he never gets the chance to try this shit again."*

"Ah. Right." She was quiet for a moment. *"I'll speak with Frey and we'll get it done, and there's good news on the Executive Director front...sort of. They've agreed to put together a committee, discuss the problem, get impact surveys done, decide if they can allocate the money for a rebuild, and then hold a vote."*

"That'll take weeks," Jin complained.

"More like months, Chief Kannon."

"We don't have that kind of time!"

"Welcome to topside politics."

"Fuck."

"Yep."

The entire world was going to fall and there were a bunch of self-important morons who wouldn't make fast moves in order to stop it? All in the name of "process?"

Insane.

"Jin," she added, *"I know this is frustrating and I can see how much you care about the team and the city, and I just have one thing left to say."*

Calling him by his first name? Oh oh. *"Uh...yes?"*

"You were a good hire."

She disconnected.

CHAPTER 36

Prender

Prender was so nervous that sweat was beading on his brow. He was about to take a massive risk, putting his life in danger, and right after he'd taken steps to solidify his worthiness to Lord Vestin, too!

His stomach churned.

Even if he succeeded in convincing Emiliano to get to the convention center, it didn't mean the PPD would win. In fact, it was more likely they'd lose. If that happened, Emiliano would certainly rat on Prender and that would spell the end of his life.

Was being the head of a thong empire really worth that kind of risk?

He thought about how Janet and Carina had already headed downtown. They were driving directly into the mouth of the beast. But that was their choice, right? Prender never asked them to do that. Janet had been the one pushing him to get his thong business thriving. Sure, he loved the idea of it, just as he had when he'd started the blasted company, but that dream was supposed to have died when Vestin crushed it.

And why did Janet care so much about it anyway?

Cash, no doubt. She was pretty money-hungry. He knew that from the way she nickel-and-dimed Vestin at every turn. She also wanted power. That's why she always had those clauses slapped into her contracts.

The only problem with his thinking was that Janet hadn't told Prender he needed to sign anything, and she'd been treating him quite nicely to boot. But why? Could it be that she found him interesting in a romantic kind of way?

Again, he thought she was attractive. There was no denying that. And he did fancy how she treated pompous people like Vestin.

It couldn't be that, though, right? They'd just met. She'd not given him any signals, and he was careful not to give *anyone* any signals.

It had to be the money, or the power, or the fame, or something.

Right?

Gah! He hated uncertainties. He wanted black and white answers. Gray areas ruined his day and had the potential for getting him killed.

What he *could* do was go in and tell Lord Vestin precisely what Carina and Janet had planned. It would solidify his position in the new world order. He would be revered, in fact. He might even be thoroughly praised!

The temptation was real as he padded solemnly back into his office and sat down at his desk. He brought his eyes back to his screen and stared dreamily at his designs while Lord Vestin continued cheering like a madman.

Was Prender truly this much of a coward? Besides, what was his life worth if its only purpose was to do the bidding of someone like Vestin? Prender's face fell as the futility of it all gripped him. His days consisted of one panic attack after another as of late, and he was tiring of it rapidly.

Vestin's laughter rang out at the falling of innocents, stinging Prender's ears and causing his head to ache. It wasn't the sound itself so much as what the sound represented. Lord Vestin was vile. He was rotten. He was a downright son of a bitch.

And Prender was serving the bastard blood wine and popcorn.

What the hell was wrong with him?

This had to change, and it had to change now. If it didn't, Prender would lose his nerve.

He got up and gingerly shut the door. Then he slid Vestin's connector device over his ear and pressed the button to contact Emiliano.

"Yes, My Lord?"

The voice sounded through vibrations in Prender's skull. It was awkward and it'd always hurt his jawbone, but he persevered.

"This is Prender, Emiliano," he replied. "Lord Vestin commanded I call to inform you that he is vastly pleased with how things are going down there. You and the army are thrilling him to no end." As if to solidify his words, Vestin cheered yet again. "I'm assuming you can hear our Lord's happiness?"

"Yep, and he's right. We're totally kicking ass here!"

"You indeed are, and our Lord wishes to provide you with a token of his appreciation."

"Oh?"

"He commands that you and all—all—of the zombies get to the convention center immediately. Carina is there and she's going to give everyone their full height back. She's also figured out a way to increase your speed and power."

"Really? That's great! Any chance he'll also allow us to quit shitting ourselves whenever we think negative thoughts about him?"

"I wouldn't push it, Emiliano," Prender replied. "You know how quickly he changes his mind about things when he feels challenged."

"Yeah, true. Okay, I'll get all the zombies to the convention center. Emiliano, out!"

Prender took the connector off his ear and carefully slid both Lord Vestin's device and his own down into the dirt of the small plant he had sitting next to the door.

Then, he straightened himself back up and went to fetch Vestin a fresh glass of blood wine.

CHAPTER 37

Carina

Carina was feeling a mixture of horror and exhilaration. She'd already stepped into the muck when she offered to help the PPD via her initial contact with Madison, but this was taking it about ten levels further. If they succeeded, it would be amazing; if not, she'd be tortured for a very long time.

She couldn't think like that at the moment, though, or she'd freeze up.

"You're doing the right thing," Janet said. "*I'm* not, but you are."

"Wait, what do you mean you're not?"

"I've got a contract with Vesturd," she answered, shaking her head. "While you might be worried about what his zombies are going to do to you, imagine how freaked out I am about what his lawyers are going to do to me."

Actually, the thought did seem to ease Carina's mind a

little. Being tortured was one thing, but being grilled by a bunch of attorneys and then having everything ripped away from you, including your dignity, was something else.

Yikes.

"Don't worry," Carina said, trying to offer Janet some measure of comfort, "this is going to work. It has to work."

Janet scoffed as she turned toward the convention center. "I'll believe it when I see it. Either way, this is the last time I'm going to throw my hat into the arena for a shit fondler like Vesdick." The car came to a stop. "I've done it for years, and I have to admit it's been a blast to call them names and watch them squirm, knowing they have no recourse, but none of them have ever gotten this close to actually closing the deal they set out to make." They ducked down in their seats as a sea of zombies rushed past them, running around the building. "This fucker's actually got a chance to succeed!"

Not if Carina had anything to do with it.

Once things died down, she started to get out of the car, but stopped as inspiration struck.

"Hey, do you know where the PPD is?"

"Yeah."

"Excellent." Carina pulled out the camera. "Madison, are you there?"

"I'm here. The chief is getting everyone to the back of the building in a few minutes. I'm working with my crew here to drop the cameras so Vestin doesn't see it."

"Perfect. I have another idea, but it's going to require you to get that partially-turned zombie you're holding down here as quickly as possible. Janet's car is already warmed up and she's on her way now."

"I am?" Janet asked, looking over at a determined Carina."I mean, right…I am!"

"She'll be there in five minutes, Madison."

"We'll be ready. I just have to shut down these cameras and tell the chief to get to you immediately."

CHAPTER 38

Jin

Madison reached out to him again and let him know that all the cameras had been disabled on Park Boulevard and East Harbor Drive. In other words, the cops and assassins were on their way.

Jin and Raina ran to the back of the building and waited for the last remaining zombies to clear out before Raina morphed into a unicorn again and carried them both down.

Carina slipped out from the shadows.

The look on her face was probably similar to how Jin appeared when he'd first seen Raina as a dark unicorn. It changed yet again when Raina turned back into her human form.

Jin could see Carina's heart beating in her throat, and he completely understood the way she felt.

"Got something to say, witch-bitch?" asked Raina, who

had apparently also noticed how Carina was studying her in shock.

"Huh?" Carina ripped her gaze away. "No! I'm sorry. I've just…"

"Yeah, yeah, yeah," Raina grumbled. "Just get over it. We're here to kick ass and you've got a job to do. If you don't fuck it up, *maybe* I'll forgive you for being an asshole."

Jin winced. "Reel it in, Raina." He then turned to the witch. "She's normally as sweet as pie, but when she turns into—"

The next second Jin found himself with his back against the wall and an iron grip around his throat. He was also looking down at Raina, meaning he was in the air a couple of feet.

"Did you just tell me to reel it in, you ass-gobbling gremlin?"

Jin tried to reply, but his vocal cords were being crushed, so he opened the connector. *"Raina, you may be a badass as a dark unicorn, but unless you want the rest of your month—when you're* not *a dark unicorn—to be spent standing in the unemployment line, I'd suggest you let go of me immediately."*

His eyes felt like they were bulging out of his head from the pressure and he knew he was going to pass out at any moment.

She dropped him.

"Watch yourself, Jin Kannon," was all she said in response.

It seemed there was enough of the actual Raina in there to recognize Jin's threat had been legit. That was something, at least. If there hadn't been, he would've been lying in a heap on the floor as his spirit flew toward the Vortex.

The thought irked him, causing his own eyes to smolder a bit.

He had to take hold of the situation fast. It was one thing for Raina to be who she was, but it was quite another for her to run over everyone who gave her shit. This wasn't some kind of democracy. Jin was the chief and his job was to keep things under control.

Therefore, he got to his feet, channeled his djinn magic and grabbed Raina by the arm, and then pulled her along to the side of the building after holding up a hand at Carina, signaling they'd be right back.

Raina struggled to pull away, but Jin wasn't having any of it.

As soon as they were out of Carina's visual field, Jin spun on Raina and allowed his eyes to go fully molten.

"Listen to me, and listen to me good," he said, lacing his voice with magic while using language a dark unicorn would hopefully understand. "I don't give a flying fuck about your situation right now. We've got a city on the brink of falling and a world that's going to follow it pretty damn quickly afterwards." He gestured at her. "Your little dark unicorn bullshit doesn't mean dick compared to that." He tightened his face menacingly. "From this point forward, all your aggression and attitude will be focused on the zombies. If you so much as give me even the slightest grit, I'll have you melted down and turned into glue, and that will be *after* I pluck your precious horn off and sell it to the highest bidder." He ramped up his magic even further. "Is that goddamn clear, Deputy Raina Mystique?"

And that's when something happened that Jin could never have seen coming.

She began bawling.

"Oh shit." Jin blinked rapidly. What the hell was happening right now? Jin reached out to her but she batted his hand away. "I…uh…oh shit."

"Do you have *any* idea what I'm going through?"

He shook his head as his eyes lost their glow. "I really don't."

"No, you don't, and yet you're treating me the way you are?"

That wasn't fair. He'd actually been doing his best to treat her nicely. It was almost like he was talking to a teenager at the moment. Not that he'd had any real experience with that, but he'd seen movies and TV shows.

"I'm sorry," he said, "but it's nobody's fault you're going through this, Raina. I know that includes you, and I'm sensitive to that. You, however, are *not* being sensitive to others in the least."

"I hate you! You're ruining my life!"

What?

He pressed forward. "Everyone understands your situation and we're all trying to be there for you, but you've got to try harder to control yourself."

For a few seconds, Raina's eyes lost their black as her face contorted. "I'm trying, chief. I really am. But it's almost impossible…" She growled and grabbed her head with both hands. "Dammit! Leave her out of this!"

Jin decided maybe he wasn't actually helping the

situation. He needed the dark unicorn to fight the zombies, even if that meant Raina was going to be a colossal bitch for the time being. What he couldn't tolerate was her attacking the crew or any of its friends.

"Listen," he said through the connector, *"you have to let go and be what you are. I get that. I respect that. Believe it or not, when it comes to certain aspects of your personality and the demons we all harbor, I understand it better than you can imagine. But where I draw the line is you potentially hurting your own team because you're being too careless."*

The PPD cars were pulling in, along with the bus transporting the assassins and Officer Kink.

"Excuse me," said Carina, holding up her hands. "I know you two wanted to talk alone, but I think I may be able to help here."

Raina growled at her, so Jin stepped between them and gave the unicorn a firm stare. She calmed slightly.

"How, Carina?"

She held out a small vial. "It's a mild calming agent. It won't take away all of her aggression, and it won't drop her power at all, but it should provide her with the ability to control where she focuses her anger."

"And you don't think there'll be any side-eff—"

Before he could get the words out, Raina reached over and snatched away the vial, and then downed its contents.

"Oh...ugh. That tastes fucking horrible."

Raina coughed a few times and dropped the bottle. It shattered when it hit the ground. She was bent over for about twenty seconds before slowly lifting her head up again. Her eyes had returned to normal, but the rest of her was the same as before.

"Wow," she said in a voice that was less grumpy, "I feel a lot better." She blinked in confusion. "Don't get me wrong, I still *want* to rip apart everything and everyone, but it's like I can *almost* control it now."

Carina was all smiles. "Glad I could help." She then grew serious. "It'll only last about an hour, though, and then you'll need another. I've got a few more in my pack, and if we get through all this, there's a huge vat of it back in my lair. It's been the one elixir I've kept building over the years to help keep my light magic flowing, meaning I have a lot of it." She smiled at Raina. "I drink at least one vial a day myself."

Raina began bawling again.

"It's all right," Carina said, giving Raina a much-needed hug. She then turned to Jin. "I have to get inside now. She'll be fine, though. Just give her a few minutes, okay?"

"Yep."

Carina nodded and took off into the building.

CHAPTER 39

Prender

Lord Vestin had taken the glass of blood wine and drained it in one shot. The man was clearly loving every minute of how his plan was unfolding. He cheered, he laughed, he clapped his hands, and he generally looked more pleased than any vampire ever should.

With luck, that would all come crashing down soon.

"That's odd," said Vestin as he calmed a bit. "Why are all the zombies slamming into Emiliano?" He sat back in his chair with a perplexed look on his face. "They should only do that if he summons them." Vestin glanced up at Prender. "But why would he summon them?"

It was obviously a rhetorical question, at least from Vestin's perspective, even though Prender actually knew the reason.

Prender wanted to spill his guts at that moment, tell Vestin what was going on and beg for mercy. If he fetched the connection device before it was too late, Emiliano would resume the killings and maybe, just maybe Vestin would allow Prender to live, after a fair bit of punishment.

Vestin picked up a piece of popcorn and held it to his lips, though not taking a bite.

"He must have some plan to…" He paused. "Ah! I see. He's going to bring everyone into the convention center and start destroying all of the normals in there." He began bouncing in his seat again, after having started to chew the popcorn. "This is so exciting. I can only imagine the upcoming war as we take over states and then countries and then the Netherworld. The battles will be epic!"

Prender was trembling as Emiliano's camera showed the zombies allowing droves of normals to escape.

That visual caused Vestin to stop bouncing. "Why is he letting them go?" He soon resumed. "Ah! It's because he wants to give chase! Brilliant!" Vestin looked up again at Prender. "Emiliano's fully aware that I'm watching, you know? He's clearly trying to give me a wonderful demonstration of the power I've brought into this world!"

It was all Prender could do to not say a word. His life was possibly moments from ending, and he had the means to stop it. He could either admit his part in all of this before it was too late, or, even better, he could throw Janet and Carina under the bus completely and claim he had no idea what was happening until just now. All he had to do was go back and fish the connection device out of the soil, claim he found it in Carina's office, and ask Vestin what she could possibly have been doing with it.

Damn. That wouldn't work. He'd contact Emiliano straightaway and learn that it was Prender who told

Emiliano to get everyone into the convention center in order to get their heights back.

Prender had trapped himself.

There was no way out now, unless Carina's plan worked and the PPD somehow managed to destroy the zombies.

But Prender could do one thing before everything became obvious. It would stop Vestin from being able to kill him while they were alone. It would also give Prender time to run, should it become necessary.

He rushed to his office after grabbing Vestin's emptied wine glass. Then he reached into the bottom drawer of his desk and fumbled around until he found the little gold box he kept hidden in the back. Opening it, he pulled out a small white pill and dropped it into the glass. Next, he walked out and filled the glass to the brim with blood wine, swirling it gently until the pill dissolved.

Returning, he said, "I believe success will soon be yours, My Lord." He handed him the glass. "It has been my honor to serve you and to watch your genius in action."

Lord Vestin lifted the glass up as if to toast Prender's words. "Yes, I'm sure it has been." Vestin then downed the contents of the glass and smacked his lips. "Delicious, Prender. A top-class blood wine here."

He turned to the screen again and slowly set the glass down on the table beside the chair.

"Is that Carina up on the ledge? It looks like her." He rubbed his eyes. "It *does* look like her, right?" Prender said nothing as Vestin yawned. "What's she doing there? Did I…." He blinked a few times. "Did I sennnd her therrre?" His voice was slowing. He shook his head, looking more and more wobbly by the second. "I don't recall sennn... sennn...sending her down there." His speech was affected badly now. "Prennnnder, I'mmm nnnnot feeeeeeeeellliing soooo wellllllll..."

Vestin collapsed in his chair, putting the final nail in Prender's coffin, should the PPD fail.

"This had better work," Prender rasped as he stared down at Lord Vestin's passive face.

CHAPTER 40

Emiliano

At first, Emiliano was thinking it'd be fine to just wait until all was said and done before bothering to increase the height of the zombies again. Then, he imagined the looks of dread and awe on the faces of the people as he and the army attacked. As it stood, everyone laughed and pointed at them until they were consumed with power and violence.

It was embarrassing.

On top of that, if Carina was able to further their power and ability to kill, he definitely wanted to take advantage of it.

So Emiliano used the one call he had at his disposal. It was a blast of scent that transferred from him to each and every zombie, telling them all to immediately rush to his position. Once it hit those nearest him, they would transfer it forward and so on until it struck every zombie in San Diego...well, at least those who were part of

Vestin's army. Even if they were miles away, they'd pick up the communication within seconds.

Unfortunately, he hadn't waited until he was in the convention center before sending it and so he was currently being crushed by all the zombies within the area.

"All right, all right," he cried. "Back up before I snap every last one of you in two!"

They backed up, only to be thrust forward again as wave after wave of the zombies arrived.

After what seemed like twenty minutes of pushing, he'd finally managed to get to the main entrance to the convention building and got inside.

Carina had walked out onto one of the balconies and he gave her a nod, but it was difficult to stay focused with all the mayhem.

Apparently the word was out on the street about how the zombies were wasting people, because everyone inside the building rushed out, screaming and toppling over each other.

"Leave them alone!" Emiliano called out. "We're all about to become tall again, and even more powerful. Once that happens, we'll hunt 'em down and waste every last one of them."

There was a look of pure hope on all their faces. It was something only another zombie could see, of course. To everyone else, they'd just look like they always did.

He was about to say something more, but to what end? His zombies didn't need pep talks. They needed to look and feel strong. Being tall again would grant them that, and it made Emiliano feel a sense of pride in knowing that his Lord was looking after them somewhat.

Maybe this was what Sofia and Alejandro felt during those rare moments when Emiliano offered them praise?

Just in case, he decided to pass it on.

"Um," he said, quieting the chatter, "you've all been doing a great job killing and turning normals into zombies." It felt incredibly odd. "I…uh…couldn't have done it without you…or something."

They were all beaming now. Again, you wouldn't have a clue unless you were a fellow zombie.

"When this is all said and done, I'll…uh…buy you a beer, I guess."

They cheered, clearly not realizing Emiliano was never actually going to buy them drinks. Even if he had, zombies and beer weren't a great combination. It made them far too gassy.

He was going to say more, but his soldiers were so busy high-fiving each other that he just decided to let it go.

Besides, he didn't want them *too* happy. They still had a lot of work to do before the night was over.

CHAPTER 41

Jin

Everyone had arrived and they were being as silent as death.

They snuck through the halls, barely making a peep. That wasn't surprising when it came to the assassins. If you couldn't sneak as an assassin, you couldn't *be* an assassin. In fact, one of the tests each of them had to endure was creeping up on seasoned veterans without being noticed. Almost nobody passed that particular test, but as long as you did well enough, it was clear you'd be able to get by your average person.

Jin was glad to see that Hector's team, Einstein and his brothers, and the crew of the PPD were all moving as silently as panthers on the prowl.

All but one of them could've passed the assassin test.

"Officer Kink," he whispered, waving the orc forward.

"Yep?" It was said in full voice.

Jin motioned for him to keep his voice down. "I don't suppose you can breathe any more quietly?"

"Oh, right, sorry. My wife says I sound like a ternordo."

"Tornado?"

"Dat's da one."

"Wife?"

"Yep." He tilted his head. "Why you ask like dat?"

Jin grinned innocently. "No reason. Would love to meet her someday."

"Oh. No orfence, but she don't like weird guys."

The grin vanished. He turned around and continued forward.

Convention centers topside were seemingly much larger than the ones in the Badlands. From the looks of the place, it could hold tens of thousands of people at once.

He kept them moving forward as quickly as possible, knowing he had to reach Carina fast while still keeping from being noticed until she got the doors locked down. Based on what he could see of the place, though, it was so huge only an outright run would get them there in time.

KLINK. KLINK. CHOINK. CHOINK. CHOINK.

"What the hell was that?" Jin hissed, pulling everyone to a stop.

"Well, I'm no witch," Raina answered, "but I'd say Carina just locked the place down."

Jin gave her a quick glance and then stared back up the hallway.

If that was true, the shit was on.

"Madison, have you heard—"

"She's cast the spell," Madison interrupted. *"Get your asses over there fast!"*

"SHIT!" Jin bellowed and started running forward for all he was worth. "LET'S GO!"

CHAPTER 42

Jin

The mass of zombies was an intense sight for Jin. He assumed it was for the assassins as well. They weren't built for armies. They were built for sneaking in, carving their way through guards, and stitching the final entry into the book of life of their target.

This was bonkers.

To make matters worse, Jin nearly jumped out of his pants when Carina suddenly appeared in front of him.

His gun was out and against her throat liquid fast, and there were multiple other guns pressed against her body by the other members of the PPD, not to mention the slew of assassins standing nearby.

"Sorry," she said, her eyes wide. "I had to use a magical cloak to get back here or Emiliano would've killed me for having duped him."

They all lowered their weapons.

"Whew." Carina then smiled as she glanced over her shoulder. "Emiliano isn't pleased at all." She looked at Jin again. "I'm going to get back down to Madison."

"It's locked, though, right? The building is locked?"

"I'm still able to get out, since it's my magic enclosing everything. Nobody else is getting out." She patted him on the arm. "Good luck, chief."

With that she ran down the tunnel.

With a nod, the crew of the PPD unleashed their mini-guns and started blasting bullets into the crowd like it was nobody's business. The sound the little guns made reminded him of the firecrackers kids set off during Independence Day in the Badlands.

"Is it just me," Raina called over to him as the team blistered the area with shrapnel, "or are the zombies not dying in droves?"

Jin had noticed that, too. The bullets were striking and ripping through flesh, but they didn't appear to be bursting on contact.

"Didn't Madison say these bullets would break apart or something?" Raina glanced over at him and tapped the side of her ear. Jin moved to speak with her via the connector. *"These bullets are supposed to break apart, right?"*

"Yeah. They're breaker bullets. That's kind of what they do, and it looks like they are *breaking once they hit the wall. They're not actually doing their job until they've made it through the zombie's bodies."* Jin heard a click that signaled Raina had added someone else to the connection. *"Madison, the bullets aren't popping and that's making for a really fuckin' pointless use-case here! What gives?"*

"They should be working just fine," she replied. *"I don't... wait a sec."*

Again, it was more than a second, proving that whenever Madison said that, she never truly meant it would be a short wait.

Jin kept firing his mini-gun, and that's when he noticed it was getting incredibly hot.

"Fuck!" yelped Rudy, dropping his gun. "Damn thing just burned the hell out of my hand!"

Jin's was starting to turn red from the heat, too. He dropped it as did the rest of his crew.

He pulled out one of his standard guns and fired it off at the nearest zombie. The thing fell over like a wet bag of cement.

The PPD gang started using their regular guns, too, which meant the bullets were again flying, only in a much slower fashion.

It wasn't going to be enough to stop the onslaught of zombies. They'd recovered from their initial shock, clearly realizing the little bullets that were originally being fired at them weren't doing much but possibly stinging a bit.

"Shit!" Madison hissed. *"I updated the breakers to only affect supers, not normals. And I'll bet most of those zombies are being identified as normals by the breaker tech. Worse than that, I made sure they would only explode in live bodies. That way you could kill one zombie with a breaker explosion and the bullet would tear through and hit the zombie behind them, doing the same thing. But—"*

"They're already dead," Raina groaned. *"Shit. Well, thanks*

to that super huge fuck-up, we're all about to become zombies, too. Thanks, Madison. You're the best!"

"Hey!" Jin cut in. *"Didn't we just have a talk about your outbursts, Raina?"* He gave her another molten look. *"Madison, don't let the Queen of Assholes make you feel bad about this. We all make mistakes."*

"For example," he mumbled to himself, "I joined the San Diego PPD for some stupid reason."

"No, she's right," Madison said, not sounding bothered in the least. It had to have been a succubus thing to be able to take such harsh criticism without getting flustered. *"Not much I can do about it now, though, so I'd suggest getting the hell out of there."*

"Can't, dipshit," Raina said. *"Carina locked the fucking building down, remember?"*

Madison didn't reply, and even if she had it would've been too late. The zombies were pushing forward, stepping over the bodies lying in front of them. Even though they were only about chest high, they could jump pretty high.

"We have to get out of here," Clive said. *"This is impossible."*

"We'll never be able to outrun the little shits and you know it," Raina pointed out, *"so what good will running away do? May as well kill as many as we can before they waste us."*

The roar of an orc sounded, causing Jin to drop to a knee in an instant. All the zombies slid to a halt as the massive body of Officer Kink landed in front of them.

They began backing away.

Interesting.

Kink glanced over his shoulder and nodded at Jin. "I got dem. You guys run!"

Jin held his gaze for a moment, thinking how fortunate it'd been that he'd brought the orc topside. It still was very unfortunate how they'd met in the first place, but sometimes the very people who came to your rescue were the ones you considered to be the biggest pains in your ass.

The orc roared again and then started swinging his massive fists. Zombies began flying off in various directions, crashing into walls left and right. When they landed, they were clearly dead.

Studying the rest of the team, he saw they'd been just as mesmerized by the sight of the orc destroying the zombies as he'd been. It put the little creatures on their heels.

In other words, they were all wasting time.

Before Jin could make a move to get people rolling, Raina took the reins and stepped ahead of everyone, turning back to face them. "The orc needs help. Rusty, you're strong and you can't be turned. Get your ass in there and fight, now!"

Rusty didn't question it. He just ran in and started crushing, and he was even more effective than Officer Kink. In fact, Jin noted the android started a little *too* strongly. His fists were literally punching through zombie bodies instead of causing them to fly off. He adjusted pretty quickly, though, and then zombies were launched away properly.

"Chimi, you're strong, too, and you've got a good head on your shoulders...when you're not fucking about with that stupid tarot card shit, anyway." She rolled her eyes at herself. "Sorry."

Chimi didn't seem pleased with the comment, but instead of grumbling something in return, she roared and rushed toward the zombies, joining the fight.

Jin had never witnessed a cyclops in battle before. It was…interesting. She picked up one zombie at a time, snapped it in half, and threw the pieces in opposite directions. Then she roared and repeated the process.

Raina continued doling out assignments. "Lacey, you've got some kick-ass magic. Use it."

"Yep!"

The leprechaun zipped over the heads of the little creatures, launching green bolts of static that caused them to slap at their own heads. Smoke was rising behind her after each strafing run. It didn't look strong enough to kill the zombies, but it sure as hell provided an excellent distraction.

"Hector—"

"We already know what to do," he said. "We've been fighting uphill battles forever. Right, gang?" Cano, Alejandro, and Sofia all nodded, and then whipped out and cocked their weapons. Hector smiled. "I guess we're going to find out if daddy was right about my ability to fight. Let's rock!"

They filed off into the fray as Einstein and his brothers moved up and looked around.

"I believe we'll stay back for now," Einstein said. "We will make our move at the right time. This particular moment, however, is not the right time."

"Whatever the hell that means," Raina replied, again

proving she was poor with diplomacy in her current form. "Rudy, what's the one thing were*roosters* can do better than any other shifter?"

"Please the ladies?"

She gave him a look. "Try again."

His face fell, proving he totally knew what she was talking about. "But I don't want to launch fire pellets."

"We *need* you to launch fire pellets, Rudy." Raina grabbed him by the shoulders and turned him to look at the fighting. "Alternatively, you can rush into that mess and show us how great you are at hand-to-hand combat."

Rudy gulped. "I can launch fire pellets."

She let him go and turned to Clive while pointing at the rafters.

"Yeah, yeah, yeah," Clive said. "I have to get up there and extend my tail across so Rudy can run back and forth shitting on zombie heads, right?"

"You got it."

"Such a waste of my talents."

"And those are?" Raina challenged.

Clive glowered at her for a moment. "I'll need to neigh so I can get the energy to roll my tail out that far."

Raina and Rudy cringed at that. Jin had heard that Clive had some kind of magical neigh, but he'd never experienced it. It couldn't be that bad, right?

"Fine," said Raina. "Get ready to do it, but hold off until I give you the signal." She then turned to face Jin. "Chief, you were a top assassin for a reason. Time to show us why."

He scanned the area, looking for his target. It was going to be Emiliano, of course, but he couldn't see him through the crowd. Leaders tended to stand near the rear of the battle, though, which meant Jin had to work his way around.

The assassins had taken up shop on the right side and were busily unleashing magic, projectiles, and all sorts of mayhem at the zombies, and they were doing it like skilled death-engineers.

It was a beautiful thing.

The PPD crew, along with Officer Kink, were keeping the front of the line in check, at least for now.

"I know what I have to do," he said to Raina.

"Yay," she replied and then looked at Clive. "Go!"

"Cover your ears, everyone," Clive called through the connector. *"I'm about to neigh!"*

The moment Clive's wailing horse call sounded, it was like being clobbered by a shockwave from an atom bomb. It was so loud that Jin's ears rang and his vision blurred. He hit the floor and convulsed for a few seconds.

Finally, he regained the ability to control his body again, at least partly. The only thing he could hear as he dragged himself forward, though, was the sound of his own blood rushing through his head.

Everyone except Clive was on the ground, and they were all writhing in agony.

"Bloody hell," groaned Lacey. *"I'm after hatin' it when ye do that!"*

"Raina commanded me to do it! And I did *tell you to cover your ears."*

"I did *cover 'em, but it only takes the blasted edge off! Bah!"*

Jin shook himself a few times to clear the cobwebs. His

head was pounding. That neigh was off the charts. He had to get moving, though. Now was the best time.

He got to his feet and snatched his hat off the ground. The world was wobbling. He fell over again.

At least he wasn't alone. The zombies were down, the assassins were down, the coyotes were down, Hector's crew was down, and even the orc was down. Most of the PPD managed to retain their footing, but they didn't seem all that stable.

Raina finally uncovered her ears, though her face was contorted in pain from the neigh.

Clive was already rising into the air, supported by his massive tail. At the same time that was going on, Rudy had gotten up and was in the process of morphing into a wererooster, though he appeared to be struggling with the effects of the yell, too.

"Make those fire pellets sing, Rudy," Raina said.

"Yep," Rudy said, before barfing. "I'm all over it."

Jin had no idea what fire pellets were, but it was apparent he was soon going to find out.

CHAPTER 43

Frannie

They arrived at the compound, ready for anything. Chancellor Frey had her knives out, prepared to carve up zombie after zombie.

Interestingly, there were none. The grounds were empty. Frannie had been to this location numerous times, especially when she was still dating Hector. It was the first time she'd found the place to be completely devoid of guards.

"Are we at the wrong house?" asked Chancellor Frey.

"No. It definitely is the main compound. Unless we're being double-crossed by Carina, this is where we're supposed to be."

Frannie had known Carina for a long time. They weren't quite friends, but they were more than mere acquaintances, too. Whatever that category of relationship was called, it was enough for Frannie to believe Carina couldn't possibly have set her up this way.

These were dire times, however, and it was clear everyone was being forced to look out for themselves.

"Okay," Chancellor Frey said, "let's sneak in and see what's going on. If it's an ambush, I'll just kill everyone and we'll move to the next house and repeat the process. Then, when all this is over, I'll split this Carina person in two and pour salt on her until the pain makes her give up the ghost."

Frannie gave her a horrified look.

"What?" Frey replied. "Too much?"

"A little, yeah."

"Huh. Okay. So I'll just kill her then." Frey shrugged. "People lack so much creativity when it comes to assassinations anymore. They just go in and shoot. Whatever happened to the days of…" She stopped as Frannie's face grew even more concerned. "Right. I'll keep the good old days to myself."

They stuck to the shadows with Frannie taking the lead. It would probably have been smarter for her to let the chancellor take point, but Frannie knew the grounds better than the assassin. Besides, if anything went sideways at this point, it'd probably start with a strike from the rear. It nearly always did when it came to *The Dogs*. In fact, they even called that kind of attack "doggie style."

The stairs were clear, aside from a lone figure who was standing there looking down at them.

"Who are you?" the man asked.

"Director Fysh, from the PPD."

"Oh, excellent! I was hoping someone from your office would arrive, but Lord Vestin was confident everyone would be downtown fighting his armies." He bowed. "I'm Prender, by the way. And please note, I've already taken care of Lord Vestin."

Frey stepped out into the light. "What do you mean you've already taken care of him? I hope you don't mean you killed him. You *don't* mean that, right?"

The look in her eyes was that of a wild banshee.

"Oh, no! I couldn't do that." Prender was backing his way toward the door. "I put something in his drink to knock him out. That's all. I swear it."

Frey dropped the attitude and returned her knives back to their sheaths. "Okidoki," she said, instantly calm and cool. "Where's he at?"

"And where are all the guards?" Frannie asked.

Prender was looking back and forth between them. "Lord Vestin is in the entertainment room upstairs and the guards are all downtown. It was assumed with everyone trying to stave off the army, Vestin would be safe here without them."

Frannie walked by Prender, likely knowing the layout of the house better than him.

Frey was on her heels, saying, "Looks like I've given Vestin too much credit over the years. No guards? Ridiculous. Trusting his tea boy? Silly."

"I'm not a tea boy. I'm a manservant."

"Do you bring him tea?" challenged Frey as they headed up the stairs to the second floor.

"Well, yes."

"Tea boy."

Frannie rolled her eyes and just kept walking.

CHAPTER 44

Madison

Carina had made it to the back of the convention center and slipped out the door. She eyed Madison, Janet, Raffy, and Petey for a moment before focusing her attention on Timmy.

"How are you feeling?" she asked the partial zombie as she knelt down beside him.

"Tired, mostly. I feel like there are a lot of people similar to me dying in there."

"There are," confirmed Carina. "How would you like to help them?"

Timmy's face contorted and he appeared very uncomfortable with her question.

"You want me to help them win?"

"No! No, no, no." Carina reached out and put her hand on his arm. "How would you like to help them heal?"

Timmy looked into her eyes. "I would like that very much."

"Excellent."

She got up and began making motions with her hands. The ground around her was swirling with varying colors, making it look like a rainbow was forming at her feet. Madison had dominated numerous magic users over her years, but none of them had ever used spells that conjured such colors. The majority of witches she'd played with were of the Dark variety, though.

"I will need some of his blood," Carina whispered to Madison.

Good thing Madison had taken what remained of Timmy's blood from the donation he'd given to Rusty and Einstein at the office. They hadn't needed all that much in order to build their vaccine, so there was an ample supply left over. On top of that, since Carina had requested they all be transported over by Janet, Madison had the feeling Timmy's blood could be of use.

She reached into her tech bag and grabbed out the vial.

"Pour it on the ground at my feet."

Madison did as she was told.

"Now," Carina commanded, "everyone back away, except for Timmy."

The crew didn't need to be told twice. When you were in the presence of magic and the wielder told you to fuck off, you fucked off.

The rainbow of colors swirled brighter and brighter, rising up in the air until they were a few feet over Carina's head. It then expanded until it engulfed Timmy and his blood. There was a gentle sound of wind, like a breeze blowing across a lake on a fall day.

Timmy began writhing, though it didn't look like he was experiencing pain. It was more like ecstasy.

Madison *knew* that look.

A sudden flash blinded them all for a moment as the world went silent.

When Madison finally regained her ability to see, she found two bodies laid out on the ground. Carina was down and so was Timmy, but Timmy now looked like a regular college-aged kid. He was no longer a zombie. Sitting between them was a large, silver container. It was filled with a rainbow-colored liquid.

Janet had rushed over to Carina and was shaking her awake. Raffy and Petey had done the same with Timmy.

As for Madison, she picked up the container and glanced back at the convention center.

CHAPTER 45

Frannie

They were trying everything to rouse Vestin, but he was completely out.

"I can't kill him like this," Chancellor Frey complained.

"I can," Frannie offered, but Frey gave her a cold look. "Orrrrr, we can wait for him to wake up."

They watched the battling on the screen. Frannie knew it was only a matter of time before the PPD fell. They just didn't have the capacity to handle all those zombies. It *was* interesting how they'd used Clive and Rudy as a team to drop wererooster pellets on the zombies. Frannie had only seen Rudy use that tactic a couple of times. It was never pleasant.

A knock sounded at the door, causing Frey to whip out her knives. The man standing there put his hands up in shock. He was wearing a white robe with a little badge that read "Dr. Ty Sanchez."

"It's okay," Frannie said. "He's just the vet for *The Dogs*."

Frey gave her an odd look. "*The Dogs* are the cartel who own this house," Frannie explained. "They're a werewolf gang."

"Ah."

The doctor reached into his pocket and pulled out a little white device that he pressed against his own throat.

"I just found my speech synthesizer," he said in a robotic-sounding voice. "It had somehow fallen behind my desk." He then looked past everyone and added, "That man looks like he is in need of assistance, no?"

"We need to wake him up," Frannie stated. "He was given a drug to knock him out."

The doctor nodded. "Everyone clear out of the room. I have an idea."

They all walked out, but the chancellor stopped and pressed one of her knives against the doctor's throat. "Try anything funny and I'll end you."

Dr. Sanchez replied with a worried smile.

Once the door was shut, Frannie shook her head and sighed. The PPD was downtown with less than minutes before they were taking flights to the Vortex.

There were a few bumping sounds from the other side of the door they'd just closed.

Less than a minute later, the voice of Lord Vestin yelled out, "IS THERE SOMETHING I CAN HELP YOU WITH?"

Dr. Sanchez rushed out while holding up a thumb with one hand and a finger with the other, and he was wiggling his eyebrows happily.

Lord Vestin shuffled after him, his pants wrapped around his ankles. "Stop, you! I'll have you tarred and feathered for…" He stopped upon seeing Frannie and Frey standing there.

He then glanced over at Prender and gulped.

"Your time has come to an end, asshole," Chancellor Frey spoke up, her knives flashing in front of his eyes. "I've been waiting years to finish Lord Zentril's contract and now that you're awake, I can do just that."

Vestin's hands went up. "Prender, did you put something in my wine?"

Prender seemed incapable of speaking.

It didn't matter anyway, since Chancellor Frey had pulled her knife back and drew in a breath of air. She was readying to end the man once and for all.

Frannie was happy about that. Vestin had caused a lot of problems in her city and it was time for him to pay the piper.

But just as Frey was about to drive home the knife, Vestin blurted, "Vampus Stopus Killus…uh…Lord Zantril!"

Frey immediately dropped the knife and let it clank to the floor.

"You've got to be fucking kidding me," she hissed. "That rat bastard gave you his code?"

"Willingly," Vestin replied, looking smug as he pulled his pants up and fastened them. "And that means you can't kill me."

Director Fysh brought her gun up. "Doesn't mean I can't."

Vestin's hands went back up.

"Actually, it kind of does," sighed Frey, "at least while I'm around. I have to protect him from any assassins now, which is technically guild members only, but it can extend to cops as well."

"What?"

Frey nodded solemnly for a moment, and then a smirk grew on her face. "I can still torture him, though." She began pushing Vestin until he was back in the entertainment room. He fell into his chair.

"What are you doing?" Vestin asked in shock as Frey climbed on top of him.

"I can't kill you, but that doesn't mean I can't do something far worse." She cracked open his mouth with her powerful hands and reached inside.

"No! Nooooo!"

The vampire began squirming around, trying with all his might to get away from the chancellor, but she barely even budged.

Two screams later, she climbed off him and unceremoniously dropped his teeth on the floor.

Vestin was unconscious again.

CHAPTER 46

Jin

Olive's tail was extended from one end of the room to the other. It was beyond stupid. How any one being could have an appendage that long confused the mind. On top of that tail, ran Rudy. He was in his rooster form and was zipping back and forth across while launching fire pellets. Basically, that meant he was shitting on the heads of the zombies, and each of those turds was like a miniature ball of flame. They were incredibly effective, each direct hit actually killing its intended target. Rudy's aim was pretty damned accurate, too.

Jin couldn't help but feel sorry for him, though, as it was obvious each pellet released was causing the poor guy pain. He was crying out, "Buk buk buk…bu-shit!", "Buk buk buk…bu-ouch!", "Buk buk buk…bu-Jesus!", and so on.

Raina had turned into her unicorn form and was kicking at zombies with a level of power that not even

Rusty could match. One of her strikes knocked two zombies back, killing them instantly and killing those behind them within a few moments. She repeated the process over and over with a level of accuracy that would make you think she had eyes in the back of her head.

Maybe it had something to do with her horn?

Jin didn't know, and he didn't really care.

The assassins had split apart, each diving into the fray in their own particular style. Jin had hoped they'd band together, thinking that to be a more effective strategy, but assassins were loners.

He got it.

To their credit, each one of them was ripping through the zombies, proving their worth. They were making a dent, weakening the lines. That was all that mattered in the long run.

Vince Viper had his blades out and was making quick work of hands, fingers, and throats. It actually looked kind of normal with him fighting the little zombies because Vince wasn't exactly tall himself. His slice-and-dice style of fighting *did* take longer than direct kill shots, though. "Death by a thousand cuts" wasn't too far off when it came to Vince.

Nina Nightshade was launching little pellets of gasses and liquids. The gurgles that came from those who'd been struck made Jin's stomach turn. He understood the concept of a knife to the throat or a bullet to the head, but there was something dastardly about alchemy. Even standard zap-magic, like the kind Lacey employed, was more palatable to him. One of the zombies caught a pellet in the eye. The poor thing screamed, clawing at his own head while Nina laughed heartily.

It was warped.

Now, Sasha Slash was more his speed. She used a combination of knives and bullets to get the job done. Plus, she wore a cowboy hat that was similar to Jin's. This had to do with the fact that he'd been one of her original trainers. She'd taken bits and pieces from each style she'd learned from various mentors, and that included their choice of wardrobe. The way she switched between guns and knives told Jin she was going to be an assassin who hit the one thousand kill mark for sure. She was just *too* good, and yet also super careful. With each shot or stab, she stepped back, reevaluated the situation, and struck again.

That was how an assassin was supposed to work.

Marco Maim was a sword-wielding hellion. He was blisteringly fast and deadly. His blade sliced through the torso of a zombie with such speed that it severed everything, moving cleanly through flesh and bone as if it was paper. The way he spun, jumped, and moved his hands made you think he was dancing to a song only he could hear.

Jin assumed the channel Marco listened to was built from a death metal playlist.

Carla Carnage was more direct in her dealings. She employed standard explosives, not bothering with long range weapons. She was similar to Nina Nightshade, in fact, except that instead of using alchemy, Carla employed engineering. She carried a weapon that looked similar to a gun, but it was far different. A thick hose hung from the bottom of it, connected to a backpack she'd slung over her shoulders. Carla would rush in, press the tip of the "gun" against the side of the nearest zombie, pull the trigger, and then jump back out again. The zombie would wince with the hit and then would start clawing at itself in a pointless attempt to remove the device Carla had embedded. Seconds later, a popping sound could be heard, which resulted in thousands of miniature explosions that systematically ripped the poor bastard to shreds.

Again, it wasn't far different from the Nightshade technique, but since it employed metal instead of magic, Jin was somehow okay with it. Jin would be the first to admit his stance was somewhat hypocritical, considering how he used magic all the time, but he couldn't help feeling the way he did.

Next up was Chuck Cutter. His name alone would make most people assume his brand of killing came from the use of blades. It didn't. He was a gun-wielder just like Jin. They *were* different, but only in the style of weapon used and the age gap between them. Jin was a fair bit older than Chuck. While Jin was more about the traditional six-shooter, Chuck preferred more modern weapons, such as the Walther PDP Compact Steel Frame 4-inch, the TISAS 1911 Night Stalker Double Stack 9mm SF, and the Baretta PX4 Storm Compact Carry 2. Even though both men worked as assassins in the Badlands, they agreed that topside weapons manufacturers were more on the ball when it came to guns. Chuck's ability to load one-handed on the fly was impressive to watch, especially since he could do it while continuing to place perfect shots with his opposite hand.

The skills employed by today's youth weren't even imaginable in Jin's younger days.

Sadly, not all of the assassins were still standing.

Jin saw the lifeless eyes of a number of them as they bled out on the ground. The fact that none of them had turned into zombies proved that Rusty and Einstein had been successful with their vaccine, at least, but it still saddened Jin to see his once-comrades fallen.

He couldn't help but feel partially responsible for it.

No, it wasn't directly his fault. They were all adults, capable of choosing to join in on any adventure or not, but they wouldn't have even known there was an option to fight zombies topside had it not been for Jin's sales pitch.

Then again, the Badlands would've been infested with zombies soon enough, so it wasn't like there'd been much of a choice but to ask them for help.

He swept his gaze across the fallen bodies, giving each of them a spot in his memories.

Zoe Zipline, Lila Lacerate, Gage Guillotine, Damon Dagger, Felix Fury, Troy Takedown, Megan Mutilator—damn, she was one of Jin's favorites—Quinn Quicksilver, and Fiona Fatal.

They would all be remembered for their attempt to save the world, even if only by him.

Jin wasn't a fan of at least half of the assassins in the Guild, but the other half were decent enough, outside of work. Megan, for example, was someone Jin had dated for a while. She was brutal in her killing style, but gentle as a lamb when it came to her daily life. He truly hated seeing her lying there lifeless.

Juxtapose that with Dexter Deathstroke, the guy who just ran by Jin. Of all the assassins in the group, Jin never understood why Chancellor Frey kept Dexter around. He was reckless, stupid, and beyond violent. Why couldn't he be lying dead instead of Megan?

The man's medium of dealing death came in the form of magic, which would've been fine if it'd been normal magic. It wasn't. It was some awkward ass blend of various types he'd somehow stumbled upon during a massive trip he'd suffered after taking one too many hits of LSD. Plus, the guy was a boisterous, opinionated asshole. He thought he was the best assassin money could buy. And he probably was, if you were looking to hire someone who didn't give two shits about destroying everything and anything.

The members of the Guild knew Dexter punched a hell of a lot of power, but everyone also understood that Dexter never knew what the hell was going to come out of his fingertips. In other words, the jerkoff had zero control, and that's what worried Jin at the moment.

Dexter had been glowing brighter and brighter, meaning he was about to unleash some heavy magic. If it worked out, it could well be the wizard would put an end to all the zombies with one blast.

Honestly, if that *did* happen, Jin would work to change how he felt about Deathstroke.

"Deathstroke's gonna blast!" Dexter yelled out, which is what he always did whenever he was about to release his magic.

Dumbass.

The man's body contorted back and forth as he rose several feet from the ground. Suddenly, beams of green, blue, purple, pink, and yellow launched from his chest, zapping down at all the zombies and hitting every last one of them. The energy struck for a solid ten seconds before finally stopping.

Dexter dropped to his feet and promptly passed out, falling straight backward, and slamming his head on the hard floor. His skull cracked open and his eyes dulled over as blood poured out of his nose and ears.

Jin squinted to look at him more closely, finding the guy had somehow managed to kill himself.

Unbelievable.

The fighting stopped momentarily as everyone wondered what the results were going to be from Deathstroke's blast.

In a flash, the answer came, and it wasn't good.

Dexter Deathstroke would forever be remembered as the prick who'd accidentally killed himself while simultaneously returning the little zombies to their full height.

"What an asshole!" Raina groaned. *"Like it wasn't bad enough when these fuckers were short!"*

It was Jin's turn to act.

It took a fair amount of focus, but he summoned his djinn magic and pulled forth his guns. The itching in his eyes told him they were burning healthily, which gave him the energy to go into speedy mode. A rush of power struck and the world slowed to a crawl. It wouldn't last forever, so he had to utilize the time it gave him wisely.

He took off around the edge of the colliding warriors, seeking his ultimate target. While he couldn't sense zombie heartbeats—since there weren't any—he *could* tell who was a normal and who was a super. Every super he passed ended up with a bullet between the eyes until he got to the back of the pack.

That's when he saw Emiliano.

The zombie looked frustrated as hell and Jin knew why. Emiliano was incapable of moving due to the mass of zombies pressing in on him from all sides. That was a problem for Jin, too. Not because he was incapable of moving, obviously, but because he had no way to get close to Emiliano.

Fortunately, he was a great shot.

Raising his gun, he targeted Emiliano's head, which was perfectly visible through the slow-moving bodies surrounding him. He slowed his breathing and steadied his arm until there was almost no shaking whatsoever. Then, with a gentle pull of the trigger, Jin released a single bullet that zipped across the room and connected with Emiliano's skull.

It was the perfect shot and the way the other side of Emiliano's head began to blow out, Jin knew his mission had been accomplished.

Not that he was done fighting, but one of the things he'd learned as an assassin was that taking out the head honcho of any organization made everyone else feel like they'd been gutted.

Or, as he liked to call it, *thunderstruck*.

It messed with their collective equilibrium.

Recognizing he only had about ten seconds left of

speedy time, Jin rushed back to be with his crew. Staying where he was would have left him at the mercy of loads of unhappy zombies. Once they figured out their leader was gone, they were definitely going to be unhappy, after first going through a level of confusion.

He dove across the last of the zombies and rolled back up to his feet just as the world returned to normal.

"Got him!" he said through the connector, but it was an unnecessary announcement.

"THE BOSS IS DEAD!" cried out one of the zombies. "I MEAN, HE WAS ALREADY DEAD, YOU KNOW? BUT NOW HE'S LIKE DEAD-DEAD IF YOU SEE WHAT I'M SAYING!"

"AWWW!" groaned the other zombies, and then they started to fight even harder.

"Good job, chief," Raina said through the connector. *"You've used your special skills to make our situation even worse."*

That he had.

Dammit.

"Guys," Clive called out, *"I just had an idea."*

"Hopefully it's better than what the chief did," Raina rumbled.

"Maybe, I don't know." Clive adjusted on the rafter slightly. *"I've left Rudy off this connection because I think we may have an edge that will require him, but he's not going to like it."*

"When's he after likin' anything?" asked Lacey.

It was a good point.

Clive ignored the comment. *"He and I hang out all the time, obviously, and he's told me all there is to know about wereroosters. It's been...interesting. Anyway, there's a legend that he shares repeatedly when he's drunk. Apparently, if you get a wererooster mad enough, they'll do much more than fire pellets."*

"Like what?" asked Chimi, though her voice was more of a growl since she was still fighting.

"He called it, reverently, I might add, 'The Lava Shits.' He always made it sound like it was one hundred times more powerful than the pellets."

To Jin, those pellets were pretty damned powerful and there appeared to be an unending supply of them.

"How would we make him mad enough?" asked Jin, knowing they needed any edge they could get.

"Well, we all know he hates being called a chicken," Clive answered.

"Meaning we have to make fun of him," Rusty said. *"I'm all for it."*

"Same," agreed Lacey.

"Okay," said Clive, *"I'll add him back into chat and we'll need to get after him something fierce. If this is to work, he's gotta be really ticked off."*

Jin didn't love the idea, that was for sure. It seemed mean. Better than dead, though? Maybe.

"Hey, chicken nugget," Clive said, *"you're doing great!"*

"Buk buk buk...bu-fuck-you. Don't call me that."

"He's right, though," Raina chimed in, "watching you shoot out fire turds like this makes me reconsider all those BBQ wings I've eaten over the years. Then again, a couple dozen BBQ wings sounds pretty tasty right about now."

"Buk buk buk...bu-up-yours-Raina!"

"Don't ye be after listenin' to 'em, ye plate full of parmigiana. Yer doin' swell!"

"Buk buk buk...bu-are-you-kidding-me-right-now?"

Chimi was next. *"You're a chicken."* She clearly wasn't great at insults.

"Buk buk buk...buh-you're-calling-me-names-too-Chimi? Buk buk buk...bu-come-on!"

"Listen up, you main ingredient in most stir-frys," said Rusty, *"I've seen your files and know all there is to know about you, including how you like to dress up like a chicken when you're on vacation."*

"Buk buk buk...buh-that's-supposed-to-be-confidential!"

The glowing of Rudy's eyes showed the wererooster was starting to steam up, and he was launching pellets at double the speed now. In other words, the plan to make him angry was working.

The rest of the crew looked at Jin, but he just couldn't do it. Making fun of one of his crew like that wasn't in his blood. At least not directly.

However, he *did* have an idea.

After a quick whisper to Einstein, the coyote nodded and spoke with his brothers.

An instant later, Rex, Rover, and Spot began to hum louder and louder, until it was almost as painful as one of Clive's neighs..

The fighting slowed on all sides, until coming to a full stop while everyone covered their ears, probably expecting the worst.

The coyotes began their tune.

Chicken pot pie and I don't care

Chicken pot pie and I don't care
Chicken pot pie and I don't care
And Rudy is a chicken!

"Buk buk buk...bu-that's-it!"

Jin glanced up and saw Rudy's eyes were glowing so brightly that he could barely see the rooster's head at this point. His wings were out and they were smoking. Feathers began flying off his back as well.

"Everyone get back!" Clive barked through the connector. *"He's gonna blow!"*

"BUK BUK BUK… BU-FUUUUUUUUUUUUCK!"

It was like watching a flame thrower in full force. The poor bird held on for dear life as flames shot from his bottom, frying the zombies below him to a crisp. All in all, there must have been two hundred killed by a single ass-blast, and many more who were slapping at themselves to put out their personal fires.

As soon as he finished, Rudy fell off Clive's tail, having lost consciousness. Good thing for him Chimi was able to reach out and catch him.

"Is he okay?" asked Jin.

"He's out, he stinks like a sewer, and his tail feathers are singed, but he's still breathing."

That's when Jin noticed that everything had gone quiet and the zombies were all down on one knee with their heads bent forward.

"What the fuck?"

CHAPTER 47

Frannie

Prender walked forward and looked down at the fallen teeth.

Director Fysh and her assassin friend were standing there, sensing Prender was feeling suddenly empowered.

"You could make him impotent," he whispered, his voice barely audible.

The two women looked at each other, and then back at him again.

"You mean, like, cut his nuts off or something?" asked Frey.

"Worse," Prender replied, standing a little taller. "Take his teeth and reinsert them backward, points first. They'll immediately heal over and he'll be as docile as a lamb. It's the worst punishment you can give to a vampire. And, it's not reversible. He'll be stuck like that until he dies."

Chancellor Frey eyed Prender for a moment and then grabbed out her datapad and started searching. "Huh. No shit. Never heard of that one. You'd think in all my years as an assassin, this request would've come up somewhere."

"It's not killing him," Frannie stated.

Frey shrugged. "We don't *only* kill. We castrate, take fingers, remove eyes, and so on." She tapped on the datapad. "This one is new, though."

"No, I mean you said you couldn't kill him. Making him impotent is *not* technically killing him."

"Ah, true. Technically." She smiled in a feral way. "As the little guy said, it's worse."

Like some kind of crazy villain, Chancellor Frey reached down and grabbed the teeth. She momentarily positioned them normally to make sure they were on the correct sides, and then flipped them over and shoved them home, points-first.

The wailing cry of Lord Vestin as his consciousness resumed was so loud that the windows in the room shattered, the TV exploded, and Chancellor Frey got launched through the air so hard she hit the ceiling before bouncing off and landing on the floor. Director Fysh had jumped out of the way just in time, or she would've been crushed.

"Ouch," Frey said, cracking her neck from side to side as she got back up.

As for Vestin, he was in the chair sobbing.

"You've destroyed me," he rasped. "Why?"

"Technically, it was all Prender's doing," Frannie said. "He drugged you and then suggested the means for making you impotent."

"Prender?" Vestin said, his face lost in confusion. He

then glanced over at the man. "How could you do this to me, Prender?"

Prender laughed. It wasn't a nice laugh, either. It was one of a man who had lost a bit of himself.

"How could *I* do this to *you*? HA! You stole my dreams, called me names, treated me poorly, and then replaced me as your second-in-command. I've dealt with your insults, your cruel words, and your meanness for a long time. You, No-Longer-A-Lord Vestin, did this to yourself."

Vestin sat back in the chair and began to nod to himself slowly.

"You're right, Prender," he whispered. "You're absolutely right. I've been a horrible person. I see that now."

Chancellor Frey had gotten back up and was busily brushing herself off. She grabbed the datapad and read over the screen again. "Yep, it clearly took. This asshole isn't a threat to anyone anymore. The only problem you're going to have with him now is that he'll be completely aimless. If someone doesn't take him in and watch over him, he'll end up dead in an alley within days." She looked up at Frannie. "Of course, you could put him in jail and he'll die sooner than that." Frey nodded toward Vestin. "He won't defend himself or even fight. Hell, if a fly lands on his food, he'll merely have a nice conversation with it."

"Flies are people, too," Vestin mumbled.

They all looked at him in confusion, and then Prender's eyes lit up.

"Actually, I have an idea for what to do with him."

"Oh?"

Prender was all smiles. "Have you ever heard of *Prender's Thong Emporium?*"

CHAPTER 48

Jin

It wasn't like the zombies were praying, it was more like they were…surrendering?

The combined front of the PPD crew, Hector's team, the orc, and the assassins all backed off, carefully stepping over the fallen bodies all around them.

The zombies began scooting over in order to open a path between them. It looked to have led back to where Emiliano had been standing before Jin wasted him.

Another zombie walked through. She was the one who'd been to the right of Emiliano.

She was waving a white flag.

Jin couldn't believe his eyes.

"Do you guys think this is legit?" he whispered.

Sofia had been standing next to him, wiping blood from her hands. "It's legit. That's Shiela. She was one of *The Dogs*. When we give up, we mean it." She then pushed

Jin forward. "Go accept her surrender before she changes her mind."

Jin glanced around at the others and then took a few steps out.

"Yes?" he said.

"You've killed Emiliano, you're wasting us in droves, and our bites don't seem to be turning any of you into zombies." She nodded at the corpse of Dexter Deathstroke. "While we do appreciate that guy giving us our heights back, we're baffled as to why he would be directed to do so."

"He wasn't," Jin stated. "He's never been able to control his magic, so it was a gamble, as it always was with him."

Shiela suddenly grabbed her chest. All the zombies did. Their bodies shook for a few moments, and then they began to gather themselves again.

"Whew," Shiela said, refocusing on Jin. "Based on what just happened, it appears that Lord Vestin has also lost his power."

Jin's eyes shot open. "He has?"

"We no longer feel his pull." She glanced around at her fellow zombies. "Can anyone sense Vestin?"

They were shaking their heads, still looking a bit drained.

Thank goodness for Director Fysh and Chancellor Frey!

"Worst of all, though," Sheila added with a grunt, "we've just been attacked by a fire-shitting chicken. That's not only horrible, it's humiliating."

"Rooster," moaned Rudy from his position with Clive. "For the love of all that's holy, I'm a goddamn rooster."

"Sorry," replied Shiela. "Anyway, we give up. Fuck Lord Vestin and fuck being a zombie. It sucks."

"YEAH!" agreed all the other zombies.

Then, as one, they cringed and grabbed their stomachs. At least, that's what it looked like they were doing.

"Everything okay?" ventured Jin.

Shiela hesitated for a few seconds, scanning the other zombies. "Yeah, I think so. Usually, we shit all over the place whenever we think negative things about Vestin. This only proves we truly are free of him." She then looked down at herself. "Except for these fucking bodies, of course."

"I can help with that," Madison called out, walking up behind everyone.

Jin turned and saw she was holding up a silver container. Walking beside her were Raffy, Petey, Carina, Janet, and a young man he assumed was Timmy.

"Carina has developed an elixir that will not only cure your zombieism, it will bring back every zombie who fell in battle."

Wow! That was awesome.

"What about the fallen assassins?" Jin asked.

"Sorry, Chief Kannon," Carina said. "I can't do anything for them. Their spirits have certainly been picked up by reapers already. Zombie spirits, however, don't head to the Vortex when they fall. Reapers may attempt to bring them along, but the way zombies are built, it's just not possible. That's good in this case, though, because it means we can reunite them with their bodies and bring them back to life." She held up a hand.

"Before you ask, yes, it will pull even the smallest cells from all over the place to reform into what each person was before all this happened."

With that, she closed her eyes and clapped her hands together.

The locks released and the doors opened.

She then nodded at the zombies and said, "One drop each, people. Any more than that and I won't be held responsible for what happens!"

Jin backed out of the way and let them get to work.

CHAPTER 49

Jin

Everyone was back to life again, and the zombies had been fully returned to their normal bodies. That was great as far as the supers went. The normals, however? Not so much.

Jin called upon the supers to keep everyone in the building and then contacted the one place he'd hoped he would never speak with again…

The Cleaners arrived within thirty minutes and started going over every inch of the area. During that time, Jin was handed a datapad to yet again sign his life away.

He hadn't bothered to read the fine print that time. It was pointless, since he had no choice but to sign anyway.

"What kind of memories do you want to give them?" the person in the Cleaners suit asked.

Jin wasn't sure how to answer that. "Uh…well…"

Janet Smith stepped over and took Jin by the arm, holding up a finger at The Cleaner. "As you know, Chief Kannon, I'm a marketing and PR person, and I'm sure I will soon be under investigation regarding how I helped Vestin."

"Probably."

"Yeah, well, I can assist you here, assuming you want to make sure the PPD, the city of San Diego, and you, personally, don't want to get sued."

"Ah. You scratch my back, I scratch yours?" Jin said. "Okay, Miss Smith, sell me."

She smiled at him. "I've been overhearing stories about a group of little people who are making a movie."

"Yeah," Jin said, searching his memory. "*Anklebiters,* I believe."

"That's it, yes." Janet glanced over at group of the little folks, and they were all wearing their zombie outfits, though their hoods were off. "Imagine how happy they'd be if it turned out this entire ordeal had been nothing but a PR stunt for their upcoming film?"

"Huh?"

"Think about it, Chief Kannon. We're in the middle of the comic convention, right?"

"Yes?"

"Everyone directly impacted by the zombies saw some horrific shit firsthand, right? Some managed to escape, some became zombies, and everyone is going to hear about it from both parties one way or another. You can't contain something this big, Chief Kannon."

Jin swallowed hard as he looked at The Cleaner again. She was right. There was no way they'd be able to contain this secret. It was going to be all over the world within hours.

Shit.

He looked back at her with worried eyes. "Help?"

She smiled again. "I've got you covered, assuming you've got me covered?"

"Deal."

Janet Smith then turned to The Cleaner and said, "Here's what we're going to do. Everyone will believe, *thoroughly believe,* this was the grandest marketing stunt ever pulled by a movie. That movie, named *Anklebiters,* is currently in post-production, and it will be released this fall in theaters across the world." She then pointed at the little people. "Those are the actors, writers, and directors. As for me, I'm the producer, which they'll believe because you'll make them believe, you understand?" The Cleaner nodded. "Excellent. My name is Janet Smith, owner of *JS Marketing LLC.*" She leaned in. "I turned in my resignation at *Turner, Turner, and Smith* this morning. Anyway, *JS Marketing LLC* specializes in creative, realistic marketing strategies for excellent, exciting movies." She pointed at the datapad where the guy was typing. "Also add in that we are currently pushing a new garment line by the up and coming company known as *Prender's Thong Emporium.*" The Cleaner looked up at her. She crossed her arms. "Do you need help spelling it?"

Jin backed away from that conversation, glad to know Janet Smith had everything under her control.

Raina was walking toward him, but it was clear she had other intentions as her eyes were focused off into the distance.

Turning around, he saw Director Fysh and Chancellor Frey, and they had two men with them. Lord Vestin had apparently arrived. Jin was going to stop Raina from doing what she was about to do, but after all that'd happened, he allowed it.

With a punch only a dark unicorn could manage, Vestin flew across the room and landed in a heap. Raina then lifted her hand at the other man, but Chancellor Frey stepped between them.

"Leave him alone," she warned Raina. "Prender here is the guy who drugged Vestin and then taught me how to make the vampire impotent. If it wasn't for him, you'd still be fighting zombies right now."

Raina lowered her hand immediately.

Director Fysh walked up to Jin, smiling. "Looks like you've done well, Jin."

"*We've* done well," he corrected her. Then he looked back at The Cleaners. "Too bad you weren't here five minutes ago. It would've been your signature on the line instead of mine."

"Sounds like it worked out perfectly, then...for me." She gave him a wink. "Why is Janet Smith talking to him?"

"She came up with a story about this all having been about a movie stunt."

"Oh! Brilliant, actually."

"Yeah, I thought so, too, but I made a deal with her and—"

"We won't prosecute," The Director interrupted while looking around. "I expected that. Was everyone saved?"

"Except for a number of assassins, yeah. Couldn't save them because they were inoculated and therefore never turned into zombies." He sighed. "In some respects, I suppose it would've been better for them to have avoided taking the vaccine."

"From their perspective, at least." She immediately pushed past Jin, her face growing dark. "Fucking Emiliano."

Jin took off, catching up to her in order to join the discussion with the man. When they arrived, though, they found Hector was already talking with him.

"...and now that I've returned to my normal self," Emiliano was saying, "I'll take back control of *The Dogs* and get everything back on track."

"Yeah..." said Hector, and then shook his head. "No."

"No?"

"You heard me, Pop. You've been nothing but bad for our community. We have better plans for *The Dogs* now, and your brand of 'leadership' is no longer welcome here."

Emiliano's face tightened into a dark scowl. "Are you challenging me, boy?"

Hector didn't even flinch. "Oh, absolutely. Well, sort of." He motioned around at all *The Dogs* in the area. "You see, it's more a case of *we're* challenging you. Now, if you think you can whoop all our asses, by all means I would suggest you start with mine. However, if you have any sense in that old head of yours, you'll wisely step aside and count yourself lucky to still be alive."

That's when Einstein and his brothers stepped up. Einstein said, "*NOW* is our time! Let's stand with our brother, boys!"

With that, the ugly little dogs growled menacingly at

Emiliano. It wasn't intimidating in the least, sadly, but there was an endearing quality to it.

After seeing all this, the look on Emiliano's face was something thoroughly unexpected.

He actually wiped a tear from his eye and sniffled.

"My boys! *Finally* you've grown to be men!" He reached out and pulled Hector into a tight embrace. "Do you have any idea how long I've been waiting for you to grow a pair?"

Following that, he knelt down and began patting the coyotes.

"Holy fuck," Rudy choked out, "the little freaks are licking his face!"

It *was* a disturbing sight.

Emiliano got back to his feet, his face radiating joy. It looked super weird on him.

"I'll get with Mr. Becarra and let him know I'm going into retirement because my boys have finally proven themselves ready to take over the family business."

He then walked away, leaving Hector, Sofia, Cano, and Alejandro to stand there in shock.

"What the fuck just happened?" asked Alejandro.

"I have no clue," replied Sofia.

"Me neither," said Cano.

As for Hector, he was unable to respond because he was too busy dealing with the lip-lock Director Fysh was giving him. Apparently, she'd decided they were going to be a couple again.

That's when Spot, Rover, and Rex broke into song.

Hector and Frannie

Sitting in a tree
K-I-S-S-I-N-G
First comes love
Then comes marriage
Then comes a baby in a baby carriage!

Ugh.

CHAPTER 50

Jin

Jin had a long conversation with Director Fysh about his future with the PPD before they headed down to join the party in the auditorium. She wanted him to stay, and she'd done her best to convince him, but he'd already made up his mind.

The place was rocking and everyone appeared to be having a great time. Watching cops and criminals hanging out together in such a way would never be something Jin Kannon could get used to. It was simply too strange. They were on complete opposite sides of the spectrum, and yet, here they were, dancing and laughing like they were long-lost friends.

Actually, when he really thought about it, *he'd* been on both sides of the fence now. Yeah, it'd only been a couple of days, but it felt like months, especially with the integration crap he'd endured. The point was that he had a unique perspective, and it told him cops and criminals weren't as different as he kept trying to convince himself they were. They shared the same story, dealt with the same issues—namely, each other—and lived and died by the sword...or the gun, as the case may be. Theirs was a life of action and adventure. It was high risk, but it was also high-reward. Cops wouldn't be around without criminals, and if it weren't for the cops, criminality would be so rampant there wouldn't even be a term for it.

So maybe seeing them all partying like this when nobody was breaking laws, or looking to enforce them, made an odd kind of sense.

He shrugged.

"It's a shame you're leaving, Jin," Director Fysh said with a sad smile. "I wish you'd reconsider, but I understand your reasoning."

She then walked away to be with Hector.

Jin felt a little down in that moment. Part of him desperately wanted to stay. He'd only known the crew for a few days now, but it was clear to him that the San Diego Paranormal Police Department, along with all of its faults, was a family. They were dysfunctional as hell, yes, but what family wasn't?

These people honestly cared about each other in their own warped ways.

It'd been a long time since Jin had felt such closeness.

Still, he couldn't lie to himself about his true goals in life. Being a cop simply wasn't in the plan. He knew that now. It took a massive zombie incursion for him to figure it out, but here he was, ready to depart his short tenure as the chief and get on with his dream of traveling.

The sound of "whipishhhhh" was followed by a "Yeek!"

Jin spun his head to the left and saw something that made him do a double-take. He even pulled his glasses down to verify his eyes weren't fooling him.

Standing there, almost completely naked, was Lord Vestin. He was carrying a tray of drinks, which was odd in and of itself. What made him *not* completely naked was the fact that he was wearing a yellow leather thong with jewels embedded around the waistline. Above his painfully small bulge was a logo that read *Prender's Thong Emporium*.

The "whipishhhhh" sound he'd heard had come from a hand-held black leather...spanker? Jin didn't know the term for it, thankfully. At the end of the spanker was a cutout in the shape of a heart. Whenever someone took a drink off the tray, they expressed their "thanks" by picking up the whipping device, smacking Vestin's ass with it, and then returning it for the next person to use. Vestin yelped each time while everyone else giggled.

Ouch.

At least they were getting to express their anger at the man in a way that didn't involve the kind of punch Raina had landed on him.

Speaking of Raina, she was standing off to the side by herself. It looked as if she was sulking. Jin wasn't surprised since she'd acted like a teenager earlier. What was strange now, though, was how the darkness had all but left her body. Her nails were still black, but everything else appeared normal again. She *was* wearing a full outfit, though, and it wasn't like Jin was going to ask her to disrobe so he could verify the completeness of her situation.

"You okay?" he asked after walking over.

Raina nodded sheepishly. "I'm soooo sorry for the way I acted, chief." She tapped on the side of her head. "It's all up here. I remember every last bit of it and I feel like a complete—"

"Raina, it's fine," Jin interrupted. "Seriously." He ran his fingers around the brim of his hat. "If I can be totally honest with you, instead of wasting your time worrying about how you get as a dark unicorn, I'd say you should do your best to cultivate a little of that darkness during the time when you're *not* dealing with a full moon."

Her eyes widened. "What?"

"I'm serious." He gave her a strong look. "You may have lost yourself there for a bit, and I can tell how much that bothers you, but when we were faced with our finality, it wasn't me who jumped into action and acted like a damn chief should." He nodded at her. "It was *you*. You pulled us together, doled out assignments, and made the team work like a well-oiled machine. If you hadn't done that, this party might have been in Lord Vestin's honor instead of a team celebration."

She glanced away, confused. "I don't know what to say, chief."

"Think about it," he replied and then took off his hat and called out, "Everyone, listen up! I've got something to say!"

The music cut off and the laughing and dancing stopped. All eyes were on him. This time, he didn't even feel a twinge in his stomach.

Progress?

"I want to thank you all for coming to the aid of the

San Diego PPD." They gave a quick cheer. "We couldn't have won this war without you. My fellow assassins, Officer Kink, Timmy, Carina, Prender, Janet Smith, and the entire crew of the PPD...all of you pulled together and helped save the day. I think we all know it simply wouldn't have been possible to defeat Lord Vestin without your help, and without the sacrifices of those who are no longer with us."

"Except for fuckin' Dexter Deathstroke!" called out one of the assassins. "Asshole."

Nobody put up an argument.

"I would like to apologize for the trouble I've caused," Vestin chimed in, his face etched with shame. He then glanced over at Jin. "Please note that I'm no longer a Lord, Chief Kannon. I'm merely a simple servant of Master Prender and Mistress Smith now."

"Quiet, you fart-felating fiend," Janet said and then gestured toward Jin. "Can't you see the man is talking?"

"My apologies," Vestin whispered before Officer Kink pulled the whip off the tray and gave the vampire a firm smack. "Yipes!"

Most of the people in the room laughed. Surprisingly, Dr. Ty Sanchez was *not* one of them. He'd walked over to Officer Kink and ripped the whip out of the orc's hand, putting a little white device to his throat.

"That isn't cool," his robotic voice rang out. "The man is a loose rectum, but he is still a person."

"Oh yeah?" Kink growled in response.

"Yeah."

They started to point fingers at each other in a menacing way but suddenly stopped. Instead of sneering, they began sniffing the air around each other's extended fingers.

Then they both guffawed at each other.

"Am you a member of da *Brotherhood of da Finger?*" asked Kink.

"Card-carrying," replied Dr. Sanchez, whipping out a card that had the image of a drawn digit with a dirty fingernail on it.

Ew.

"Wow! Dat's great. I am da superveezer at da customs place in da Netherworld. You wanna job?"

Dr. Sanchez rubbed his finger under his nose for a few moments and then glanced back at Hector questioningly.

"Go ahead," Hector said. "I'm sure nobody on *The Dogs* will mind."

"NOPE."

The orc and the doctor shook hands as Jin shook his head.

It took all kinds.

The doctor turned back around, smiling, caught sight of Rudy, and put the device back to his throat. "Buk buk."

Clive grabbed Rudy before he could dive toward the doctor.

"Anyway," Jin continued, "I thank you all again for your assistance."

Another cheer sounded.

"Now, you may all stay in here and party for a while, if you please, but I'd like the members of the PPD to come upstairs for a few minutes. We have some things to discuss."

He waved at Raffy, Petey, and the coyotes to join them as well. Catching Carina's eye, he signaled her along, too.

She set her drink down and nodded.

The entire crew was walking toward the exit, laughing and mumbling to each other. All but Chimi, anyway.

"Where's Chimi?"

Raina, still subdued, said, "She's upstairs doing one of her readings. She always does them after we finish a mission."

"Hmmm," Jin said. "I was just up there and didn't see her."

"Whenever she does the larger readings, she goes into one of the side rooms where it's nice and dark."

Interesting.

CHAPTER 51

Jin

He was going to wait for Chimi to finish her readings, but Lacey pointed out that she'd been working for a few hours and would get seriously grouchy if anyone interrupted her.

"It's like she's havin' to restart or somethin'," Lacey explained. "I'm not knowin' the ins and outs, I've just learned to leave her be until she's after finishin'."

"Kinda like Clive's mom learned to do whenever he was in the bathroom for too long as a teenager," Rudy said.

"Fuck you," Clive replied, though he was laughing when he said it.

Yep, they were definitely a family, and that was going to make this all the more difficult. But Jin had to do it. His pros and cons list had far more cons on it than pros and there was a reason for that: Jin Kannon was *not* cop material. He wasn't assassin material anymore, either.

After all these years, Jin had become simply a guy who liked wearing cowboy garb and who wanted desperately to travel and see the world. Being a cop didn't support that dream.

Director Fysh and Chancellor Frey walked into the room a few moments later. The Director had Hector on her arm.

"Gang," he said, removing his hat and setting it down, "after a nice long chat with Director Fysh, I've decided to step down as chief."

Their faces fell instantly.

He'd be lying if he didn't say he wasn't pleased to see that was their reaction. It was sad, yes, but it also proved they felt the same way about him as he'd felt about them.

"For more years than many of you have been alive, I killed people for a living." He sniffed and grinned. "In all that time, I've never been involved in a shitstorm that even came *close* to rivaling what we've been through in the last couple of days. That wasn't what I was expecting when I took the job. I thought it was going to be a pretty laid back gig, giving me ample time to hit the beach and watch sunrises and sunsets and all that."

"It's not like it's this way all the time, chief," Rudy said. "I mean, sure, sometimes things get kind of hairy, but never *this* bad. Mostly, though, we're dealing with piddly shit."

"He's right," agreed Clive and then bobbed his head back and forth a few times. "I mean, it *has* been happening more frequently over the last few years, but even now it's only like, what, once every two months?"

The rest of the cops nodded.

That wasn't as bad as Jin had thought, but he'd already made up his mind. He didn't want this life, even if it consisted of doing nothing more than handing out parking tickets. Jin wanted freedom. He wanted to go wherever he wanted, whenever he wanted. He'd worked hard over the years, giving up all the world had to offer, and now was his chance to seize the day and explore every wonder he could find.

Staying on the force wasn't going to help him accomplish that.

"I appreciate you all," he said. "I honestly do. But this isn't for me. That said, I have learned a lot about you all in the short time I've been here and I've made a few recommendations to Director Fysh." Everyone glanced back at her and then returned their curious eyes to Jin. "Since I'll be stepping down, it's up to me to name my successor. The normal thing to do is go through resumes and do interviews, but since it's my call, I already know who should replace me." He turned and looked at Raina. "Therefore, it's my honor to announce that Deputy Raina Mystique is, as of this moment, *Chief* Raina Mystique."

Everyone cheered, clapping their hands and whistling. Raina's face turned completely white. There wasn't a shred of dark unicorn left that Jin could see. Again, he wasn't going to do a full check to verify that.

"Me?" she rasped.

"You're far more qualified for this role than I am, Raina," Jin said. "You just need to let some of that dark unicorn surface all the time."

"Damn straight!" Lacey called out. "Good on you, Raina! You're after deservin' it, sister!"

"I don't know what to say," Raina replied. "I'm humbled."

"Well, you may want to get over that pretty damned fast," Jin laughed. "After only a few days acting the role of chief, I can assure you being humbled right now is nothing compared to what's in your future."

Before things got too emotional, he whispered, "And while it's completely up to you who you want as your second-in-command, I personally think Lacey would be a good choice."

Raina nodded her head. "I think she's the perfect choice, chief," Raina said and then caught herself. "I mean…Mr. Kannon?"

"Jin."

"Yeah, that's weird," Raina replied with a sour look. "I'll stick with 'chief' for now."

"Whatever makes you feel good…chief," Jin replied with a grin.

Raina shuddered. "That's going to take some getting used to."

"It really does," Jin agreed.

"Lacey," Raina said, "you're my new deputy."

"Hell yeah!" She quickly pointed at Raina. "That means I'm no longer after havin' to answer the damn phones, right?"

"We'll talk about it," Raina replied with a smile.

Jin leaned over and whispered into Raina's ear. She shook her head, whispered back, and then glanced toward the back of the room and whispered more. This went on for almost two minutes as everyone looked on with curiosity.

After including Director Fysh in on a private connection to verify everything would work out as Raina had suggested, Jin gave her a nod and gestured for her to take center stage.

"It's *your* team now, Chief Mystique," he said, "so these should be *your* announcements."

Raina stepped up, looking a bit nervous.

"Um...I..." She cleared her throat and let out a few quick breaths, psyching herself up. "I think we all know the guards downstairs, especially Guard Snoodle, desperately want to be cops, but they need some serious help to get there. It takes a willingness to put your life on the line to be effective at this job. They're too afraid to do so, but I think they can be helped. Because of that, we're going to put together a small training program for you and your guards. It will be run by Clive and Rudy."

Clive and Rudy jolted at that news.

"Sweet!" Rudy said. "Finally, some damn recognition for how awesome we are, eh Clive?"

They high-fived as Clive said, "Fuckin-A!"

"Speaking of putting one's life on the line," Raina continued, "I think everyone knows we wouldn't be alive to even have this discussion if it wasn't for Carina, so I'd like to offer her an entry-level position on the force." Carina blinked in surprise. "Chimi's going to need a new partner to mentor, and she's used to working with magic users, so it's a good fit, if you're interested."

"Wow," Carina said. "I honestly don't know what to say."

"How's about ya get your witchy' ass after sayin', 'yes,' so we can get on with it?" Lacey quipped, winking at her.

"You stuck yer neck out, Carina. Ya didn't even blink about it, as far as we know. We need people like that on the squad."

Carina swallowed hard. "I'll think about it. I'll seriously think about it."

They all clapped for her.

"Great," Raina said, her voice getting stronger. "I'd also like to invite Einstein and his brothers to the team in some capacity, though I'm not sure what we can have you do yet. You've all been such a help to the city and…" She stopped, noting Einstein was shaking his head. "Something the matter?"

"We appreciate the offer, Chief Mystique," Einstein said, "but we've already accepted positions at Janet Smith's new company. We're going to be writing loads of marketing material, running campaigns, and producing videos. It just better fits who we are." He then shot a look at Lightbulb, who was busily pleasuring himself. "Blast it, Lightbulb! How many times do I have to tell you to quit doing that in public?"

"Phmorry."

Jin winced at the visual, turning his attention back to Raina.

"Well, then," she said, "we wish you the best. Should you ever need anything from us, we'll be here for you." She then turned to Raffy and Petey. "As for you two, you've been great informants over the years, but the last couple of days have shown how valuable you can be in the realm of technology."

"Aside from the burning mini-guns with their

pointless ammunition, at least," Rudy pointed out and then scrunched up his face. "Sorry. I'm…sorry."

Raina glanced over at Madison. "You want to tell them or shall I?"

"I'll do it," Madison said. "I'm leaving, too."

They all drew in their breaths at her news. That included Jin. He knew she hadn't been all that happy, and she *had* mentioned she would love to travel the world with him, but he assumed she'd only said that because they both assumed their lives were coming to an end.

"I know, I know," she said, putting up her hands to quiet them down. "I'll miss you guys a lot, but it's time for me to go. I've felt that way for a while. I just couldn't do it because there was nobody around I'd felt confident could take over for me when I left." She pointed at Raffy and Petey. "You two have shown me things I didn't even know were possible."

"She's talking about my junk," Petey mumbled to Raffy.

"Like, I totally doubt that, man."

"Anyway," Madison pressed on, "if you're willing to take on the role of leading the San Diego PPD tech department, that would give me ample time to go traveling with my new boyfriend." She reached out and took Jin's hand. "If he'll have me, of course."

"Boyfriend?" Jin said with a gulp.

"Might wanna buy some steel undies, chief," Rusty said with a chuckle. "Trust me, I *know* what I'm talking about!"

Everyone busted out laughing at that.

"Raffy and I will take the job," Petey yelled over the laughter, "but only if we can still smoke weed."

"Like, yeah, man. No weed, no work. Ya dig?"

Raina inclined her head. "We'll put in a provision."

"Hey," Rudy asked, "while we're putting in provisions, how about adding something to my contract that says you fuckers can't keep calling me a chicken?"

"Buk buk buk…bu-why?" chided Clive.

"Dick."

Raina grinned. "We'll talk about it, but I have a feeling it's not going to happen. Maybe we could do a 'Calling Rudy a Chicken' jar or something. Every time someone calls you that, they have to put in a dollar."

"Like a swear jar," Rudy said, nodding. "I like that."

Clive pulled out his wallet and cracked it open. It was loaded with hundreds. "You *do* remember I come from a wealthy family, right?"

"Fuck."

Rusty put up his hand and interrupted the discussion. "Hey, guys, I'm also going to be leaving."

"Wait, what?" Lacey said. "No fuckin' way. If he goes, who's gonna be after answerin' the damned phones? Already said it ain't gonna be me!"

"Calm down, Lacey," Rusty said. "There's a version of me in the databanks that's in the process of being installed as we speak." He glanced over at Madison. "I've taken the liberty of removing some of *her* more submissive code, but I think you guys will like her." He then called up at the ceiling. "Riley, are you online yet?"

"I am, Rusty, and I'm ready to get to work, though I do still have a number of patches to install before I'm fully functional."

"Swell," he said and then turned to Raffy and Petey. "Take care of her, dudes. She's all yours now."

"Sweet," said Petey.

"Where are you going?" Jin asked Rusty.

In response, he walked over to Chancellor Frey. "I'm going to train up as an assassin. After tonight's fight, the chancellor is down a number of members. I can handle a lot more than an average person. Right, baby?"

"Meow," Chancellor Frey replied in a hungry voice.

Ew.

Rusty grinned at that and gave Madison a quick look. "She really likes the ExtendoPackage 1000, so thanks for building that out when you designed me."

"Yes, indeed," the chancellor agreed, her face aglow. "Thank you *very* much for that."

Again, ew.

Jin shook his head, fully recognizing Rusty would hit the one thousand mark faster than any assassin in history. All he could hope was that the android carefully chose his contracts.

"You approved this, Director?" Jin asked in a direct connection.

"Signed, sealed, and delivered. Chancellor Frey may have put in a few words with the Executive Directors, too, of course."

Of course.

"I see that look in your eyes, chief," Rusty said, interrupting Jin's connection with Director Fysh. *"Don't worry, I've already told Ivy I was going to be choosy about who I'd kill."*

Ivy, eh? It was the rare person who'd been given the okay to use Chancellor Frey's first name.

"That's great, Rusty. I'm proud of you. If you ever need

anything, find me...unless someone has a contract on my head, of course. Then, don't."

Rusty gave him a smirk in response.

The sound of stomping feet rang out as Chimi came running out into the room.

"Oh good, you're all here," she said, looking ragged. "I've been working on all the predictions and I have some heavy news to share."

Raina smiled at her. "Go on."

"Okay," the cyclops said. "First off, it seems the chief is going to be staying with us for a long time, so that's good. Secondly, Raina and Lacey, I'm sorry but you're both getting demoted. Third, Raffy and Petey are heading back to the beach to resume their duties as informants." She frowned and looked at Raffy. "I kind of hoped we could work together, but the cards don't lie."

She must have noticed everyone was smiling at her.

"Why are you all happy? This is terrible news." She quickly caught herself. "Except the part about the chief staying, of course. That's great!"

"They're, like, smiling man because you've got it all backwards," Raffy explained. He then turned and shook his head at everyone in the room. "You guys are, like, not cool, man." Raffy stepped over to Chimi. "Look, man, read your cards again, but, like, say the opposite of what their tellin' ya, dig?"

"Really?"

"Yeah, and like, so you know…I think you're, you know, like, pretty and stuff."

"REALLY?"

He tapped on the cards.

Chimi started again, though she was clearly flustered by Raffy's admission.

"Um, the chief's leaving, Raina and Lacey are getting a promotion, Raffy and Petey are staying to work in the tech department, Rusty's going to..." She stopped and stared out at everyone again. "You guys already know all this stuff, don't you?" They nodded. "Oh, the hell with this." She threw the cards on the ground and turned back to Raffy. "What's this about you thinking I'm pretty?"

The crew all laughed, making Jin feel like he was walking away at the perfect time. They were a great squad, and they would be just fine without him.

In time, he would be okay without them as well

"I know the last few days have been pretty rough on you, Chief Kannon," Director Fysh called out, "but that's nothing compared to all the paperwork you're going to need to fill out about what happened." She gave him a better-you-than-me smile as everyone on the squad shook their heads in misery. It seemed they were going to be dealing with paperwork as well. "And, yes, you *will* have to complete it before you can officially step down from your position as chief."

"Don't worry, chief," Rudy said with a groan, "it shouldn't take more than eight to ten hours, if we're lucky."

Jin sighed, having hoped he could just step out and catch the sunrise. He glanced up at the clock. Well, if Rudy's timing was correct, at least he'd finally catch the damn sunset.

"Swell," he said finally. "Where do we begin?"

CHAPTER 52

Jin

It'd taken all day to finish up the paperwork and Jin's head was spinning. Hell, that portion of the job alone made him realize he'd been right about stepping down. It was one thing to fight zombies, but quite another to plant his ass in a chair for hours recounting each and every instance. Plus, he had to sign an additional sixteen—SIXTEEN!—documents about how he was responsible should any legal proceedings arise from the ordeal.

How was it *his* fault that all this happened? Vestin should be the one suffering, not him.

That brought back the memory of seeing Vestin in his new situation. Okay, maybe Vestin's punishment *was* worse than the potential of Jin being sued at some point.

Maybe.

But none of that mattered now. It was all over. Jin

Kannon was no longer the chief of the San Diego Paranormal Police Department.

He'd even officially gone through handing over the reins to Raina, which brought a smile to his face. She looked incredibly happy, and rightfully so. If anyone deserved the "Chief" title, it was Raina.

Jin had slipped out of the building and breathed in the air. He then walked across the street and down to the ocean, just in time to *finally* catch the sunset he'd been dreaming about all these years.

A quick scan of the area told him the beach was all his, and it was amazing. Peacefully watching the sun sink over the horizon had been a dream forever and he was going to damn well enjoy every second on it.

He shut off his heightened senses and focused one hundred percent of his being on simply existing with nature, pushing himself to bathe in all of its glory.

The fiery orange globe sank slowly, casting a warm, golden hue across the ocean. The sky transformed into a vibrant canvas of colors, including streaks of red, purple, and pink, all blending together in a harmonious dance of perfection. The waves crashed on the shore like a gentle soundtrack to the breathtaking visual.

It was even better than Jin could have imagined.

Unfortunately, there was a nagging in the back of his mind that wouldn't let go.

Had he made the right choice? Was leaving such a paradise really the smart move here? Sure, there'd been a massive zombie invasion, and there'd been a vampire who'd attempted to take over the world, and having to fill out all that paperwork was an absolute nightmare, and there'd been numerous undignified moments—most notably the orc-finger incident—but looking out at the sunset might've made it all worthwhile.

Okay, so not the orc-finger part, but everything else had been acceptable.

Right?

Yes and no.

There was no doubt Jin would always hold fond memories of the crew of people who worked at the San Diego PPD, and even a few who didn't. But ultimately he had to be true to himself.

Jin wasn't a cop. Hell, he wouldn't even classify himself as an assassin any longer. He longed for a more peaceful existence, one that allowed him moments like the one he was experiencing right now. The sunrise, while probably mundane to the majority of people who lived at the beach all their lives, was nothing short of a miracle to Jin Kannon.

He wanted more of *that* in his life.

Besides, Raina was the new chief now and she was going to be awesome. The crew would stand behind her through thick and thin, and even through her monthly dark unicorn phase.

Jin shuddered at the memory. It had been some scary shit, and he'd seen a lot of scary shit in his day. Still, with Carina's help, and Jin's firm attitude, Raina had managed to keep herself *mostly* in control during the entire thing. She'd proven beyond the shadow of a doubt that, even in her darkest moments, she always put the team first. To Jin, that was how a true leader acted.

He smiled to himself as the sun continued its descent.

It was such a beautiful vision, not disappointing him in the least. He'd always considered it gorgeous while seeing it on the television, but watching it firsthand proved to him it was nothing short of a miracle. The way the light danced along the tips of the distant ripples alone was almost reverent.

Slowly, night began to swallow the day, leaving a serene twilight glow as a sense of calm covered him. It was somewhat of a metaphor for Jin's current station in life.

He had been surprised to find that Madison had asked to join him on his travels. He liked her…a lot. He also knew she was a succubus, which would very likely bring along a slew of problems. But somehow he didn't care. Everyone had their skeletons. Jin had one thousand confirmed ones living in his memory, for instance. The point was that Madison would be who she was just as Jin would be who he was, and as long as both of them were able and willing to support those idiosyncrasies, they'd get along just fine.

At least they didn't have to worry about Rusty being a thorn in their sides.

Jin actually smiled at how the android had grown. If only everyone had the ability to adjust their own programming, the world might just be a better place. Of course, since Rusty had chosen to become an assassin… maybe not. Regardless, the guy was going to be a natural, for obvious reasons. Rusty made it clear he'd only allow himself to take jobs that focused on truly nefarious targets, too. That made Jin happy. On top of that, Chancellor Frey seemed to have finally found her soulmate…or at least someone who could withstand her style of loving.

He took off his hat and set it on the sand before running his hand through his hair, letting the gentle ocean breeze blow across him.

This was the life.

Yeah, it was obvious that Jin had made the right call. He didn't fit in here. His new vision consisted of traveling the world, visiting the wonders of nature, and reveling in every charm until his dying day.

He'd always remember being "Chief Jin Kannon" with fondness, of course, but he was now the outgoing chief and Raina was the new chief.

An instant later, the sunset disappeared and the world went completely dark.

That had nothing to do with the sun completing its journey beyond the horizon.

It'd happened because a burlap bag had been slipped over Jin's head as rough hands gripped him, holding him in place.

It made him rethink the logic of turning off his senses, but that was water under the bridge now.

"Sorry, Jin," said a voice that he instantly recognized as Hector's, "but you're the outgoing chief and, well, tradition is tradition."

"Yep," Jin replied with a sigh. "Should've seen that comin'."

~

THE END

~

BONUS: Short Story

Jenn wrote up a fun little short story that follows what happened next with Jin. The ReaderTeam thought it was a hoot, so we've decided to include it here, too.

All you have to do is turn the page. ;)

DUMBSTRUCK CHAPTER 1

DUMBSTRUCK

Jin

The fact that Jin hadn't anticipated his current predicament left him dumbfounded and more than a little pissed. And yet again, he'd been screwed out of seeing the sunset....the fullness of it, anyway. It took every ounce of his self-control not to drop-kick these morons into the surf, but deep down, he knew this was his fault for letting his guard drop. He sighed deeply and resigned himself to letting Hector's goons do what they'd come to do.

Now that Lord Vestin was no longer a threat and Hector's father had been neutered, Hector had the unenviable job of proving himself worthy of running the San Diego Dogs. Jin genuinely liked the guy and saw no reason to make things more difficult than they had to be.

Besides, he doubted the Dogs meant him any serious harm.

Once the hood was securely over his head and someone had hold of him by his arms, they started to move.

They left the sand, replacing the sound of crashing waves with the clomping of heavy feet on the pavement. Next came a door sliding open, and then one of the Dogs gave him a gentle shove inside a vehicle, slamming the door closed behind him. A few moments later, the engine started, and tires chirped as they pulled into traffic.

They'd only been moving a few seconds when Jin caught the scent of something putrid. He was still trying to figure out what it was when Hector offered another apology.

"I really am sorry about this, Jin, but Becarra's in town, and as I said earlier, tradition is tradition. You have my word that we'll cut you loose the second he's gone. Until then, we'll do our best to make your stay as comfortable as possible. Don't hesitate to ask if there's anything you want or need."

Jin grunted. "You can start by telling me what the hell that stench is."

Several voices groaned in unison, and Hector barked, "We talked about this earlier, you guys. We may be old Dogs, but we're learning new tricks."

It didn't take Jin long to realize that the "you guys" Hector had addressed were his usual accomplices: Sofia, Cano, and Alejandro.

"Sure, Boss, we heard you," Alejandro grumbled, "but you gotta admit, they smell like ass."

"I admit there are still some minor adjustments to make, but the concept is solid."

There was an awkward pause in the conversation, but Jin's curiosity was now more piqued than his nose was offended, so he asked, "Can we circle back to explaining the smell?"

"Oh, right." Hector sputtered. "It's matcha mayo. Those damn zombies kept us so busy the last few days that I forgot there was a case of it in the van. The heat caused the seals on the jars to fail, and we lost the whole batch."

Jin knew he would regret asking, but he'd come this far and decided to see it through. "I have no idea what matcha mayo is, but why would anyone need a whole case of it?"

Sofia, Cano, and Alejandro groaned even louder this time.

"I'm glad you asked, Jin. As you're aware, I am *not* my father. It took some doing, but with Janet Smith's help, I was able to convince Mr. Becarra that taking the San Diego Dogs legit was in everyone's best interest. Turns out he loved the idea of creating a new revenue stream that didn't require giving up part of the profits to pay anyone off."

"Okay?"

"The matcha mayo is a topping for our newest business venture, *San Diego Dogz*. That's dogs with a Z, not an S. They're healthy, alternative-meat hotdogs made from tofu and zucchini. The matcha mayo topping is optional, of course, for vegans and those who don't do eggs."

Jin's stomach suddenly and loudly protested the mere

thought of such an abomination. Unfortunately, Hector misunderstood the gurgle.

"Great, sounds like you're hungry! When we get you back to the compound, we'll stash you in the kitchen with Jason. He's tinkering with the base recipe and would love to have a willing taste tester. We'd keep you with us, but Janet Smith and my stepbrothers are coming over for a final pitch meeting. If all goes well, we'll be converting all the houses except the main compound into production facilities and dispatching our new fleet of food trucks across the county within weeks."

Jin had so many questions he didn't know where to start, so he went with the least stomach-churning one first. "By stepbrothers, do you mean the coyotes?"

His question was met with another series of groans, followed by more chastising from Hector.

"Look, you guys, they may be ugly little bastards, but they have some serious talent. They've also been given the shaft by my old man, and nobody knows how demoralizing that can be more than I do. I'm gonna do right by them even if it gives all of us nightmares for years."

Jin wasn't sure what would give him worse nightmares, the coyotes or the thought of those damn hotdogz, but he was sure that the rest of his questions were better off left unasked.

DUMBSTRUCK CHAPTER 2

Raina

Raina sat behind her new desk, letting the last few hours sink in. Subconsciously, she was also redecorating. It wasn't that either of the former chiefs had poor taste, but Chief Kannon hadn't occupied the office long enough to redecorate, and Director Fyshe's choice of decor was a bit too nautical for Raina's taste.

What this place needed was some sparkle. Something glittery and positive, like her. It seemed fitting, considering she was a mystical fucking unicorn and the newest chief of the San Diego PPD. Just the thought of that made her so giddy that she whipped the chair around in a circle and was still spinning and happy dancing when she noticed Madison and Rusty standing in her doorway, watching her with amusement.

Well, Madison was, anyway. As usual, Rusty's sour expression made it look like he had a four-foot-long piece of rebar up his ass. That thought painted a mental picture so disturbing that Raina had to shake it off or risk spraying her newly acquired desk with sparkle-speckled barf.

"Don't let us interrupt," Rusty said with his usual snark.

Raina took the high road and ignored him.

"Is there something I can do for you, Madison?"

Madison sauntered in, hopped up on the corner of the desk, and smiled.

"Nope, just came by to say congrats and good luck. No one deserved this more than you."

Raina laughed. "You better not let Chief Kannon… I mean, *former* Chief Kannon hear you say that."

Rusty sneered and then muttered something, earning him a reproachful glare from Madison. He wilted under her gaze faster than spinach tossed in hot bacon dressing. Raina almost felt sorry for him.

Almost.

"So, speaking of our former chief, any idea where he is?" Raina asked. "Snoodle stopped by, looking for him. He claims he wanted to say his goodbyes, but you know Snoodle. He's completely by the book, so it's more likely he wanted to remind Jin to turn in his ID badge before leaving."

Madison chuckled. "He'll be back eventually. He just wanted to see the sunset over the ocean one time by himself before leaving San Diego."

"Makes sense." The words had barely left her mouth when Raina was struck with a terrible thought. "Wait, did you say by himself? Please tell me he isn't alone right now."

Madison's eyes narrowed as the look of recognition on her face matched what Raina was thinking.

With a rasp, Madison said, "They wouldn't."

Before Raina could answer, Rusty sighed. He was shaking his head, carrying the smirk Madison had lost. "They already did. I just accessed the parking lot cameras nearest to where he was going, and it appears that Hector and his crew stuffed him into a white van about five minutes ago."

"Are you sure it was him?"

"Yes, Raina, I'm sure." Rusty gave her duck lips. "I could see him brooding through the black hood."

Madison lunged from the desk, closing the distance between herself and the android in less than a second. "It's Chief Mystique to you, and you better drop the assitude and tell us everything, or I'm going to yank that ExtendoPackage 1000 out and shove it so far up your artificial anus that you'll be crapping wires for a week."

Raina knew Rusty was no longer under the influence of Madison's wily ways, so the look of fear on his face was genuine.

"Uh," he started and then centered himself, cutting the sarcasm out of his voice. "Unless there's more than one person on Hector's to-be-kidnapped list who wears a long black trench coat, boots, and a wide-brimmed hat, then yes, I'm certain it was Jin."

"Where are they now?" Madison snapped.

"Headed South on the 5, just shy of Imperial Beach. If I

had to guess, I'd say they're taking him to Hector's compound."

Raina nodded. "Safe bet, but just in case you're wrong, you two are riding with me."

Technically, neither of them were part of the PPD any longer since they'd resigned along with Jin, but Raina knew that Madison would want to rescue the man. She'd obviously become enamored with Jin over a very short period of time. Love at first sight? Raina wanted to believe in that, but it was a challenge. *That* was the key word here: challenge. If anything, Raina assumed Jin Kannon was someone Madison wanted to conquer.

Rusty was also still getting used to being his own android, which meant he'd likely follow orders if given with authority. That was proven by how Madison was still capable of bossing him around. To be fair, most everyone succumbed to Madison at one point or another.

The three of them rushed into the squad room, and Raina silenced the room with a double pinky whistle.

"Listen up, team! As much as it pains me to say this, Hector isn't so different from his father that he'd let the cartel's traditions die."

Lacy dropped an F-bomb. "Are ye after saying what I think ye is?"

Chimi lifted up a card and smiled. "Says here the chief is going on an adventure." Her eye went wide. "Sorry, meant to say the *former* chief."

Raina nodded. "For once, your card is correct, Chimi."

"For once?"

"The Dogs have kidnapped Jin."

"Oh."

Seconds later, the entire team was on their feet and headed toward the door. Any disappointment she may have felt for not seeing the obvious before it happened was quickly replaced by the pride she felt at seeing her team jump into action.

DUMBSTRUCK CHAPTER 3

Hector

As they pulled into the driveway, Hector's heart skipped a beat. He blinked twice, hoping his eyes were deceiving him. They weren't. Janet Smith and all five of his brothers were standing on the veranda chatting up Mr. Bacerra.

"Crap. They're early."

Alejandro grunted. "Yep. Do you think that look on Bacerra's face is horror or annoyance?"

"Probably both," Sofia replied, then snorted.

"Alright, enough with the chit-chat." Hector wasn't usually this tough with them, but his stress level had jumped to the next level at seeing Mr. Becarra. "Drop me here, then drive around back. I don't want our guests asking any unnecessary questions. Once Jin's safely in the kitchen with Jason, get your asses up to my office so we can get this meeting started."

With that, Hector took a deep breath to center himself

and casually exited the van. He tugged nervously on the cuffs of his sleeves and forced a smile as he greeted his guests. It wasn't easy.

"Janet. Fellas. It's great to see you, and you're early, too. You must be as excited as I am about this venture." He then gave Mr. Becarra a respectful bow. "It's genuinely an honor to have you here, sir." There was no response. "Well, Janet, why don't we all head inside and show Mr. Bacerra what you and your team have come up with?"

After herding them toward a set of large double doors that led to his office, he quickly pulled the doors open and motioned for everyone to enter. Once inside, he offered his desk to Mr. Bacerra and took a seat next to Janet on the large sofa opposite the desk, leaving the remaining chairs for his brothers. He was about to start when a confused look crossed Bacerra's face.

"Wait," the kingpin said, "shouldn't there be five of those things?"

Hector did a quick head count and realized that only four of his brothers were present. He was embarrassed to admit it, but he still couldn't tell them apart. In his mind, he just thought of them as the smart one, the stupid one, and the three who sang. Fortunately for him, the smart one was not the one who was missing, or at least he assumed not since one of them stood up and said, "Worry not, I've got this."

All eyes followed the coyote as he trotted over to the double doors and yanked them open. Parked directly on the other side of the doors was his missing brother, who appeared to be snout-deep in some sort of personal moment. The slurping and snarfing sound almost made

Hector barf. It had quite the opposite effect on Janet Smith, who was doubled over laughing hysterically while the other brothers broke into song.

Our brother Lightbulb
May not be too smart
But when it comes to hygiene,
He takes it quite to heart
Though it's often embarrassing
because he loves cleaning his—

Hector had never been more relieved in his entire life than he was when the coyote nearest the door turned around and shouted, "Stop! Don't you dare finish that song!"

They hung their heads in disappointment but stopped short of finishing.

Hector let out a sigh as Bacerra shook his head in disappointment.

Unfortunately, Janet Smith wasn't as easily controlled as his brothers. Once she regained her composure, she looked directly at Bacerra and blurted, "Dick. They were going to say that cleaning his dick is his favorite part." She let out another cackle. "Aren't these guys a hoot? Best jingle men I've ever met."

Before Hector could regain control of the room, the smart one bellowed, "Lightbulb, stop that this instant and get in here!"

With his mouth still full, Lightbulb mumbled, "Thorry, I'm phcoming."

Hector certainly hoped that meant he was on his way inside and not the other possibility.

Everyone had just gotten settled when Sofia, Cano, and Alejandro finally showed up. Hector waited once again for everyone to get seated and finally turned the meeting over to Janet Smith.

That's when his nerves really jumped into play. Everything hinged on how Mr. Becarra felt about Hector's plan. If he liked it, there was a solid chance the San Diego Dogs would become a legitimate enterprise, bringing the community together while building a business that would catch fire. If he didn't like it, Hector was going to have to learn to accept that his life would be spent selling drugs and crushing heads.

Thankfully, five minutes in, Janet had Bacerra hanging on her every word. Even Cano, Sofia, and—most shocking of all—Alejandro were sitting on the edge of their seats. It was actually quite impressive.

When the presentation was done, Hector gave Bacerra a few minutes to digest everything before asking, "So, what do you think, Sir?"

Bacerra leaned back in his chair and stared up at the ceiling for what felt like an eternity before answering. "I tell you what, I'm impressed with what you've laid out here, but I'm still not sold on the concept of artificial meat. I'd say we head down to the kitchen and let my mouth decide where to put my money."

Hector gulped, then flashed his crew a nervous smile. Alejandro and Sofia were clueless, but thankfully, Cano understood and quickly excused himself to go make sure everything was as it should be in the kitchen. He did his best to stall his guests on the way to the kitchen, hoping to buy Cano enough time to get Jin out of sight.

As they entered the hallway leading to the kitchen, Hector spotted Emiliano sitting at one of the tables, reading a book. Squinting at the cover, he saw the name *Soul Snatcher*. It showed a bulky guy with a mohawk, a thinner guy wearing a vest and shades, and a rather pudgy dog. The author's first name wasn't visible, hiding behind Emiliano's meaty hand, but the last name was definitely Mitchell.

"Emiliano?" said Mr. Becarra. "What are you doing here?"

Emiliano set the book down, giving Hector the ability to see the author's full name was Jenn Mitchell, and the series was called *Danny Tarot's Pawn Shop*.

Honestly, it shocked Hector to see his father was interested in reading urban fantasy, but not nearly as shocking to find out that his father could even read.

A split second later, they were all assaulted by a wretched stench. Bacerra glanced at Hector and asked, "I know you're no longer running the show here in San Diego, Emiliano, but do you really feel that gives just cause to stop showering?"

"That's not me," Emiliano grumbled, "it's that genie from the PPD."

Hector chuckled nervously. "Pay no attention to the old man. He's been a little strange in the head since being unzombified."

He quickly rushed everyone toward the kitchen, glancing back to see his father's annoyed look.

The moment they busted through the kitchen door,

Hector immediately regretted his play. The stench doubled in potency, and everyone began to gag. He also spotted Jin sitting on a stool beside Jason, and he looked to be higher than a kite.

As for Cano, he was nowhere to be seen.

"I sent Cano down to let you know we were coming," he choked out. "I guess he got lost."

Jin and Jason both laughed. "No, he was here, but he didn't stay long." Jason pointed toward an open door leading to the parking lot. A terrible retching sound like a cat coughing up a fist-sized hairball could be heard from outside.

"Cano?"

Jason grinned and nodded his head just as Jin released a heinous air biscuit that almost singed Hector's sinuses.

His eyes were still watering when Bacerra turned to him and said, "I sure hope that boy hasn't been eating those hotdogs you're trying to sell me on."

DUMBSTRUCK CHAPTER 4

Jin

Jin apologized and then reached for another hotdog. He slathered it with matcha mayo before sliding his plate toward Jason. "Like, hit me, brother."

The chef grabbed a plastic bottle of amber-colored sauce and squirted it across the top of the hotdog, then added several slices of something green. "Order up."

Jin downed half the hotdog in a single bite, then lifted a cheek and blew ass again. With his mouth still half-full, he muttered, "Like, Hector, my dude, these things are righteous. I can't stop foodin'."

"Foodin'? Dude? Righteous?" Hector turned toward Jason. "What *else* did you put in these? He's clearly stoned and I told you to put nothing but all natural ingredients in there."

Jason appeared affronted. "I assure you that everything in that is one hundred percent natural."

"Oh?"

"It's weed, bro," Jin said, grinning. "Top quality plant, too. I haven't felt this good in years."

That was true, too. He felt amazing. It'd never really been an interest of his to get high, but boy was he, and it was great. Gnarly? Heh heh…maybe.

Hector was still holding his nose. "How many of those have you eaten?"

Jin shrugged. "At least a dozen, bruh. The hot honey and pickled jalapeños were my idea. Smokin', right?"

"I'll say."

"Totes. It really cuts through the funk and gives them that little somethin' extra they were missing, ya dig? No doubt it causes quite a rumble in the old back carriage, though. That's why we decided to call this version the *Kannon Fire Dog*."

He'd no sooner finished speaking when the coyotes broke into song again.

You'll love the Kannon Fire Dog
Made from tofu and zucchini, not processed hog
It's a guilt-free treat
With a heat that's sweet
But be careful how many of them that you eat
Or you'll be shooting fire out your cannon hole

"Heh heh. Righteous."

Janet Smith let out another cackle and slapped her thigh. "Ha, see, what did I tell you? These guys are priceless."

Her hysterics were cut short by the sound of several vehicles screeching to a stop in the driveway.

Alejandro lumbered to the doorway, looked out, then turned back. "Uh, boss, looks like the calvary has arrived."

Jin reached for another hotdog as his former team charged past Alejandro and into the kitchen. Rusty was the first to protest the smell.

"Holy shit, if I had an actual stomach, I'd be out there hurling with Cano." His eyes fixated for a moment. "There, shut off my sense of smell routine. But, seriously, what the hell is that? If this is your way of torturing prisoners, Hector, it should be considered a human rights violation."

Jin watched in amusement as Raina glared a hole through Rusty's forehead. "Shut it down, bolt brain. We're here to rescue Jin, not start a turf war." To be fair, though, her eyes were watering.

Hector held his hand up in mock surrender. "No need to rescue him, you're more than welcome to have him back as long as you get him out of here before he shits himself."

A look of confusion registered on Raina's face but quickly changed to disgust as Jin ripped off another face-peeler.

"Oh my lord, is that smell coming from you?" the unicorn asked before raising a hand to cover her nose. The rest of her team was now gagging and backing slowly toward the open door.

"Where are you guys goin'?" Jin asked. "Seriously, man, you gotta try one of these *Kannon's Fire Dogz,* they're, like, amazing."

Raina took a few steps back. "Um, no thanks. We're good, but you feel free to stay here and eat until you're full. We'll just head back to the station and send Snoodle by later to pick you up." She turned and practically shoved Alejandro over, trying to get out the door.

Hector ran after her, yelling, "Wait, you guys, you forgot Jin. I'm begging you, please don't leave him here."

Raffy, however, walked over and grabbed a hotdog, taking a sniff of it. "That's some high quality ganja, like, you know?"

"Dude, like, totes," Jin replied.

Jin heard several replies, none of which sounded as if his former team was too concerned about his abduction. Finally, Bacerra yanked a white towel off the counter and strutted toward the doorway, waving it above his head like he was surrendering the Alamo.

Hector rushed out the door behind him as Jin and Raffy continued munching down on their respective yummies.

"Chief Mystique," Mr. Becarra called out, "please listen! As of today, we're turning over a new leaf and will no longer honor old traditions. Going forward, the San Diego Dogs will never again kidnap an outgoing chief. We are now reputable business owners and law-abiding citizens. On top of that, I formally give you my word that I will personally see to it that the San Diego PPD is given ten percent of our profits…if you'll *please* just take that damn gasbag with you right now!"

"Not worth the money!" Raina called back.

"Twenty percent?"

"Nope."

"Fifty?"

There was a brief delay. "Fine, fifty, but you also have to allow us to use your horse trailer, 'cause he's not getting in my car."

"Deal!"

Jin grinned at Jason and Raffy. "Sounds like it's all settled, bruh. Drag, but it's time for me to head out. Think I can get a couple of those smokin' *Kannon Fire Dogz* to go?"

"Like, can I get some, too?" Raffy asked.

"Totes."

~

THE END

~

Thanks for Reading

If you enjoyed this book, would you **please leave a review** at the site you purchased it from? It doesn't have to be a book report… just a line or two would be fantastic and it would really help us out!

John P. Logsdon

www.JohnPLogsdon.com

John was raised in the MD/VA/DC area. Growing up, John had a steady interest in writing stories, playing music, and tinkering with computers. He spent over 20 years working in the video games industry, where he acted as designer, programmer, and producer on many online games. He's now a full-time comedy author focusing on urban fantasy, science fiction, fantasy, Arthurian, and GameLit. His books are racy, crazy, contain adult themes and language, are filled with innuendo, and are loaded with snark. His motto is that he writes stories for mature adults who harbor seriously immature thoughts.

Jenn Mitchell

Jenn Mitchell writes humorous Urban Fantasy from the heart of South Central Pennsylvania's Amish Country. When she's not writing, she enjoys traveling, crafting, cooking, hoarding cookbooks, and spending time with the World's most patient and loving significant other. She also writes Cozy Mysteries as J Lee Mitchell.

CRIMSON MYTH PRESS

Crimson Myth Press offers more books by this author as well as books from a few other hand-picked authors. From science fiction & fantasy to adventure & mystery, we bring the best stories around!

www.CrimsonMyth.com

Made in the USA
Columbia, SC
25 October 2024